DUDLEY POPE

The Ramage
Touch

FONTANA/Collins

First published in 1979 by
The Alison Press/Martin Secker and Warburg Limited
First issued in Fontana Books 1980

© 1979 by Dudley Pope

Made and printed in Great Britain by
William Collins Sons & Co Ltd, Glasgow

THE RAMAGE TOUCH

LORD NICHOLAS RAMAGE, eldest son of the Tenth Earl of Blazey, Admiral of the White, was born in 1775 at Blazey Hall, St Kew, Cornwall. He entered the Royal Navy as a midshipman in 1788, at the age of thirteen. He has served with distinction in the Mediterranean, the Caribbean, and home waters during the war against France, participating in several major sea battles and numerous minor engagements. Despite political difficulties, his rise through the ranks has been rapid.

In *The Ramage Touch*, his tenth recorded adventure, Post Captain Ramage and his captured frigate *Calypso* return to the Mediterranean, and the Italian coast where he held his first command.

DUDLEY POPE, who comes from an old Cornish family and whose great-great-grandfather was a Plymouth shipowner in Nelson's time, is well known both as the creator of Lord Ramage and as a distinguished and entertaining naval historian, the author of nine scholarly works.

Actively encouraged by the late C. S. Forester, he has now written nine 'Ramage' novels about life at sea in Nelson's day. They are based on his own wartime experiences in the navy and peacetime exploits as a yachtsman as well as immense research into the naval history of the eighteenth century.

The Alison Press will publish his new novel, the eleventh Ramage story, in 1980.

Available in Fontana by the same author

Ramage
Ramage and the Guillotine
Ramage's Diamond
Ramage's Mutiny
Ramage and the Drum Beat
Ramage and the Freebooters
Ramage and the Rebels

FOR ROZ AND DAVID

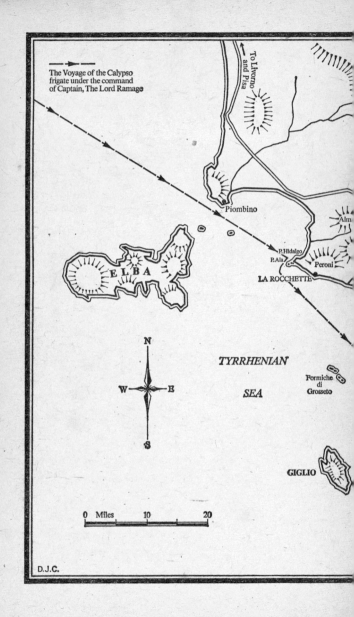

The Voyage of the Calypso
frigate under the command
of Captain, The Lord Ramage

To Livorno
and Pisa

Piombino

P. Hidalgo
P. Ala
LA ROCCHETTE

ELBA

Alm

Peroni

N

W — E

S

TYRRHENIAN

SEA

Formiche
di
Grosseto

GIGLIO

0   Miles   10   20

D.J.C.

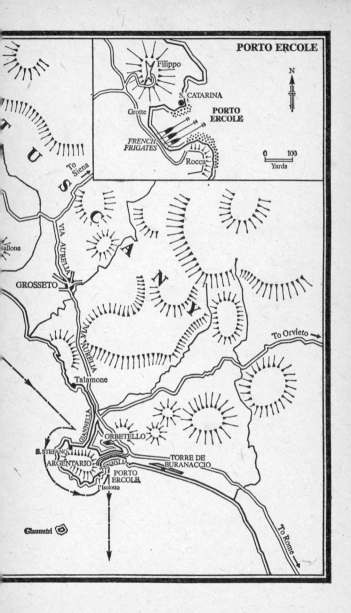

CHAPTER ONE

When Ramage eventually succeeded in focusing the night-glass on the two distant ships, because it showed an inverted image they were faintly outlined against the stars and looked like bats hanging side by side and upside down from a beam.

Southwick and Aitken stood beside him at the quarter-deck rail attempting to conceal their impatience. The vessels had been spotted ten minutes earlier by a mast-head lookout, who had seen them momentarily against a rising star. The master was the first to give up trying. 'Frigates, are they, sir?'

'No.'

'Nor ships of the line?' Southwick's voice indicated more hopefulness than fear, even though the *Calypso* herself was only a frigate.

'No,' Ramage said sarcastically, although secretly amused at the old man's pugnacious attitude, which was obviously under a strain because they had been back in the Mediterranean for several days now without firing a gun, except at exercise. 'As soon as I identify them, I'll tell you. Or you can take this – ' he offered the nightglass, which was the only one left in the ship because the other had been broken within hours of leaving Gibraltar, 'and go aloft to look for yourself.'

Southwick patted his paunch and grinned in the darkness. 'I'll wait, sir. Sorry, but it makes me impatient . . .'

'Don't get too excited,' Ramage warned. 'Although they're damn'd odd-looking ships they're small. And they're steering for the coast.'

'You mean we won't catch 'em before they reach it, sir?'

'Not with this whiffling wind. Either they've spotted us and are going to run up on the beach and set themselves on fire because they can't escape, or they haven't and, because they can't make headway against wind and current, have decided to edge in and anchor in the lee of Punta Ala. They can stay there until the wind strengthens, or veers more to the north. In fact, I doubt if they've seen us and are waiting for a veer. They must be as sick as we are of tacking in this light southerly.'

Ramage looked up at the sails, great rectangles, blotting out whole constellations of stars, but there was so little wind that there was only a slight belly in the canvas. For once he was grateful that for the moment there was not enough chilly downdraught to make him turn up the collar of his boat-cloak. He could see the quartermaster was dancing from one side of the binnacle to the other, watching the luffs, while the men at the wheel felt the ship almost dead in the water.

Once again Ramage steadied his elbows on the rail and once again held his breath to lessen the movement of the glass as he pressed it to his eye. The eastern horizon was jagged with cliffs and hills, black humps and odd shapes that made up this part of the Tuscan coast. Yes, there they were, tiny, angular black bruises against the night sky. The strangest thing was the position of the masts, although their angle made it certain they were steering in for the north side of Punta Ala . . . It was no good straining his eyes any longer: at that moment the ships slid into the dark background of the Tuscan hills as though a door had closed behind them. Ramage put the glass in the binnacle box drawer.

'We'll go in after them,' Ramage said briskly, explaining that they were out of sight.

'Shall I send the men to quarters, sir?' Aitken asked eagerly, reaching for the speaking-trumpet.

'There's no hurry; it'll take us an hour or more to get within sight of the beach. When is moonrise?'

'Another hour,' Southwick said promptly, having just put his watch back in his pocket. 'And it'll be a few minutes late by the time it has climbed up from behind those mountains. The – er, those two ships, sir . . .'

'The devil only knows,' Ramage said. 'There are so many odd local rigs out here in the Mediterranean, from caiques to xebecs, that I can't even guess in this light. These two look like ketches, except for the masts: they are set so far aft. The mainmast is where you'd expect the foremast to be stepped; the main looks like a mizen. They seem to have tall rigs considering the lengths of their hulls, and unless the light was playing tricks they have long jibbooms.'

'Could they be timber carriers?' It was a sensible question from Southwick because a ship carrying lumber needed long hatches to load decent lengths in the hold.

Ramage shook his head. 'Not in the Mediterranean. In the Baltic and North Sea, with long mast timber being moved, yes; but down here the trade is in what the shipwrights call "short stuff"; larch and the like, and the occasional oak.'

'Wine?' Aitken asked, managing to put into the word all the disapproval of a stern Scottish upbringing.

'Neapolitan wine-carriers?' Ramage expanded the question, knowing Aitken was a stranger to the Mediterranean. 'Or even olive oil? No, I've been thinking of them but they're beamier; they sit squat in the water like Newcastle colliers and don't have a very high rig. In fact I doubt if they could maintain steerage way in this breeze.'

'They must be transports of some sort,' Southwick grumbled, removing his hat and shaking out his flowing white hair as though spinning a dry mop. 'Troops, guns, horses, infantry, powder and shot . . . The French have to supply the garrisons in Italy.'

Ramage had already considered salt fish being brought down from Genoa or Leghorn, and military cargoes that could be travelling up and down the coast. He had a vivid picture of the *Calypso* frigate boarding one French transport and discovering at the last moment that she had five hundred well-trained troops waiting on board, with another five hundred in the consort coming up to the rescue. Likewise a few broadsides fired at close range into a transport laden with casks of gunpowder might well make a very loud bang that none of them would survive to hear for more than a second.

There was only one way of finding out what it was all about. 'Allow a knot and a half of northgoing current,' he told Southwick, 'and give us a course for Punta Ala. If you don't see those ships bursting into flames before moonrise, you can reckon they're just anchored to wait for a wind veer.'

Still thinking of the strange shape of the two ships after they had slid into the shadows, Ramage reflected that every country's coast had its own characteristic smell and noise when approached from seaward at night. With experience you can recognize it. The Italian coastline here just south of Elba was just as he remembered it from three or four years ago – but very different from the West Indies he had just left.

Oddly enough there was not so much physical difference in daylight: the high but rounded, breast-shaped Tuscan hills and more distant mountains, scorched brown by the summer drought and with trees only on the lower slopes, were very similar to those of several West Indian islands. Apart from the startling blue of the Caribbean sea and sky, the Virgin Islands, St Christopher, Nevis, St Bartholomew, St Martin and even Guadeloupe and Martinique, could have been part of Tuscany – except, of course, for the noises and smells.

In Italy the *carbonaio* was always busy cutting thick shrubs and lopping branches from trees and at night he tamped down his ovens with turf so that random draughts did not make too much heat and burn the wood to ash instead of baking it into charcoal. The smoke coming up from the hummocks, like autumn mist starting in a valley, drifted off to leeward with its own distinctive smell: of neither bonfire nor blaze, open grate nor bushfire. When the offshore breeze came up at night in settled weather the smell of the charcoal burning could be detected many miles out to sea, a signpost pointing homeward for the local fishermen but a warning signal to the unwary navigator. Mingling with it but sweeter yet sharper than the charcoal was the smell of herbs: sage, which covered many of the hills, thyme, rosemary and origano.

Among the West Indian islands the effect of the trade winds blowing regularly from the east was that the west side of each island had this almost permanent smell, and it was one which became stronger as you went on shore and entered the little towns: the sellers (usually women) would have their small piles of charcoal under the shade of a big tree. Plump women in colourful but never garish dresses, chattering with each other in shrill voices, occasionally quarrelling but mostly laughing, eager to tease a bargain-hunting buyer who went to a rival.

Ramage shivered in the darkness. Smell, noise – and temperature. If you had been serving on the stormy Channel

Station for a few years, a move to the Mediterranean seemed blissful because (apart from a few weeks in mid-winter) it was so much warmer. Then you went to the tropics and for the first few weeks the heat seemed stifling, damp and draining off one's energy. Soon you learned tricks like always standing in the shade when the sun was at its zenith, and you discovered the cooling breeze of the trade winds, so that you became accustomed to it. No doubt soldiers on duty inland found it scorching for an hour either side of noon but, to a sailor in a ship anchored in a quiet bay, places like the West Indian islands seemed to have the perfect climate.

The Caribbean climate *was* perfect, Ramage thought, and there had been no pleasure leaving the tropics this time, particularly because the *Calypso* was not bound for home. As the frigate sailed north from Tortola, heading for Bermuda, which was one of the first stepping stones across the Atlantic going eastward towards Gibraltar, the temperature had dropped one degree for every degree of latitude made good northward. He had been thankful when they sighted the Azores and began the long final sweep that would take them down into the Gut, as the Strait of Gibraltar was always known to the Navy.

He pulled his boat-cloak round him and with another shiver unconnected with temperature realized how a fox must feel as it paused to watch the pack of hounds sniffing the air, seeking its scent, because those two black shapes he had been watching could be a trap. They could be two hens waiting to be snapped up; they could also be two Trojan horses. All he could do was close with them and hope that sharp eyes and the nightglass would give him enough warning. After all, he told himself sharply, that was why he was here, one of the few King's ships now in a Mediterranean from which the Navy, stretched beyond its capacity, had almost completely withdrawn its strength which was needed more urgently from Brest to the Texel, from Jamaica to the Skaw. The Navy's task of blockading the French was like a cooper trying to prevent an old cask from leaking: no sooner was one leak stopped up with a small blockading force than another was spotted.

Of course, that was one of the reasons why Their Lordships in their wisdom had sent off orders from the Admiralty saying that the *Calypso* was to leave the West Indies 'and make the best of her way' to Gibraltar (a time-honoured phrase). At Gibraltar, Ramage had found fresh instructions waiting for him – he was to provision for four months and enter the Mediterranean. The instructions went on in immaculate copperplate for several pages, but boiled down to the fact that Ramage was being sent into the Mediterranean with the *Calypso* for four months to create as much havoc as he could along the French and Italian coasts, disrupting shipping, transport, communications . . .

Ramage was at first hard put to know why he and the *Calypso* had been chosen: it was unlikely that Their Lordships were concerned that he spoke French and Italian fluently and sufficient Spanish. Perhaps they remembered that he knew the Italian coast very well – but Their Lordships rarely bothered themselves with such considerations, reckoning that any officer with a decent chart was as well off as someone who had sailed the coast a hundred times. Or – and he guessed this was the real reason – they wanted a former French frigate.

The *Calypso* was French built, with a distinctive French sheer and the French cut of sails. With French colours hoisted, a French sailor fifty yards away would not know that the British now owned her. She could pass through a French fleet without arousing suspicion; she could sail into a French-held port and anchor and no one would think anything of it, recognizing the cut of her sails. Signals would be no problem because Ramage had recently captured another French ship and secured a copy of the latest French signal book.

Ramage had captured the *Calypso* frigate, making her present ship's company (most of whom had sailed with him for two or three years and more) comparatively wealthy, thanks to the prize money. It was appropriate therefore that he should command her for this freebooting expedition into the Mediterranean, although Their Lordships would never let any sentimental considerations affect their decision. In fact, he guessed as he held his cloak closer round him, the answer was probably that they could take a frigate away from the commander-in-chief at Jamaica without too much fuss (Admirals always let out a howl of dismay when they lost a frigate) because the *Calypso*, being a recent capture, was an extra, a consolation prize. If the commander-in-chief grumbled, the Admiralty could quite reasonably reply that he still had the usual number of frigates.

Slowly, as the *Calypso* steered inshore, a dark headland which he could just make out to the south divided into four sections. The eastern one was Punta Ala itself, and the three smaller were the islets extending westwards, as though a giant had rolled three great boulders off the end of the peninsula. The *Calypso* had sailed in just far enough to reveal the gaps between them.

A figure approached him in the darkness, padding along the deck like a tame bear. He recognized the bulky shape of Southwick, the *Calypso*'s master.

'The islands have just opened up, sir,' he said.

'Yes, I saw them.'

'The moon should be up in twenty minutes or so. In fact I'm sure I can see a hint of it behind the mountains.'

'Yes,' Ramage said, lifting his nightglass again. 'I can just about make out Monte Amiata over there. It's three or four thousand feet high and must be thirty miles inland of us.'

Southwick gave a characteristic sniff. He had various sorts which described different attitudes and each of which, for anyone who knew him well, represented a whole sentence, sometimes a paragraph. Ramage recognized this one as a prelude to a nostalgic remark; even the preliminary to some sentimental reminiscence. Southwick, now well into his sixties, was tending to become more sentimental as the years passed, and a return to somewhere like the Tuscan coast was sure to stir up old memories.

'Deck there! Foremast here!' came a hail from aloft.

'Deck here!' Southwick shouted back, before he had time to make his remark, and Ramage was thankful he had kept a couple of lookouts aloft throughout the night, though it was customary to bring them down at nightfall and station them round the deck with more men, six pairs of eyes searching the darkness for enemy ships (there was little chance of sighting a friendly one) or breakers on a shoreline.

'I think I can make out two ships anchored in the lee of that headland, sir.'

'Very well – someone'll be up with a bring-'em-near.' Ramage realized that he was mellowing; a couple of years ago he would have reprimanded a man for the 'I think', telling him either he could or he could not.

The master looked round and an American seaman, Thomas Jackson, seemed to materialize from the darkness. Ramage held out the nightglass. 'Aloft, m'lad; you know what to look for.'

He then murmured to Aitken: 'Send the men to quarters – but do it quietly.'

17

The usual beat of drum would carry for miles on a quiet night like this and the regular 'Heart of Oak' could hardly be mistaken for a French Revolutionary song.

'Guns run out, sir?'

'No, loaded but don't trice up the port lids.'

Ramage was not quite sure why he wanted the port lids left down. A vague idea was lurking in the back of his mind, like a half-remembered dream, so vague that he knew there was no point in trying to hurry it out.

'Quarterdeck – masthead!'

It was Jackson's voice and Southwick answered.

'Two ships, sir: both anchored close inshore, just a few hundred yards from the beach.'

'North or south side of the headland?' Ramage asked. The little castle of La Rocchette stood on another small headland to the south and the French might have a garrison there and a few guns. If the ships were lying on the north side of Punta Ala then the headland itself hid them from La Rocchette.

'North side, sir, but I can't make out the type of ships. Two masts, but they're not brigs. The foremast is set so far aft. It may be the way they're lying to the wind,' he added doubtfully.

'Very well,' Ramage shouted back, 'stay up there and report anything else . . .'

Round him men were gliding to their places for battle: water was being sluiced over the deck and men sprinkled sand on it in the ritual that would soak any stray grains of gunpowder and prevent men slipping on the deck planking. Gun captains were tightening the two wing nuts securing each flintlock and attaching the trigger lanyards, careful then to coil up the long lines and place them on the breeches of the guns.

Aitken, the Scots first-lieutenant, hurried up to ask:

'Roundshot, grape or case, sir?'

'Grape in the carronades, roundshot in the rest,' Ramage said briefly. It was going to be interesting trying out the carronades; they had only just been fitted in Gibraltar, six 12-pounders with the new slides that (so the master armourer in the dockyard assured him) made them easier to run in and out and doubled the rate of fire. They certainly looked effective, each sitting on a sliding wooden bed, instead of being fitted on a carriage with wide tracks like small cartwheels. Everyone on board was familiar with the effectiveness of carronades – they were devastating at short range but useless at anything over five hundred yards.

Young boys were hurrying past, clutching the wooden cylinders with close-fitting lids in which were carried the powder cartridges for the guns. They had collected them from the magazine and now each boy would squat along the centreline out of the way behind his gun, waiting for the gun captain to call him.

Meanwhile the quartermaster kept an eye on the two men at the wheel, frequently glancing down at the binnacle window, where a shaded candle lit the compass, and then up at the luffs of the sails. East by south was the course given to Ramage by Southwick, and east by south the man steered, neither knowing nor caring that the *Calypso*'s jib-boom now pointed towards places whose names sounded like music or were famous from Roman days and earlier – Vetulonia and Montepescali, Roselle and Vallerona, the mountain named Elmo with Acquapendente beyond it, and the hill town of Orvieto, perhaps the loveliest of them all.

For Ramage the names along the coast had a magic ring, even though he knew them by heart: just beyond La Rocchette was Castiglione della Pescaia, the Portus Traianus of the Romans, and overlooked by a medieval castle with square towers. Then Talamone, then Argentario, almost an island but connected to the mainland by narrow causeways. Beyond the causeways was the old Etruscan town of Ansedonia, now ruined, and close to the Lago di Burano, the lake with the tower beside it, the Torre di Buranaccio.

Neatly spaced all along this coast were the fortified lookout towers watching seaward, built by the Spaniards two centuries ago (mostly by Philip II, who sent the Armada against England); and even now perhaps keeping a lookout for Barbary pirates, Arabs from the northern coast of Africa and still known to the Italians generally as *Saraceni*. A coast of memories! His own would not be really strong until he was down towards the Torre di Buranaccio, where there was the memory of an enemy musket shot for almost every foot of beach.

In the meantime the downdraught from the mainsail was now chilly on his neck, telling him that the breeze was increasing, and the ship, whose deck had been almost deserted a few minutes ago, was teeming with men, soft-footed and certain in their movements despite the darkness. Watching the topsails and topgallants as black squares stark against the star-spattered sky, Ramage tried to recognize some of the constellations which were now partly obliterated. Orion's Belt was very low in these latitudes; in the West Indies it passed almost overhead.

Aitken came up to report: 'The ship's at general quarters, sir; all guns loaded but none run out.'

Ramage led him to the binnacle, took the chart from the binnacle drawer, and unrolled enough in front of the candle-lit window to show the first-lieutenant the stretch of coast ahead of them.

'Jackson reports two ships here – just beyond Punta Ala and behind this second little headland, Punta Hidalgo.

You see how the bay then makes a great sweep inland –
sandy beach, good bottom? Just the place to anchor and
wait for a fair wind.'

'Aye, sir,' the young Scot agreed. 'And it tells us yon
ships are even less weatherly than we thought: there's
enough breeze come up now for us to make a couple of
knots . . .'

'I expect these Frenchmen like a good night's sleep at
anchor,' Ramage said, 'and you can't blame 'em for not
wanting to tack down this stretch of coast at night. Here
– ' he pointed with a finger, 'you can see this reef between
Castiglione and the island of Giglio, the Formiche di
Grosseto. They wouldn't want to run into that. *Formiche*
means ants, so you can guess how many rocks there are.
And if they reached that far south before the moon rose
they'd find it difficult to round Argentario – the mountain
is big enough to throw a large wind shadow, and they'd get
becalmed in the lee of it . . .'

'So you don't think they've anchored inshore because
they're suspicious of us, sir?'

Ramage shook his head. 'I don't think they even saw
us: don't forget, only our masthead lookouts first sighted
them – we never saw a thing from the deck. I doubt if the
French keep lookouts aloft at night in whatever vessels
they are. If we *had* frightened them, they'd have anchored
here, under the guns of La Rocchette – the castle covers
the anchorage on either side of the headland – not off
Punta Hidalgo.'

There were faint shadows across the deck now and
Ramage glanced up from the chart to see the top edge of
the moon just peeping up to the east, the hills and mountains of Tuscany making a horizon jagged like torn paper.
With the anchored ships and Punta Hidalgo over to the
east, they would soon show up well against the moonlight

21

while the *Calypso*, approaching from the dark west, would
not be seen until the last moment. When it was brighter in
fifteen minutes or so the golden disc of the moon would
make enough light to pick up the *Calypso*'s sails, but what
sort of lookout would the French be keeping?

As if reading his thoughts, Aitken said in his soft
Highland voice: 'We can hope they all had a good tipple
of wine before they turned in for the night. With a bit o'
luck any lookouts will be stretched out on the hatches,
fast asleep.'

'If they have lookouts . . . We're probably the only
British ship within a thousand miles. They can treat every
ship they see as a friend. Of course, that makes it much
easier for us – every ship *we* see is an enemy.'

'Deck there!' Jackson hailed, and when Ramage answered he reported: 'Now the moon's up I can see both
ships anchored abreast of each other, sir, a cable or so
between 'em, and a cable from the beach. Can't make out
what they are, though; just that the foremast is set well
aft. Maybe it gives a bigger forehatch for cargo.'

Ramage could just make out the vessels now, so there
was no need for Jackson to stay aloft with the nightglass.
At general quarters he was usually the quartermaster,
watching the men at the wheel, the wind direction and the
set of the sails. Ramage called the American down on deck
again.

Two enemy ships anchored off the beach and a couple
of hundred yards apart . . . Even if they *were* keeping a
lookout, the men would see only a French frigate approaching out of the darkness. The moon would show
enough for them to recognize the cut of the sails and the
sweep of the sheer. They would have no suspicions.

He looked at the chart to get some idea of the depth
in which the ships were anchored and then put it back in

the drawer, motioned Aitken to stay and called to Renwick, the Marine lieutenant, who was just inspecting his file of Marines now drawn up at the after end of the quarterdeck. Even in the darkness the difference between the two men was striking: Renwick was stocky, round-faced and bustling. His every movement seemed military, like the jerkiness of a wooden puppet on strings. Aitken was slim and moved quietly – Ramage had no trouble imagining him stalking a deer in the hills of his native Perthshire, moving silently to avoid breaking a twig and always making sure he kept the animal to windward. Or even hanging silently over the bank of the Tay, reaching down into the chilly water to tickle a trout and knowing the water bailiff was close by.

Both Renwick and Aitken were brave men, one a fine soldier and the other a fine seaman. Both had sailed with Ramage for long enough to know that he hated gambling with his men's lives: he would take a chance when necessary but only after reducing the odds as much as possible. Many captains of frigates reckoned promotion depended on the size of the butcher's bill after a successful action – losing a third of their men killed could mean getting a larger and newer frigate, or even a pat on the back from the commander-in-chief.

One good thing about Mr Ramage, Renwick thought to himself, his last year in the West Indies had been quite fantastic – frigates and schooners captured, a whole French convoy seized, the surrender of the Dutch island of Curaçao taken and a Dutch frigate blown up – and all without losing more than about a dozen men killed. Mr Ramage himself had nearly been killed in the Dutch business, though; and the scars of the two other wounds still showed. Apart from those lucky captains capturing an enemy ship carrying bullion, few had made so much prize

23

money as Mr Ramage in so short a time. All the *Calypso*'s officers now had enough money put by in the Funds so that when the war ended (*if* it ever ended and *if* they survived it) they could retire and live comfortably. Every seaman, marine, petty officer, warrant and commission officer had more money than he had ever dreamed of. Mr Ramage always made sure that the prize agents he chose were honest. All too often one heard of a capture earning a lot of prize money, but when the division was made the prize agent had managed so many 'deductions' that he was the only one left satisfied.

The irony was that Mr Ramage was not really interested in prize money for himself. Too many captains (particularly of frigates) thought only of capturing the kind of enemy ships that yielded a good haul in prize money. Renwick had heard of several cases where they had avoided action with French men o' war, preferring to go after the rich merchantmen they were escorting. They were often tacitly encouraged by their commanders-in-chief. The 'commander-in-chief upon the station' and his second-in-command took an eighth of the total prize money, so that it was only human nature for an admiral to send his favourite young frigate captains cruising where they were most likely to take the prizes that would increase the wealth of both admiral and captains at no cost to the government. Indeed, both could always claim to be fighting the King's enemies.

At first Mr Ramage had been far from popular with the two commanders-in-chief under whom he had been serving in the Caribbean, at Jamaica and the Leeward Islands. They gave him the unpleasant jobs while sending their favourites after the prizes. But time and time again Mr Ramage had returned to port with rich prizes. It had been luck half the time, good planning the other. The commanders-in-chief had had to put a good face on it because although Mr Ramage was not a favourite, they had their share of the money ...

Renwick listened carefully as the Captain gave him his orders for the Marines. They were straightforward enough, and thank goodness it was going to be almost entirely a Marine action. There was nothing wrong with the *Calypso*'s seamen, of course, but he found it very satisfying for the Marines to be left alone to do a job. With a sergeant, two corporals and thirty-two men, he had a reasonable force; more than enough for the job in hand. The sergeant, a corporal and sixteen men would go in the green cutter; himself, the other corporal and sixteen men in the red. No muskets, Mr Ramage was most emphatic about that, and Renwick had to admit he was probably right: muskets were clumsy weapons and for close-range work a pistol was easier to handle, quite as lethal, and just as accurate in a mêlée.

Aitken was thankful that Renwick had grasped Mr Ramage's plan so quickly, even though the Captain seemed to be placing overmuch reliance on the Marines. They were good enough fellows, but he had never met one that was not possessed of three left feet the moment he climbed down into an open boat; and whose uniform was not covered with loops and beckets which caught the triggers or cocks of muskets or pistols and made them fire prematurely, or sent a cutlass clattering on a dark night, so that the enemy was alarmed and all surprise was lost. Brave enough fellows, but for an operation like this one he could not help thinking it was like sending a young bullock along a burn to stalk a wary deer.

At least Mr Ramage's plan was simple; that was the

beauty of most of his plans. Double the number of details, Mr Ramage said, and you quadrupled the chance of mistakes. Men became excited going into action, and excited men had bad memories. Aitken had already learned an important lesson – never put a *plan* down in writing. By all means give written orders, otherwise officers might suspect their captain was trying to avoid responsibility if anything went wrong later, but if the plan was so complicated that its execution required to be written, it was too complicated. All too often the bulk of any plan had to be carried out by seamen and Marines who lacked nothing in courage or initiative but who might not be able to read or write. They acted instinctively; usually they could be relied on to do the sensible thing. But, as Southwick once said emphatically: 'Don't stitch up anything fancy.'

Ramage told Aitken: 'Orsini will command the red cutter and Jackson the green.' A moment later he added: 'You'd better send Rossi and Stafford in the red cutter, too.'

'Yes, sir. Young Orsini's got to get experience, but there's no need for him to take too many risks.'

'I'm not concerned with Orsini's personal risks,' Ramage said sharply, 'but he'll be responsible for eighteen Marines and the ten seamen at the oars.'

'Of course, sir,' Aitken said hurriedly, knowing Ramage's strict rule that Orsini should receive no favouritism. The Scot knew only too well that the result was very unfair on the lad because Orsini had a far harder time than any other young midshipman. But the nephew and heir to the ruler of the state of Volterra was cheerful, absurdly brave, quite useless at mathematics, apparently a natural seaman, and a favourite with most people on board. Southwick – old enough, as he said on one occasion when trying to din

26

some mathematics into him, to be his great-grandfather – liked him, so did Alberto Rossi, the Genovese, an able seaman who kept his history in Genoa a secret (most people were sure that he had stabbed a man) but whose casual remarks from time to time gave glimpses of a lurid past. The man who had struggled through boyhood in the back streets of Genoa and the fourteen-year-old aristocrat who was the heir to a state, seemed to share the same practical approach to life. Perhaps it was really a practical approach to death.

'Very well, Mr Aitken, we'll heave-to now and have a good look round before we get the cutters hoisted out.'

Ten minutes later the *Calypso* was stopped in the water, her foretopsail and foretopgallant hauled round until the wind blew on the forward side, trying to push her bow one way while the wind on the after sails tried to push her bow round the other. Southwick had trimmed the sails so that the opposing thrusts were equal and the ship, balancing like a pair of scales with similar weights in each pan, sat on the water like a gull so that when the order was given the two cutters could be hoisted out by the stay tackles. Once in the water the boats were led aft and streamed astern, where both crews would wait by the rope ladders which were ready to be rolled down from the taffrail. The boats would be visible from the French ships, but it was not unusual for a frigate to tow a boat or two in reasonably calm water.

'We'll go in closer,' Ramage said. 'Half a mile.'

The moon was rising higher, making an ever-widening silver path to the French ships. Southwick gave the orders for the foreyards to be braced up; the sheets and braces were hauled home – there was very little weight on them – the tacks settled, and the water began chuckling under the *Calypso*'s bow as the frigate gathered way again. On the fo'c'sle a group of men under the bosun were rousing out a cable and preparing an anchor.

As he watched through the nightglass for the moment when one of the two ships would be right in the path of the moonlight, Ramage tried yet again to distinguish the type. Was he taking all this trouble just for a couple of leaky galliots laden with casks of Marsala, or local craft from the Adriatic come round to the Tyrrhenian Sea collecting marble from Carrara, or delivering salt fish from Leghorn, or gunpowder from Toulon? He would know soon enough.

He could hear Aitken giving softly-spoken instructions to Paolo Orsini and Jackson concerning the two cutters, while behind him Renwick gave orders to the Marines in the kind of breathless bark he adopted when the men were on parade. Presumably having them drawn up in two ranks at the after end of the quarterdeck qualified them for the parade ground voice.

Four seamen were dragging up a wooden chest of pistols for the Marines, and Aitken was making sure that each of the seamen who would be at the oars also had a pistol in his belt and a cutlass ready to put under the thwart, just in case.

The *Calypso* was gliding through the dark waters like a marauding shark: in the lee of Punta Ala the sea was almost flat and, now approaching the beach at an angle with the two anchored ships fine on the starboard bow, it seemed as though she was sliding diagonally across a narrow looking-glass reflecting the full moon. There was no sign of movement in either French ship; the sails on their yards were furled untidily and neither showed any lights. The two masters must be asleep by now, not carousing in their cabins.

Southwick ambled up, buckling on his huge meat-cleaver of a sword just as Jackson came out of the darkness and gave Ramage two pistols to tuck in his belt, and a seaman's cutlass. As the Captain's coxswain, Jackson knew that Ramage had no time for what he called 'fancy swords'. If there was going to be hand-to-hand fighting, and the two scars over the Captain's right eyebrow (which he rubbed when puzzled or angry) showed he spoke from experience, fancy swords were useless.

Ramage slipped the wide leather band of the cutlass belt diagonally over his shoulder, obeying his own orders that when the ship went to general quarters officers should wear swords and at least one pistol. The quickest way to encourage seamen and petty officers to take short cuts or ignore captain's standing orders was for them to see their captain or officers doing it.

It was a typical moonlit Mediterranean night with a gentle breeze turning the sea into hammered pewter. As Ramage looked across the bay, with the Tuscan hills and mountains beyond like petrified waves, it seemed a time for lovers. Instead the Calypsos were within minutes of the time for duplicity and perhaps death. If they were lucky, the duplicity would save lives – their own and the enemy's. Ramage shrugged his shoulders: he knew from bitter experience that a captain becoming too obsessed with saving the lives of his own men could act timidly and ignore one of the most important rules of war – that the boldest move was often the safest.

'About three-quarters of a mile to go, sir,' Aitken murmured, recognizing that Captain Ramage was absorbed in his own thoughts.

Ramage blinked, looked ahead and lifted his nightglass once again. He made a tiny adjustment in the focus. He was beginning to have a suspicion of what those two ships were, even though they seemed to be hanging upside down, ready at any moment to drop silently into some dark pit.

In the meantime he needed only topsails to manoeuvre: the topgallants could be furled. He gave the order to Aitken and a few moments later topmen were scrambling up the ratlines and out along the topgallant yards high overhead. Sheets and tacks were eased, yards braced to spill the wind, and the quartermaster gave quick orders to the men at the wheel to compensate.

By now the *Calypso* was sailing along almost parallel to one end of the great semi-lune of beach towards the two ships lying head to wind at anchor, fine on the starboard bow. The wind – still little more than a breeze in here – was broad on the beam, so the frigate could stretch along comfortably. There was plenty of water; the Frenchmen were anchored in at least six fathoms, and there were three and four fathoms to within a hundred yards of the shore.

Then, like a pickpocket leaving a crowd, the idea that had been lurking at the back of his mind, crowded in there but mercifully not lost, managed to slip out. He examined it carefully, as a parson might consider a subject for next Sunday's sermon; he looked across at the anchored ships and the gap between them. He knew the depth of water in which they were anchored; he guessed that by now the *Calypso* would be in sight of them if they had any lookouts.

Tense at the quarterdeck rail and looking over the whole forward part of the *Calypso*, he could now see every detail in the moonlight. His men were standing to the guns, with tubs of water between them ready for mops to be soaked, the trigger lanyards were coiled on the breeches like springs, the topsails were drawing well with just enough wind to press them into gentle curves with the silver of the moonlight making the cloth of the sails look white

instead of the warm sepia and raw umber of Admiralty
flax. The waist was clearer now, with the two cutters
which had been stowed there towing astern.

There was only one question, which was how deeply
did drunken men sleep, and the answer to that was it depended how deeply they had drunk. He could only guess
that French seamen after a few days' beating in light airs
would, the moment they were safely anchored in a secure
lee like Punta Ala, drink deeply. Anyway, he found his
mind was made up, and it meant scrapping entirely his
plan and cancelling the orders he had already given. Later
he might be accused of risking his men's lives in a joke
– that would be if he failed.

He called to Aitken, Renwick and Southwick, explained
what he intended trying to do, and after the three men
had considered it for a few moments, he knew they liked
the idea. From the point of view of discipline it mattered
not at all whether they liked it or not, but Ramage had
long ago learned that men put their hearts into a plan they
liked, whereas only their bodies went into something
in which they did not have much confidence.

Southwick, although the oldest of the trio, was always
the one who was first to accept some unusual idea, and
just as Ramage had guessed, Renwick was the last to see
the merits of this one. Hardly surprising, Ramage admitted,
since it took whatever glory there might be away from
Renwick's Marines . . .

The three men left Ramage at the rail and moved about
the ship, giving new orders. As he stood there alone,
draped in his boat-cloak, he listened idly as the bow wave
chuckled under the cutwater. It *was* a chuckling: Ramage
could always imagine a group of small boys down there
chuckling away at some trick they had played. The ship

seemed to be happy at this comfortable progress and wanted to share the fun.

The French vessels were approaching fast, or rather the *Calypso* was approaching them quickly. No lights, no sudden shouts, no startled challenges – either the Frenchmen were all asleep or it was a well-planned trap. Which was it?

They were asleep, he decided. They were damned odd ships, and all the men were asleep, snoring in that strangled and staccato way of men who had been drunk when they toppled into their hammocks. They seemed to have less than six gunports a side. Yet dare he risk what Their Lordships would regard as an irresponsible joke if it failed? Always the second thoughts . . . It would do the Calypsos good. They had somehow lost the edge they had had in the West Indies. It was not slackness – they still reefed and furled as though an admiral was watching – it was rather that they were slowly losing their zest. There was less skylarking now, fewer jokes, a heavier atmosphere. This was true of their captain, too, Ramage admitted; he too found the Mediterranean chilly and damp after the tropics. The moonlight view over the *Calypso*'s bow was some compensation: the sea and landscape combined looked like a painting by an artist, one of the more imaginative of the early Italians who fully understood that strange and (if you have not seen it) unbelievable Tuscan light and managed to capture it.

CHAPTER TWO

The *Calypso* seemed to be gathering speed in the moonlight but he knew it was an illusion: time was playing tricks, as it always did when there was a whiff of danger in the air. Sometimes it speeded up and at others it slowed down. This time it was speeding up. Ramage watched the dogvanes, a string of corks on a stick, each cork with white feathers stuck into it. Flying from above the hammock nettings, they were fluttering just enough to show that the breeze, which was even more fitful in the lee of the cone-shaped peak called Peroni, was still from the south. Perhaps it was an offshore breeze distorted by the mountains because the sky looked settled enough, with no hint of a sirocco.

The two vessels, lying near the beach at the end of their anchor cables, were like cattle standing almost side by side facing the hedge and waiting to be milked. Two hundred yards to go to the first one and the *Calypso* was moving almost silently: the occasional creak of the rudder, the squeak of a sheet or brace rendering through a block, the unavoidable flap of a sail, like a massive dowager puffing out a candle.

Ramage stared at the space between the two ships, now on the starboard bow, estimated it at two hundred yards, and held up a warning finger to the quartermaster, who hissed towards the men at the wheel to attract their attention. Southwick was now standing on the fo'c'sle, facing aft and watching Ramage, whose shadowy figure he could see through the network of cordage made by the rigging.

Men stood by at every port lid, holding the lanyard that would trice it up, allowing the guns to be run out. The Marines, instead of waiting at the taffrail to stream down the rope ladders into the cutters, were now lined up on either side of the quarterdeck, ready to act as sharp-shooters. The plan was all changed but the *Calypso* was ready.

One hundred yards . . . seventy-five . . . fifty . . . you needed to know precisely the turning circle of your ship when only the rudder was acting . . . twenty-five yards and Aitken was glancing sideways at him: he could just see the movement out of the corner of his eye . . . ten yards: then he snapped the order to the quartermaster and the great wheel began to spin as the men clawed down at the spokes.

The *Calypso*, her sails starting to flap but the yards creaking as they were braced sharp up, began to turn to starboard, heading straight for the beach and for the gap between the two anchored French ships. Not a word was being spoken; language might not have been invented as far as the *Calypso* was concerned.

As the frigate carried her way and glided in a curve towards the gap between the two French ships, Ramage watched carefully while the foretopsail was backed, the yard being hauled round so that the wind now blew on the forward side, slowing down the ship instead of driving her forward.

He continued watching as the *Calypso*'s stem came level between the two French ships and the frigate continued her glide towards the beach. Was she making a knot now? Barely, and slowing down fast. She would stop in just about the right place – there, she had: the bowsprits of the two ships were just abaft each quarter of the *Calypso*, and he could see Southwick gesticulating to the boatswain at the starboard bower anchor: it was already hanging down only a few feet above the water. Suddenly it was let go and the cable began racing out, and within moments Ramage smelled scorching from the friction of the rope against the wooden rim of the hawsehole.

By now Aitken was standing beside the binnacle to give whispered instructions to the men at the wheel because as the cable ran free the foretopsail remained aback, pushing the *Calypso* astern and reversing the action of the rudder. The bows of most ships paid off to leeward as they anchored and Ramage wanted to be careful not to alarm (or intimidate) the French ships by getting the *Calypso* stuck athwart the bow of either of them, causing a splintering crash which would smash the bowsprit and jibboom.

Now men aloft were furling the maintopsail, leaving only the foretopsail moving the *Calypso* astern, and at that moment Southwick on the fo'c'sle gave the order for the cable to be snubbed, digging the anchor in by dragging on it and forcing one of the flukes down into the sandy bottom.

Ramage had told Aitken and Southwick that he would be listening to the French ships, rather than watching them. In fact he had done both because the whole operation had, so far, gone very smoothly. But listen as carefully as he might there had been no hail, no challenge, no shouted question – nor any greeting, for that matter : it was as though both vessels were deserted.

The *Calypso*'s anchor was holding, and at a signal from one of the lieutenants close to Southwick, topmen swarmed along the yard and furled the foretopsail as the *Calypso* came back on the full scope of her cable to lie abreast the two French ships. From the shore the *Calypso* must look like a large dog with a half-grown but plump pup on each side.

Aitken came up to Ramage and said softly: 'It's

almost unbelievable, sir. I'd have thought that at least the splash of the anchor would rouse 'em out.' He shook his head. 'They must be sodden with the wine,' he pronounced. Coming from Aitken, being sodden with the wine was akin to standing in the antechamber to Hell with Lucifer topping up the glasses.

While Ramage examined the vessel to larboard with his nightglass, still trying to decide why both the masts were set so far aft, Aitken looked over the other one. Ramage could see no sign of movement but just as Aitken gave a warning hiss, a sudden intake of breath, Ramage turned to see a man at the taffrail of the ship to starboard. The man seemed to be trying to scramble over the taffrail, as though making a hurried escape, but he paused after a few moments and began relieving himself. He then hiccupped and went to turn forward to return again whence he came, but in turning he caught sight of the *Calypso*'s great bulk almost alongside and lurched to the main shrouds, holding on to one of the ropes as if it was all that stopped him falling over the edge of a cliff. After a couple of minutes' bleary inspection he asked in French, his voice slurred and barely raised above conversation level: 'When did you arrive?'

'Half an hour ago,' Ramage answered in French. 'Is the captain asleep?'

'I *am* the captain,' the man said, struggling with his dignity as he swayed.

'I look forward to your company,' Ramage said. 'For dinner tomorrow, perhaps? I have a saddle of lamb that might interest you . . .'

As he had hoped, the Frenchman took the bait. 'I am at your service, *m'sieur*, but we have to sail south at daylight,' he said vaguely, adding: 'We are several days late with these light winds. Have you found any winds to the north? I mean the south.'

'I've come from the north,' Ramage said. 'I must have been close behind you. I couldn't see any point in continuing to chase after puffs of wind, so I decided to anchor in the lee here and wait for the weather to change.'

'It's never going to change,' the Frenchman said gloomily, his voice becoming more slurred. 'Becalmed . . . we're all becalmed . . . sleeping close to the beach . . .'

His voice died away and now Ramage could not see the man any more: he must have quietly subsided on the deck. But his voice had not roused anyone else.

Ramage saw Southwick coming up the quarterdeck ladder, white hair flowing in the moonlight and seeming silver. He was still wearing his sword but from the grin on his face he must have guessed the last part of the conversation with the Frenchman.

'I can't see them getting under way at daylight, sir,' the master said cheerfully. 'Their heads will be throbbing so badly they'll think it's drums beating to quarters! Shall we send away our boarders?'

Ramage had been considering it carefully. He pictured Renwick and his Marines trying to force twenty or thirty drunken Frenchmen to wake up, stand upright, and then climb down into a boat to be ferried over to the *Calypso* as prisoners. It would be like trying to shovel up smoke.

'No. I think we'll wait for the Frenchmen to wake up. They'll have such bad headaches, they'll think they've been wounded. Trying to get them under control now means sobering 'em up . . . they'll be falling over like skittles. A really drunken one may want to fight. They'll wake up eventually and find a French frigate between them.'

Aitken gave a dry laugh. 'Aye – the *Calypso* looks French enough and they won't be able to see the name on the transom anyway. I'll tell the men not to shout, so the Frenchmen won't hear any English.'

Ramage nodded when asked if the men should stay at general quarters, with permission to sleep beside the guns.

At number six gun on the starboard side, sitting down on the deck below the level of the bulwark and with his back resting against the carriage, a Cockney seaman, Will Stafford, was finding a ready audience for his stories about three people, Captain Lord Ramage, the Marchesa di Volterra, and her nephew, Paolo Orsini, serving as a midshipman in the *Calypso*.

'Yers,' he said with an airy wave of an arm towards the north-east, 'all that land over there belongs to the Marchesa, and if she don't 'ave no sons, then 'er nevvy, Mr Orsini, inherits the lot. When we get it back from Bonaparte, o' course.'

'What akshully 'appened, Staff?' enquired one of the seamen who knew something of the legend but realized he now had a chance of hearing the true story from Stafford. If not the true story, then one which would pass for true once the trimmings had been removed, like pulling off the outer leaves of a cabbage.

'With the Marchesa? Oh, we rescued 'er,' the Cockney said matter-of-factly. 'Jackson, the Capting, a few others and me. This 'ere Bonaparte was marching 'is army down Italy and the Marchesa – she rules this state of Volterra, yer know – she an' some uvvers was escaping. Our frigate was sent to rescue 'er, got sunk by a French ship o' the line, and Mr Ramage – he was the only orficer left alive – took us in one of the boats to finish the job. Rescue the Marchesa, I mean.'

'Is it true she's very beautiful?'

'My oath,' Stafford exclaimed, and for a moment it

seemed he might be at a loss for words, but he managed to get a grip on himself. 'Well, she's about five feet 'igh, long black 'air, the air of an empress when she feels like it, she teases everybody, always seems to be laughing and her face – well, it ain't beautiful like they 'ave in paintings; it's – well, she's all that a woman should be only she's the only one I've ever seen who *akshully* is.'

'Where's she now, then? Where'd you take her after you rescued her in the boat?'

'Oh, all that's too long a story for now, but she's living with the Capting's family in Cornwall.'

' 'E's supposed to be in love with 'er, ain't 'e?' another seaman asked.

' 'E is,' Stafford said firmly. ' 'E don't seem ter be doin' much abart it yet, but – ' he lowered his voice and tapped his nose with his index finger ' – there's problems. One is she's a Catholic, I think. The other is 'is father, the admiral. 'E's the Earl of Blazey, and when 'e dies the Capting inherits the title and a big estate.'

'What's that got to do wiv 'im marrying this Marchesa?' the seaman persisted.

'I dunno,' Stafford admitted frankly, lost in the aristocracy of Volterra and of the United Kingdom. 'All I know is, if it was me I wouldn't 'esitate. She still remembers us – whenever she writes to the Capting, she mentions me an' Rossi, an' Jackson an' Mr Southwick. Funny, she speaks ever so good English but she can't get 'is name right; "Souswick" it was at the start and "Souswick" it remains.'

'Where did all this rescuing 'appen, then?'

'Why, just down the coast 'ere a few miles. There's a big sort of island – well, it's not a real island, 'cos a couple o' causeways join it to the mainland – but just beyond, on the coast, there's a tower. We picked 'er up there.'

'So yer been along this bit o' the coast. But what are we doin' 'ere, Staff? Ain't many o' our ships around, not from wot they said in Gibraltar . . .'

'Why, the Capting knows this coast like the back of 'is 'and,' Stafford said contemptuously, baffled that anyone could be stupid enough to ask such a question, but unable to deal with two aitches in succession. ' 'E speaks the lingo, and that's why we got these orders,' he added mysteriously.

'Wot orders, Staff?' At that moment Rossi joined the group, just in time to hear Stafford's answer.

'My oath, you chaps don't know nothink. Our orders are to capture or sink every French or Spanish ship we find. We got to make a bleedin' nuisance o' ourselves, like a fox in an 'en run.'

'Well, we've 'ad it quiet enough all the way up from the Gut,' another seaman said. 'We seemed to be keeping away from the Spanish coast to avoid trouble, not make it.'

'Ah, that's just it,' Stafford said triumphantly, accidentally guessing that it had been part of Ramage's orders. 'We got to get well into the Mediterranington afore we start cutting up rough. That way it takes longer for the Frogs and the Dons to get the glad news and send ships from Cartagena and Toulon, and it gives us more time to break the crockery.'

'I say, Staff,' said a timid voice, 'do they 'ave poisonous snakes 'ere?'

'Snakes?' Stafford exclaimed scornfully but stumped for a moment. 'Why, they 'ave 'em ten feet long. Not all of them are *poisonous*,' he added reassuringly. 'Some just bite and crush the bone.'

'*Accidente!*' Rossi commented calmly, 'what a liar you are, Staff. If only you sing like you tell stories – ah, the opera we should have. La Scala would be the nothing by comparison!'

'La Scala?' Stafford asked suspiciously.

'An opera house in Milan,' Rossi explained. 'They sing there.'

'Yus, they do in opera 'ouses in England, too,' Stafford said sarcastically.

'Belay all that talking,' a boatswain's mate growled, his interest now waning, 'you're at general quarters.'

An hour later, with the *Calypso* lying to her anchor cable and occasionally swinging gently in unison with the vessel on each side as the breeze changed direction slightly, Ramage stood on the quarterdeck alone with his thoughts, the ship's officers purposely keeping clear of him and the men lying beside the carronades remaining silent.

The *Calypso* seemed to envelop him: the decks beneath his feet, the masts overhead, the guns loaded and with scores of men waiting beside them. The ship was silent and there was no movement, yet it needed only one shout from him and thirty-six guns and the carronades would be blasting the darkness.

It was all here, he marvelled; the contradictions of peace and war. The moonlight sparkled like idly tossed diamonds as a wave curled up lazily on the sandy beach; the cone-shaped peak of Peroni stood a thousand feet high like a Tuscan symbol, and farther round and twice as high, one segment dark in the moon shadow, was Ballone and beyond was Alma, within a few feet of the same height. And forming the background were the Apennines. He was back in Italy and it seemed as unreal as a dream.

As they approached the anchored vessels Southwick had murmured, 'It was somewhere near here that you

41

rescued the Marchesa, wasn't it, sir?' and he had grunted a bare acknowledgment. But of course it was nearby; just a score miles or so along the coast.

Southwick, like the rest of them – Stafford, Rossi and Jackson – was always waiting to hear that he and Gianna had become engaged. They did not know enough to realize that the answer was obvious: Gianna, Marchesa di Volterra, was the rightful ruler of the kingdom of Volterra. When this long and damnable war ended and the French were driven out of Italy, she would return to rule her people. How would they feel if she came back married to a *straniero*? Curious that in Italian the nearest word one could get to 'foreigner' was 'stranger'. To an Italian a *straniero* was anyone who came from somewhere else – another village, another province, another country: someone who was not of the same place as the speaker and, by inference, not to be trusted.

Gianna did not accept the existence of these difficulties, of course; Volterra would accept him because, *Mama mia*, he would be the husband of the Marchesa . . . There were religious difficulties as well, but . . .

He shivered because that part of his personal future was uncertain; possibly insoluble. Anyway, for the moment he was within yards of his second home.

Second? Where was his first? Presumably England in general and Cornwall in particular. Yet if he was honest with himself – and being anchored like this in the lee of Punta Ala, having just nosed round Elba, was as good a time as any to be that – he was slowly becoming a man without a real home.

St Kew, the village forming the family estate in Cornwall, had been owned by the Ramages for five or six centuries, but for many generations the successive heads of the family had spent more time abroad than at home, usually on the

King's business. His own father used to be away at sea for three or four years at a stretch, latterly as the commander-in-chief on various distant stations. Now Admiral the Earl of Blazey spent all his time in retirement at St Kew, happily being the squire, and also the Lord-Lieutenant of Cornwall and Custos Rotulorum.

Meanwhile his son stayed at sea, still one of the youngest and nearly the most junior of the captains on the post list. He had not seen the latest Navy List, but presumably a few more lieutenants had recently made the leap to the post list, and because a captain's seniority dated from the time of his appointment, there would now be some names below his, so that they pushed him higher (*slightly* higher, and very slowly!). The two most important things speeding your move up the ladder of seniority were captains going off at the top of the list on promotion to admirals, some dying, and more lieutenants being 'made post' below you.

Ramage suddenly felt guilty about Paolo, whom he could see going quietly from gun to gun, checking that all was well. He had a cutlass in a belt over his shoulder, and his dirk at his belt, a weapon he loved to use as a *main-gauche*. The boy must be fourteen years old now, and it was a couple of years since he had finally managed to get away from Volterra, escape through Naples and then reach a British ship of war. The voyage to England to join his aunt had decided the boy that he wanted to serve in the Royal Navy. Ramage could recall the arguments only too well: Gianna had simply announced that Paolo would serve with Nicholas. Because Captain Ramage was allowed to take up to six 'young gentlemen' to sea with him as midshipmen, it was simple, she said; Paolo would be one of the six. Except, of course, that Captain Ramage did not like having too many midshipmen on board, and certainly did not want to be responsible for the safety in battle of the young nephew of the woman he loved.

Still, it was useless talking to either aunt or nephew about danger; both had already faced death several times and, as far as he could make out, and he had watched Gianna on a couple of occasions, they greeted it with an airy wave of the hand. So the boy had gone to sea and it seemed to work; Paolo had already been in three or four actions against the French where the only thing that saved his life was the quickness of his own cutlass or the dirk, and once Thomas Jackson had saved him from a French sword.

His use of the dirk as a *main-gauche* had started many of the seamen practising it – probably inspired by Will Stafford who, first hearing the phrase and not realizing it was French for 'left hand', had asked: 'What *is* a mango?' thinking, no doubt, that it was another variety of the fruit. After that Ramage had often seen seamen, a long piece of wood in the right hand as a cutlass and a short piece in the left representing the dagger, practising fencing, each trying to use the cutlass to swing his opponent round and leave his right side open, so that a dagger held in the left hand could be plunged in. The *main-gauche* was generally regarded by the British as not the sort of thing a gentleman would use. However, the Italian fencing master who had begun teaching young Paolo just as soon as he had learned to walk without staggering, was obviously a more practical man who considered that if relations had become so bad that men fought with swords, the object was to kill the adversary and stay alive oneself, and a *main-gauche* could often be an ace of trumps.

Ramage had been so wrapped up in his own thoughts when he first saw the Italian mainland once again the previous day, a distant blue-grey hint on the horizon, that he had not given a moment's thought to Paolo, who was seeing his homeland for the first time in several years and with the knowledge that it was still occupied by the enemy. Even the most optimistic of men could not guess when the French army would be driven out of Italy. Bonaparte occupied Europe from the North Sea to the Mediterranean, and, apart from occasional defeats at sea, seemed invincible. Paolo had borrowed a telescope, looked for two or three minutes, commented to Alberto Rossi that he had never previously seen Tuscany from seaward, and handed back the telescope. Unfeeling, self-controlled or indifferent? Ramage did not know.

In fact Paolo, almost overwhelmed with nostalgia, had been nearly in tears, but was imitating the Captain in hiding his feelings. Beyond that blue-grey blur the boy had pictured the many towers of the city of Volterra, tall, slim rectangles, and round it the cone-shaped hills with tiny towns perched on top, the dark green of the cypress trees covering the countryside, lining tracks and sheltering houses from the winds, and looking just like the broad blades of spears stuck hilt-first into the ground.

He recalled his own room in the palace and the armoury with the splendid collection of pistols – including some of the finest examples ever made in Pistoia, only a few miles away and the town which had given the world the word 'pistol'. It was when he commented on this recently to the Captain that Paolo had learned that the English word 'bayonet' probably came from the French town of Bayonne, where the short swords fixed on to muskets had first been made. The Captain had known about 'pistol' and 'bayonet' but could not tell him where the word 'dirk' came from, except to mutter something about Scotsmen.

CHAPTER THREE

Shortly after dawn Ramage was back on the quarterdeck watching the curious outline of the two French ships emerging more sharply as daylight spread across the bay. They were not Mediterranean vessels; he was sure of that. They seemed to be typical galliots of the French Channel ports – except that the mainmasts were set so far aft, and the stays from the mainmast to the stemhead, bowsprit and jibboom seemed fewer than usual but comparatively massive. Odd-looking vessels, obviously, built for a special purpose, but for what?

He looked carefully, beginning at the bow. A comparatively short bowsprit and a long jibboom, three headsails lying in heaps at the foot of the stays, and he could just make out the upper curve of the drum of the windlass. It was a normal windlass and not a capstan, and to be expected. What was that? It looked like the rim of something canted at an angle. The muzzle of an enormous gun? A mortar perhaps? His eyes ran aft past the mainmast and there, just forward of the mizen, was another. These weird vessels were bomb ketches!

What on earth were bomb ketches doing here, along the Italian coast? They were not properly designed bomb ketches, specially built in one of the naval yards, but merchant ship hulls which had been adapted – strengthened to take the weight of the mortars and their enormous recoil, the mainmast stepped farther aft, and the rigging simplified so that no shrouds, halyards, sheets and stays went across the fields of fire or, equally important, were close enough to the muzzle flash to catch fire.

Southwick, freshly shaved, hat four-square on his head with wisps of white hair sticking out like hay beneath a nesting hen, his face settled in a cheerful grin, walked up to Ramage as he stood at the binnacle and said: 'A couple of Dunkirkers, eh?'

'I don't know about Dunkirk,' Ramage said, 'but built fairly close. Notice anything else?'

Southwick took off his hat and scratched his head, a typical gesture, like someone tidying the head of a mop. His forehead wrinkled as he concentrated on looking at the ship to starboard. He took Ramage's proffered telescope and adjusted the focus. 'Ah,' he said finally. A few moments later he repeated it. 'Ah. Two mortars.' He walked to the larboard side to look at the other ship and came back almost immediately.

'Bomb ketches. Or a couple of galliots turned into bomb ketches. I wonder where they're bound? What do the French want to pound to pieces along this coast? I thought they'd occupied most of it already.'

Ramage shrugged. 'We'll soon find out.' He tapped the French signal book lying on the top of the binnacle. 'We'll hoist the signal for the commanding officers to report to me on board here. They can tell us.'

Southwick was already looking round for seamen to collect the correct French flags from the special locker when Ramage held up a restraining hand. 'We'll wait an hour or two for them to recover. They've no suspicions — they might even be alarmed at receiving orders too early!'

'Where do you think they're bound, sir?' Southwick persisted.

'Probably not Italy at all. They might be on their way to the eastern end of the Mediterranean on some wild scheme of Bonaparte's. Don't forget he tried to capture Egypt;

in fact he'd still be there but for the Battle of Aboukir Bay.'

Southwick pretended to shudder. 'Don't mention the name, sir; when I think we missed that action . . .'

'We'll have to make do with what we've got. The Battle of Punta Ala – or do you prefer the Battle of Punta Hidalgo, that's this point close to us.'

'Ala,' Southwick said firmly. 'Hidalgo sounds foreign. It's not an Italian word, is it, sir? Seems more Spanish to me. Haven't I heard it in connection with horses, or estates or something like that?'

'Gentleman. Just a gentleman. Perhaps you're thinking of a gentleman riding round his estate on a horse.'

'Why should there be a Punta "Hidalgo" here, then?' Southwick asked, gesturing towards the headland to seaward of them, which had Punta Ala beyond to the westward.

'Not so long ago the Spanish owned all this. Most of these castles and watch-towers along the coast were built by the Spanish, by Philip II. Just down the coast here, at Santo Stefano, there's one of his splendid fortresses which is named after him, the Fortezza di Filippo Secondo.'

'But what did the Spanish want with all this land in Italy?'

'The Spanish want land wherever they can get it! Anyway, the Grand Duke of Tuscany is a Habsburg. He's a weak man who just buckled under to Bonaparte. Don't mention his name to the Marchesa! Her mother reckoned that every Habsburg should be hanged with a thin rope from a tall tree.'

Ramage picked up the French signal book and began flicking over the pages. He had a personal rule never to trust his memory, so he looked through the signals again. There was only one that could be applied, '*All captains to report immediately to the flagship.'* The *Calypso*, even while pretending to be French, was certainly no flagship; but obviously her captain was by far the senior officer present – at most the galliots would be commanded by lieutenants and if the one that had emerged briefly during the night was anything to go by, they were former mates or even bosuns of coasting craft pressed into the Navy to serve the new Republic.

Ramage held up the book and pointed out the flags to Southwick. 'You're right; I suppose we might as well hoist them now. The captains will be wakened eventually and they'll get nervous because they won't know how long the signal's been up.'

Southwick sniffed, a quiet but contemptuous sniff which in one brief indrawn breath revealed his opinion of the French Ministry of Marine, French naval officers in general, and commanders of galliots in particular. 'When do we let them know we're British, sir? I mean, do you want all the officers to wear trousers and shirts, not uniforms?'

'Yes, then they need not stay out of sight of the ships. Marines had better dress as seamen. I could send Renwick over now with his men, but we might just as well make it a bloodless capture. Renwick won't thank us, but we're more likely to find out what we want from the French officers this way, because the alternative is being put back on board their ships and having one of our broadsides follow them.'

Leaving instructions that he was to be called the moment there was any sign of movement on board either ship, Ramage went below to shave, change into a shirt and nankin trousers, and have his breakfast. One thing that could be said in the Mediterranean's favour was that, as in the West Indies, it was easy to get fruit and vegetables – in the summer, anyway.

Ramage had just finished shaving, in cold water because the galley fire was out, and was tying his stock when Southwick called down the skylight: 'Couple of fellows moving about on deck in the galliot to starboard, sir. They haven't noticed the signal.'

His steward was handing Ramage his shoes (the fourth best pair with silver buckles) when Southwick reported a man relieving himself over the side of the other ship to larboard without, apparently, even noticing the *Calypso*. Ramage had just finished his breakfast and was dawdling over a cup of green tea when Southwick called down that there were now half a dozen men on board the vessel to starboard and they had just noticed the signal.

'I hope you're not in uniform,' Ramage said, irritated that he had not finished his tea.

'Pusser's shirt and trousers, sir,' Southwick answered. 'I look as though I've just been elected by a Revolutionary committee. Ah, that looks like the master, or captain. Yes, he's gesturing to have the boat lowered. Seems to be in a fine fury. The boat in the transom davits seems to be the only one they have. Yes, he's run down to his cabin — back he comes with his hat. And rubbing his face with a wet cloth. Hah! Sword in one hand, wet cloth in the other, and his headache thudding, too, I'll be bound. Phew, they let the boat drop with a run — marvel it hasn't stove in some planks. The captain heard it and he's fairly dancing round with rage. In fact he's just hit a man with the flat of his sword. Now the rope ladder's been let fall . . . he'll be on his way in a few minutes.'

Some ten minutes later Southwick whispered a hoarse warning through the skylight and then the sentry gave a double knock and pushed the door open. A slim man with a wrinkled, tanned face and wearing a faded blue shirt and well-patched white trousers, a broad leather cutlass belt diagonally across his shoulders, walked nervously into the cabin, looking left and right like a bird fearing a trap.

The Frenchman had reached this far without anyone speaking a word: as he came up the side he had been met by Southwick, who pointed to the companionway, and then the sentry had pointed at the open door.

Suddenly the man caught sight of Ramage sitting at the table, a cup and saucer in front of him. He smiled uncertainly, careful as he walked towards Ramage not to bump his head on the deck beams above. There was considerably more headroom than in his galliot, but still not enough to allow him to stand upright.

'Renouf,' the man said by way of introduction, *'lieutenant de vaisseau . . .'*

Ramage stood up with just the right pause to be expected from a captain in the Revolutionary Navy. 'Ramage,' he murmured, giving his name its French pronunciation and turning an old Cornish surname into the French word for the music of birds. He held out his hand and the Frenchman shook it as though it might bite him and then sat in the chair to which Ramage had gestured.

'You have your orders?' Ramage asked in French with suitable brusqueness.

Renouf burrowed into the pocket sewn inside his shirt and brought out a twice-folded sheet of paper. He opened it, smoothed it carefully on his knee and then handed it to Ramage.

The orders told Renouf, commanding *Le Dix-Huit de Fructidor*, bomb vessel, to proceed to Candia, on the island of Crete, and there await further orders. (Ramage was amused to notice that despite the Revolution, French orders were written in the same dead language contrived by British government officials.) Each ship was commanded by a lieutenant, but the two were treated as a little squadron of which Renouf was the senior officer.

The paper was coarse, and at the top was a circle with an anchor in the centre surrounded by 'Rep. Fran. Marine' with 'LIBERTÉ' in capital letters printed separately to the left and 'EGALITÉ' to the right. The unbleached paper, an economy measure or perhaps just poor papermaking because it soaked up the ink like cloth, had a faint greyness as though the colour of communications from *Le Ministre de la Marine et des Colonies* in Paris was always like this, even when the actual orders came from the *Chef d'Administration de la Marine*, Brest (although given in the name of the Minister and *la République une et indivisible*).

The orders were dated – Ramage paused, working out the new French calendar – four months ago. It had been a long voyage for the two galliots, all the way round the Spanish peninsula from Brest. *Le Dix-Huit de Fructidor* . . . that name was a special date, but what the devil was it? The first of September was the fifteenth of Fructidor, so the eighteenth was the fourth of September. What had happened then? It did not give the year, either. The new Revolutionary calendar began on 22 September 1792, and introduced a ten-day week. So the 18 Fructidor could be the birth of the galliot's original owner's mother-in-law.

Ramage searched his memory. Several years ago Robespierre had fallen and the new government had exiled to Devil's Island everyone suspected of being lukewarm towards the Revolution. Within a year or so there had been revolts against the Revolutionaries (the Convention, rather) . . . Then there was the Paris rising, which was put down when a young General Bonaparte fired on the Paris rebels with grapeshot, and a new Constitution came into force. The currency collapsed, food prices went up like celebration rockets, and never came down again. The new Directory was not popular. Then General Bonaparte returned from Italy, marched on the capital and scores of deputies were arrested and exiled to Devil's Island.

That *coup d'état,* or whatever it was called, had been on 4 September 1797, which was le dix-huit Fructidor in year five of the Revolution? Well, *Le Dix-Huit de Fructidor,* galliot, named after the event, was herself going to suffer a *coup d'état* within the next half-hour. As far as she was concerned the Revolutionary wheel would have turned a complete revolution. The thought made him smile, and he realized that Renouf was smiling back rather uncertainly, wise enough to know that junior officers *always* smiled when their seniors smiled.

Renouf, however, was looking too comfortable. The narrow Gallic face with its olive skin, the hair black and wavy, the queue long and tightly bound, the eyes brown but bloodshot and trying to avoid the glare from the rising sun now beginning to come through the stern lights behind Ramage, needed shaking up. Renouf needed reminding that his head throbbed, that he felt shaky from the night's wine bibbing. He had to be unwary and weak: unwary while he still thought that the *Calypso* was French; weak when he found that he was a prisoner.

Ramage coughed in the way that most superior officers did before finding fault or blaming juniors. Renouf glanced up nervously to find that the *Calypso*'s captain had folded the page of orders and was using it to tap the table top.

'Citizen Renouf – you seem to be taking your time over this voyage. When the *Chef d'Administration* at Brest gave you these orders, I'm sure . . .'

'But the additional orders,' Renouf protested. 'From Toulon – they modify those.'

'What additional orders?' Ramage demanded heavily, deliberately sounding doubtful, as though accusing Renouf of lying.

Again the Frenchman ferreted around in his pocket and, with the clumsiness of a man not used to handling papers, came out with another folded sheet, which he handed to Ramage after opening and smoothing the page.

Obviously the bomb ketches had called in at Toulon to repair damage or get supplies, instead of making the passage to Italy direct from the Strait of Gibraltar, and, all navies being the same, the unexpected arrival of a couple of extra ships had to be turned to some advantage, however brief. Then Ramage read the extra orders again more carefully and discovered that his first glance had given him the wrong impression. Apparently the ketches were far more important to the French than he had thought, and they were to be escorted by two frigates. These frigates would meet them just down the coast on the other side of Argentario at Porto Ercole. He cursed the Revolutionary calendar but worked out that it meant in five days' time. The two frigates were going there after landing some stores at Bastia, in Corsica. The ketches should by then have watered, taken on what provisions they needed (and which were available locally), and then be waiting at anchor outside the harbour because the frigates would then enter to water as soon as they arrived and embark cavalry, infantry and field artillery and transport them to Crete while escorting the bomb ketches.

Ramage considered the dates as he folded the letter. It was now the 8th, and the two bomb ketches had to be watered, provisioned and anchored outside Porto Ercole by the 13th, when the frigates were due. By then cavalry and field artillery would have arrived at Porto Ercole from somewhere nearby, ready to be embarked. Presumably they would bring forage for the horses. But why on earth were the French sending a couple of bomb ketches and a couple of frigates to Crete with cavalry and artillery?

'You have the charts for Crete?' Ramage asked casually.

Renouf grimaced expressively and shook his head. 'The frigates are bringing one. I don't even have a chart showing where it is; just a latitude and longitude written down.'

'You sound as though you do not even know *why* you're going to Crete!'

'I don't,' Renouf said bitterly, thinking that Ramage's little trap was an expression of sympathy. 'All I know is that since we left Brest we've sailed as far as across the Atlantic by the southerly route, and we still have a long way to go. They must have some important fortresses to knock down in Crete, that's all I can think.' He scratched the back of his head and added viciously: 'I hope so, anyway; we deserve to have something to blow up, after all this sailing.'

'Crete is larger than Corsica,' Ramage said casually. 'A squadron of cavalry, a few field guns and two bomb ketches are not going to make much impression. You'll probably meet a fleet there and go on somewhere else. Back to Egypt, perhaps ...'

Renouf looked alarmed at the mention of Egypt. The defeat of the French fleet there – Nelson had captured or burned eleven ships of the line out of thirteen – and Bonaparte's narrow escape (at a cost of abandoning his Army of Egypt to its fate) was still fresh in every Frenchman's memory, and the prospect that the *Dix-Huit de Fructidor* and the *Brutus* might be part of a new plan by Bonaparte to return to those scorching sands (even though the Royal Navy had quit the Mediterranean) did not appeal to him. Then he composed his face – it was an expression Ramage had often read in books, but he had never previously seen someone actually doing it. Clearly Renouf had suddenly realized the danger of letting a senior officer glimpse his feelings: charges of treason made as the result of a look, let alone a careless word, had led to a man making the short walk to the guillotine or the long voyage across the Atlantic to Devil's Island, just a few miles north of the Equator. 'The convoy to Cayenne', meaning transportation, was as common an expression in France these days as 'taking a ride in a tumbril' and 'marrying the Widow' were for being guillotined.

Renouf saw that his companion was nodding and smiling understandingly, so no harm had been done, but the mention of Egypt was enough to turn a man's stomach. One could not trust such a fellow as this too far, however. He was from Paris, judging by his accent, or maybe from the Orléans area. Obviously once an aristo – Renouf could tell that from his voice. But he, or his family, must have done good work for the Revolution, or else paid a lot of money, to keep his head on his shoulders, and even more to have obtained and kept command of a ship like this frigate.

Renouf admitted that the ship was in good order: he had seen enough while being rowed over, and the decks were spotless: he had noticed that in the brief walk from the entry port to the companionway. As scrubbed as they always said English ships were!

Still, the damned man might at least offer him a drink. His mouth tasted as coppery as a moneylender's leather pouch. There was something he did not understand about this young man. He had the face of an aristo: high cheekbones, a slightly hooked nose, dark brown eyes very deepset under thick eyebrows. Not really a French face – but then what *was* a French face? Long and narrow with crinkly black hair and a boasting tongue like a Gascon?

Leathery, the body wiry, like a man from one of the provinces along the Pyrenees? Or stocky, round-faced from too much eating, like those living close to the Swiss border, neither men of the mountains nor the plains? There was no really typical Frenchman, but nevertheless this *capitaine de vaisseau* looked different. Perhaps his mother was a foreigner.

Renouf decided that the eyes were disconcerting: they seemed to look right through you. The two scars over the right eyebrow must be sword cuts – one newer than the other. He held his left arm as though the muscles were slightly wasted. He must be recovering from a wound. Renouf always warned his men that if you had a wound in a limb, you could say goodbye to it. At least this fellow had escaped the surgeon's saw.

This frigate, Renouf thought, was not one of the two that were supposed to meet him at Porto Ercole since the Captain knew nothing of his orders. Curious that there should be a third frigate in such a small area. Perhaps this fellow was trying to catch him out; trying to make a case against him for wasting time? No, there was no doubt about the Captain's surprise when he read the second set of orders.

Renouf was startled by a double knock at the door, which had been left open. He heard uneven footsteps coming down the companionway and a moment later the lieutenant commanding the *Brutus* entered. The fool was drunk; Renouf spotted that immediately although someone who did not know Michelet so well might take a few minutes to realize it.

Renouf stood up at once. 'Captain,' he said hastily, 'may I present Citizen Jean-Pierre Michelet, commanding the *Brutus*, who is not only a fine seaman but a man of considerable skill in the use of the mortars.'

Renouf had not fooled the Captain, who nodded towards a chair and said sarcastically: 'Citizen Michelet had better sit down: he finds the ship is rolling rather heavily at the moment.'

Certainly Michelet had walked in as though trying to keep his feet in a rough sea, and now he turned and headed for the chair. Renouf guessed that Michelet could see three chairs and hoped he would sit down in the middle one. But the drunken lieutenant must have seen four and sat on the third because a moment later he fell over backwards. The startled look on his face before he hit the deck made Renouf think of a man who found himself falling over a precipice.

The Captain did not move, did not smile and did not start cursing. Nor did he threaten Michelet. In fact he did not even look down at him as the man struggled to his feet.

'Does he often do that?'

The eyebrows were slightly raised and the question might be facetious, or it could be serious. The voice was quiet enough. Renouf knew it could bode ill for the two bomb ketches, because commanding officers had been court-martialled for much less. Travelled in a tumbril for less, because Michelet was on duty, and sleeping or being drunk on duty was punishable by death.

'Er, no, sir.' He had not intended to say 'sir', but the Captain had an odd effect on him. Renouf thought of him as 'sir' and the old phrase had slipped out. 'No, Citizen, but we have had a long voyage and I'm afraid we all celebrated last night.'

Renouf tried a conspiratorial grin and hoped that the Captain would not smell the fresh wine on Michelet's breath nor appreciate that Lieutenant Renouf shared the responsibility for Michelet's condition, even though he was himself now sober. There was a noticeable tremor of the hands, a redness of the eye, a queasiness of the stomach, but he was sober, the smell of wine on his breath being old and stale from last night's wine. Admittedly he had been pulling a cork when a seaman shouted into his cabin that there was a frigate alongside, and then he vaguely remembered a conversation with someone on board a strange ship the previous night.

'Citizen Michelet reeks of fresh wine; in fact the front of his shirt is still damp from where he spilled it.'

Again, Renouf was puzzled because the Captain's voice was a straightforward observation and gave no indication of his view of Michelet's absurd behaviour. The Captain was in fact talking to Michelet through him, as though Michelet when drunk spoke a foreign language only understood by Renouf, who was expected to translate.

'Has the lieutenant brought his orders?'

Renouf relayed the question by repeating it and hurried across the cabin to collect them as Michelet wrested them from his pocket.

The strange captain opened both sheets, glanced over them to make sure they were the same as the others, and handed them to Renouf, who went back to return them to Michelet and made sure he accidentally stood on the man's foot, hoping the sharp pain would help sober him, but Michelet swore violently, and there was little doubt that the Captain saw what had happened. Nor did the episode help sober up Michelet, who now he was sitting properly in a chair looked pop-eyed, like a freshly-landed cod.

'When was the lieutenant last drunk while in command of the *Brutus*?'

What a question, Renouf thought, as he tried to think of an answer. Michelet was very drunk at least every other day, fine weather or foul, and slightly drunk all the time, and of course a captain was always in command of his ship, unless he was away on leave or official business. Because they had left Brest four months ago, Michelet must have been drunk one hundred and twenty times, if not more, because anniversaries of great victories, birthdays and even landfalls were good enough reasons for him to have extra celebrations. The worst of it was he forced some of his officers and petty officers to join him. One petty officer who came from Caen (which, being the centre of Calvados, meant the man was hardly a stranger to liquor) had finally gone off his head, leaping over the side one night screaming that the guns had broken loose and were running after him. That had been hushed up and described in the log as an accident in which the petty officer had been killed by a fall down a hatchway.

'I don't know, sir – I've never been on board his ship.'

'But you are his senior officer; the two ketches form a squadron.'

'Yes, Citizen, but . . .' he could not think of a 'but' and realized that Michelet's head was drooping; his chin was resting on his chest and he was dribbling, his whole body shaken every minute or two by a prodigious hiccup.

There was no point in trying to save Michelet now; anyone who was not only fool enough to come on board a senior officer's ship drunk but then allowed himself to fall asleep (or drop into a drunken stupor) while being questioned deserved whatever punishment came his way. But in all honesty it might have been me, Renouf thought.

Now the Captain was looking at Renouf as though he could read his thoughts and it was like staring at the muzzles of two cannon. That fool Michelet had scuttled the pair of them. If the Captain started questioning *Fructidor*'s men about their commanding officer there were two or three who would be only too willing to exaggerate and say Renouf drank too much, just because he had flogged them a few times. No doubt the same went for Michelet.

'Neither of you will be drinking wine again for a long time . . .'

He will have to court-martial us, and no court has yet sentenced a man not to drink, Renouf thought.

'. . . because of course you are now both prisoners of war.'

What was that? Renouf repeated the sentence to himself. It had been spoken clearly enough. The accent was indeed Parisian – 'because of course you are now both prisoners of war'.

'*Prisoners*, Citizen? How can we be *prisoners*?'

'This is a British ship of war.'

A joke! Not a very good one, but now was the time to laugh, and he had to laugh for Michelet as well. The Captain was not laughing. Not even smiling. In fact he looked serious and might even be sneering.

Now he was calling an order. Was it in English? *Mon Dieu*, it sounded like it! Renouf had heard English spoken by fishermen before the war. Through the door came the sentry, holding a cutlass and a pistol. Not a French design of pistol. And the man was gesturing that he should go to the door.

'This man is going to take you up on deck so that you can see this ship is flying British colours . . .'

'But, Citizen . . . Citizen, she is a French frigate! I recognize the class!'

'She *was*, until the British captured her in the West Indies. She is now the *Calypso*, one of His Britannic Majesty's frigates.'

'But ... but ... I can't believe it!'

'I commanded the ship that captured her, but just go up on deck with this Marine sentry. If you don't believe the evidence of our colours, you are free to speak to any man you see.'

Renouf heard the Captain give a quick order to the man, who took him by the arm after stuffing the pistol back in his belt, and led him out through the door and up the companionway. On deck the sun was just warming the planking and Renouf glanced aft, by now knowing what he would see. There were the British colours, the cloth barely moving in the early morning breeze. He looked across at each bomb ketch in turn and saw that they had not noticed the colours. The fools! Then he realized that although the frigate's port lids were not triced up, all the frigate's guns were manned. One broadside would destroy the *Fructidor*, the other broadside would reduce the *Brutus* to kindling.

This aristo of the Royal Navy had brought the *Calypso* into the bay in the darkness, anchored so that his ship was perfectly positioned between the two ketches, and then patiently waited for the Frenchmen to wake up. Renouf suddenly felt cold as he turned and walked back down to the cabin, followed by the sentry. This captain was a cool one. He must have confidence and a droll sense of humour. But if he intended to kill them all, obviously he would have fired broadsides at first light. Then, as Renouf went back to his chair and sat down again and looked up at the Englishman, he was not so sure.

He suddenly remembered why the name Ramage had seemed vaguely familiar. He had been thinking that he knew it from some French circumstance, but now he remembered the Royal Navy captain who had started off by rescuing that Italian woman aristo from somewhere close to here, and later in the West Indies had completely destroyed the convoy intended to relieve Fort de France, in Martinique.

Now it was coming back to him like a flood tide: that was where Ramage had captured this very frigate. Four frigates had been escorting the convoy and Ramage sank two and captured two. The cabin began to move in the most curious way, as though it was swaying, and then it went blurred, as though he was looking at it under water, and then night suddenly fell.

'Sentry!' Ramage called, 'this blessed Frenchman's just fainted. Get him out of here.'

CHAPTER FOUR

Ramage walked round the *Dix-Huit de Fructidor* with Aitken and was impressed by what he saw. The ketch was about sixty feet long, with both masts set well aft. The mainmast was almost amidships, the mizenmast halfway between it and the taffrail. Just forward of each mast, though, there was a circular hatchway, looking like an enormous cartwheel lying flat on the deck and inset several inches. On top of this, instead of spokes and an axle, there was a thick circular wooden disc, or bed, and on this bed was mounted a large mortar. The circular bed revolved on the hatchway, or wheel, so that the mortar could be trained all round the compass.

In fact great care had to be taken to make sure that a mortar shell did not damage any rigging or the masts, so that effectively each could be trained through about 130 degrees on either side – from twenty degrees ahead to 150 degrees on the quarter. Then neither the mortar shell itself nor the muzzle flash would do any damage.

Aitken pointed at the bed on which the mortar revolved. 'They must turn it with handspikes when they want to train it round.'

Ramage saw that the bed was constructed differently from the usual type built into a British bomb ketch because the French constructors had to adapt the already-completed hull of a merchant ship. Ramage looked at the paint on the woodwork and said: 'It's more likely that they lock the mortar on a bearing, probably forty-five degrees, and then to train it they turn the whole ship by putting a spring on the cable. That would be a more accurate way of aiming the gun. I wonder if this one has ever been fired in anger?'

The first-lieutenant shook his head doubtfully. 'I can't remember ever hearing of the French using bomb ketches – not in this way, anyway. This would be the first time. Interesting things, aren't they, sir?' he commented. 'Must be the very devil to elevate a mortar accurately.'

'You don't. It's like hitting a ball with a stick. You can hit it hard from underneath so that it goes high in the air but no great distance, or you can hit it on the side so it flies lower and flatter but covers the same horizontal distance. In each case you usually correct your aim with the second shot. It's the same with a mortar. You train the gun in the right direction with the spring on the cable – at a fort, for instance. Then, with the barrel pointing on the bearing of the fort you have to hurl the shell over the walls and into the middle. You do that by increasing or decreasing the amount of powder used to launch the shell. Like a child's peashooter, in fact. A boy points the peashooter in the general direction of his target and controls the parabola of the pea by blowing harder or softer.'

'So the most important items on board a bomb ketch are a good telescope to spot the fall of the shell and a large scoop to measure the powder,' Aitken said with a grin. 'As we have a bring-'em-near and scoops to spare it seems a pity that we have to scuttle these two vessels, sir.'

'It does,' Ramage said thoughtfully, 'but a bomb ketch's drawback is that it's not much use for anything else. These two go to windward like haystacks. They'd never keep us in sight for more than six hours, let alone stay in company, and we have a long way to go.'

Still, it shocked Aitken's thrifty soul to scuttle or burn two well-built ships. There was no chance of treating them as prizes – with Malta in French hands the nearest prize court was in Gibraltar, a thousand miles away, and both vessels would be recaptured long before reaching it because the Mediterranean was now swarming with French and Spanish ships.

''Tis a pity we can't use them to bombard somewhere,' Aitken said almost fretfully. 'Anyway, could we not have some practice, sir? I've never seen one o' these shells burst. I think it's knowledge I ought to have,' he added hopefully. 'And the men, too.'

'It's knowledge you ought to have already,' Ramage said with mock severity, having served in a bomb ketch for a brief three months when a young midshipman, although she had never fired a shot.

'I know, sir,' Aitken said contritely. 'I was hoping that . . .'

'You're like a child with a new toy,' Ramage said amiably, going to the ship's side and gesturing to Aitken to climb down into the waiting cutter so that they could return to the *Calypso*. One of the few advantages of being the senior officer was that you were the last to enter and

65

the first to leave a boat, and as he had always been impatient, he welcomed promotion.

Back in his cabin and sprawled in the one comfortable chair, his sword and hat tossed on the settee, Ramage quietly and amiably cursed Aitken. The Scot was a fine seaman, extremely brave, with a whimsical sense of humour and an extraordinary devotion to Ramage which had recently led him to decline the command of a frigate (and thus promotion to the post list) so that he could stay as the first-lieutenant of the *Calypso*. But this product of Perth – of Dunkeld, anyway, which was just to the north, alongside the Tay – had unintentionally jabbed a finger on a tender spot.

Since he had ordered the Marine sentry to drag Renouf away after he had fainted, Ramage had been trying to make up his mind about the two bomb ketches. Having read the French orders, he now knew what they were supposed to be doing, and all the Frenchmen were on board the *Calypso*, guarded by Marines. Even the *Brutus*'s commanding officer had eventually been sobered up with the help of several buckets of sea water hurled by a couple of gleeful British seamen.

The French plans could be wrecked by burning or scuttling the ketches, but for the moment young Paolo was temporarily in command of the *Fructidor*, striding up and down the tiny quarterdeck in his second-best uniform, dirk hanging at his waist, telescope tucked under his arm, and trying to keep his prize crew of half a dozen men busy coiling ropes and swabbing the decks. Aitken had forbidden him to start the men scrubbing and holystoning, though the planking was as stained as the floor of a bankrupt wine shop.

The *Calypso*'s new fourth-lieutenant, William Martin, was temporarily prizemaster of the *Brutus*, and he too had been dissuaded from setting his men to work to remove a year or two's grease and wine stains. Ramage thought that Martin was settling in well – apart from his confounded flute. It was hardly surprising that his nickname was 'blower'; he must have lungs like a blacksmith's bellows.

'Blower' Martin had joined the ship at Gibraltar, replacing a bag o' wind called Benn who had taken only the voyage from Jamaica to the Rock to decide that the *Calypso* was not for him. It was not really the poor fellow's fault . . . Benn, something of a sea lawyer, had been one of the admiral's favourites in Jamaica, and being promoted from a midshipman in the flagship to fourth-lieutenant (and no one's favourite) in a frigate had been a shock.

Ramage still missed Baker. When they had captured the island of Curaçao he had a good set of officers: William Aitken was first-lieutenant, Baker second, Wagstaffe third and young Kenton fourth, with Renwick commanding the Marine detachment. Considering that the *Calypso* herself had not been engaged, but only a boarding party, the casualties had been heavy – himself bowled over with a musket ball in the left forearm and a scalp wound, Renwick with a ball in the right shoulder, and Baker killed outright. So Aitken had remained first-lieutenant, he had made Wagstaffe second, Kenton third, and this elegant young nincompoop Benn had been sent across from the *Queen* by the commander-in-chief as the new fourth. He was, he made it quite clear to all and sundry, one of Admiral Foxe-Foote's favourites.

Ramage was not sure what had gone on in the gunroom during the *Calypso*'s Atlantic crossing, but Benn had been quick to ask for permission to leave the ship on arriving in Gibraltar, and Aitken, when asked by Ramage about what was a very unusual request, merely smiled and

said he supported it. So Admiral Foxe-Foote's favourite
had left the ship and thrown himself on the mercy of the
port admiral at Gibraltar in what Ramage soon discovered
was, for Benn, a very unwise move.

When Ramage had reported to the port admiral next
day and asked for a replacement, the admiral had bellowed (he rarely spoke in anything less): 'Count yourself
lucky to have got rid of that lapdog of Admiral Foote's.
Wonder you accepted him. Still, your fellows made his life
a misery – and now I'm landed with him. There's no
commanding officer I dislike enough to inflict with him, so
he goes back to England as a passenger by the next ship
and Their Lordships can find him a berth – if they con-
firm his promotion. Now you want a replacement, eh?'

Ramage had agreed politely that the *Calypso* stood in
need of a fourth-lieutenant.

'What happened to your original one?' the admiral
demanded.

'Promoted to third, sir.'

'What happened to the third, then?'

'Promoted to second.'

'And the second?'

'Killed in action, sir.'

'Hmm. So you can't be as bad as your late fourth-
lieutenant implied. He told me you were always changing
officers. I'm asking because you are going to be landed
with one of *my* favourites. He's a good lad, passed for
lieutenant five months ago, plays a flute – '

'A *flute*, sir?'

'Yes, you know, a hollow stick with holes drilled in it.
You blow into it with your mouth like this.' The admiral
gave a passable imitation of an old dowager sucking a
bitter lemon. 'Very tuneful.'

'Er – I'm just wondering, sir,' Ramage said warily, 'if

this young man really is suited to a frigate: after all, it – '

The admiral roared with laughter and slapped the table in front of him with a hand the size of a leg of mutton. 'Damme, Ramage, if you don't have the sheepish look of someone trying to jilt the parson's daughter! Don't fret – this lad's a favourite o' mine because he's good and because his father is the master shipwright at the Chatham yard. He built his own skiff when he was eight and rowed all the way to Sheerness on its maiden voyage.' The admiral looked directly at Ramage. 'I have fresh orders for you from Their Lordships, and I know what they are. I want you to take this lad because he can learn a lot from you – if he lives long enough.'

'Those sort of orders, sir?'

'What? Oh no, I'm thinking of the lad. He's too keen, if anything. You've learned already there are two kinds of keen officers – those who get killed in a blaze of glory, and those who *survive* in a blaze of glory. I see new hair growing over a pink patch on your scalp, there are a couple of scars over your right eyebrow, and you're holding your left arm stiffly, so you've been wounded a few times – unless you were careless when getting out of some trollop's bed. I'd say you haven't made up your mind yet – or fate hasn't, rather – exactly which of the two you are. If you survive, and young "Blower" Martin does, too, I hope he'll go a long way with you.'

'Blower' Martin had since proved to be a very capable and popular young officer: his nickname was intended to tease because he could make a flute do almost everything except actually talk, and many an evening as the *Calypso* struggled eastward along the Spanish coast against light head winds young Martin had started playing with perhaps a couple of people listening, and ended up with nearly every off-watch seaman in the ship squatting nearby, perched on guns or just lying back on the deck planking. Sometimes they danced, applauding themselves between tunes.

Thin-faced with wavy brown hair, slightly built and nervous and jerky in manner, Martin seemed out of place in uniform – until you watched him on deck. His eyes were never still. They would run along the horizon, up to the luffs of the topsails, along sheets and braces, to the compass card . . . the restless eyes of a true seaman, someone unlikely ever to be caught by a white squall, a badly trimmed sail, a stuck compass card, or an enemy ship sneaking over the horizon. Now, after not more than a few days, he had his own command for a day or so.

Like Paolo, he had to make the best of a prize at anchor, but that would be exciting enough. Ramage recalled the first time he had ever been sent off in command of a prize as a young midshipman. For a few hours he felt the greatest sense of freedom that he could ever remember – but the feeling had lasted only until sunset. Then the prospect of a long, dark night had brought doubts and fears . . . confidence had vanished, black clouds on the horizon looked like the outriders of the most terrible storm, the sea had suddenly become vast and the prize had shrunk. His confidence returned with daylight, and he found he had learned his first real lesson in leadership – that it was a lonely business, but no more difficult in the dark.

Lonely, but exhilarating: here he was sitting in an armchair in the coach of a frigate he had captured and now commanded, and he was back in the Mediterranean with the kind of orders he had always dreamed of getting. They said, in effect, that for four months you sail round the Mediterranean and sink, burn or destroy everything that presents itself . . .

An idea flitted across his mind and he took out his keys as he went to the desk and removed the canvas bag in the locked drawer. The neck of the bag had several brass grommets worked into it, so that the line passing through them could close it up. Inside was a small ingot of lead weighing three or four pounds – enough to sink the bag and its contents if it was thrown over the side in an emergency. Some captains preferred a wooden box suitably weighted and drilled with holes, but he liked a bag: it was easier to throw and more certain to sink. There was the story of a captain who threw the box containing all his secret papers into the sea but forgot to lock it so that the lid popped open when the lead weight sank it just as the enemy boarding party approached. The signal book, the private signals for three months and his order book had all floated to the surface, where they were fished out by the French. The captain had been court-martialled as soon as the French exchanged him, and dismissed the service. The Admiralty did not give you a second chance where secret papers were concerned . . .

He took out his orders and read them again. They had been worded very carefully by Their Lordships, who knew only too well that most officers went over them searching for loopholes which would give an excuse for doing either more or less than was written. Ramage considered that there were two aspects to a set of orders – the wording and the spirit. You could ignore the precise wording and act in the spirit, though if you failed you were court-martialled on the precise wording. He ran a finger along the appropriate lines . . . yes, these orders had a loophole.

An appropriate word, loophole: it meant the slot or

loop in the wall of a fortress through which you could
fire down at the enemy, whether using a bow and arrow
or a musket. Or, in this case, a bomb ketch. The orders
had a loophole big enough for two bomb ketches to sail
through because Their Lordships referred only to 'the
enemy' without specifying (as they usually did) 'enemy
ships and vessels'. He folded the single sheet, slid it back
into the canvas bag, pulled the drawstring tight, replaced
the bag in the drawer and turned the key.

'Pass the word for Mr Aitken,' he called to the sentry.
It was time for the *Calypso* to sail under French colours
again – or at least stay at anchor under them. There was
time for them all to learn more about firing mortars.
French shells, French powder . . . plenty of target practice
at no expense to Their Lordships; the gunner would have
no forms to fill in though this would not stop the miserable
wretch grumbling; he grumbled in the same way that a
damaged cask dripped . . . There were no villages within
ten miles of this stretch of beach; the nearest French were
probably at the little fort of La Rocchette – if they bothered to garrison it. There might be a few Italian fishermen
or hunters in the area, but whoever they were, French or
Italians, they would not become alarmed at seeing ships
with French flags firing on to deserted beaches in what was
obviously target practice. A passing cavalry might pause
and watch the fall of shot, and no doubt comment on the
Navy's skill with mortars, or lack of it.

Lieutenant William Martin was just twenty-three years old,
celebrating his birthday on the day he joined the *Calypso*.
He celebrated it quietly, keeping the fact to himself, because no one in his right mind joining a new ship as the
most junior lieutenant would announce it was his birthday;
that would be asking for everything in the history of gun-

room practical jokes to be played on him.

Twenty-three. Eight years at sea as a captain's servant, then midshipman, and then he had passed for lieutenant. Not a brilliant pass (not that they gave marks) but he was one of only three that passed out of the nine hopefuls presenting themselves at Gibraltar to the specially convened board of four captains. All four captains knew his father; all would no doubt be taking their ships into Chatham at some time or another, requiring work done in the dockyard. All would no doubt expect favours from his father as a result of passing his son.

All four, William Martin thought with satisfaction, would be disappointed, because he had not told his father their names. He was not ungrateful, but when he discovered from the other midshipmen the kind of questions they had been asked and the answers they had given, he knew he would have passed whether or not he was the son of the master shipwright at Chatham. None of the captains had offered him a berth as a lieutenant, so he owed them nothing. He had had to wait another three years, serving as a master's mate, until the *Calypso* gave him a chance and now he was serving with Mr Ramage he was prepared to admit the wait had been worth it. They had not done anything very much up to now, but the gunroom gossip was that Mr Ramage's orders were to make as much trouble in the Mediterranean as possible in four months, which was like giving a bull his own china shop.

Peter Kenton, the third-lieutenant, although a year younger had served with Mr Ramage in the West Indies and just about worshipped him. So did Wagstaffe, the second. Mr Aitken was remote and did not mix much and certainly rarely revealed his feelings unless he was angry. But it was obvious that he respected the Captain, and Mr Aitken was the kind of man that most people in turn respected. Yet Mr Ramage was hot-tempered, impatient, had a caustic tongue, and obviously did not stand fools gladly. The lads told some remarkable stories about Admiral Foxe-Foote, the commander-in-chief at Jamaica and a fool among fools.

Apparently Mr Ramage had rescued an Italian marchesa from somewhere nearby, and Paolo Orsini, the *Calypso*'s only midshipman, was her nephew. Well, Orsini was a bright and eager youngster. Some of the men who had helped rescue her were still serving with Mr Ramage and, according to Southwick (who also knew her), these seamen had formed themselves into a special guard, without Mr Ramage knowing it, and now they also kept an eye on young Orsini, half because they knew how upset the Marchesa would be if anything happened to the boy, but also because they seemed to regard the Captain, the Marchesa and Orsini as a family to which they owed their loyalty. It sounded a bit like some Caesar with a – what was it called, he had learned it at school? Praetorian guard? Something like that.

It was all a long way from Rochester. This stretch of Tuscan coast was beautiful, with the big rounded hills becoming more pointed and mountainous as they went farther inland. He had grown up amid the flat marshy land on either side of the River Medway; he had been a boy of the saltings, trapping wild duck over the marshes and bringing home sea kale which they were thankful to boil as vegetables, because there was never enough money in a family that included three brothers and four sisters.

His father had let him roam in the dockyard; he had watched many a 74-gun ship grow from a baulk of timber until it was a great thing of beauty and menace sliding down the ways to the cheers of hundreds of people, launched with a bottle of port wine. Frigates, sloops – aye, even some bomb ketches – had been built and launched at Chatham, but no launching had excited him more than that of the *Bellerophon*. There was, of course, a 74-gun ship called the *Bellerophon*, better known to her men as the Billy Ruff'n, but his *Bellerophon* had been seven feet long, a cross between a punt and a skiff. He had made her from scraps of timber and copper rivets and roves which he had cadged from the shipwrights.

His father and the shipwrights had prepared a surprise for him: they had taken over one of the vacant building slips, carried the skiff to it overnight and fitted it on to a small, weighted carriage which, when a line was jerked, would run down into the water and launch the skiff. One Saturday morning at the midday break he launched the *Bellerophon*, tossing a tankard of good Kentish ale over her bow as he named her, and going red with embarrassment as she slid down the ways and the shipwrights gave him and the skiff each three cheers and a tiger. And then, with the *Bellerophon* floating in the water, he had suddenly realized that his father was still standing there with his men and they were all grinning. It was then he remembered he had built the boat but forgotten to make oars.

Then, from behind a nearby shed, a shipwright had brought a pair of oars and given them to his father, who had presented them to him amid even more cheers. They were beautiful oars, made from ash and perfectly balanced, with strips of copper sheathing protecting the tips of the blades. With that he had rowed round to Hoo, thankful that it was nearly high water so that he could get the skiff up to the stretch of gritty beach in front of their house – at low water several hundred yards of smelly mud separated them from the river – and his mother, admiring the boat, had agreed that next day he could miss church and take half a loaf and a piece of cheese and row down the river towards Sheerness.

His eldest brother, in a burst of enthusiasm, had said he could borrow his gun and have some heavy shot so that he could try for a duck or two. Early on Sunday, the Medway still misty and the sun not yet up, he had rowed out, passing the old and new ships of the line, frigates and transports lying on moorings, and the ancient forts of red brick and of grey stone. He had planned to start off just before the top of the tide and carry the ebb all the way, resting to eat his bread and cheese at slack water, and start back with the first of the flood. And that was what he had done. He had rowed along the high-banked channels of the saltings and often let the ebb drift the boat along – so that it slowly grounded a few yards from some ducks dabbling away, tails in the air, in their eternal hunt for food. Slowly he had collected his trophies – the banks seemed to muffle the heavy blam of the gun firing, so that within fifteen minutes or so ducks had settled again. By the time the flood took him back to Hoo he had seven plump duck lying on the bottom boards, and a heap of fresh sea kale to go with them. His eldest brother's only comment as he took the gun back was that he might have plucked the birds while he waited for the tide to turn . . .

Although he had enjoyed rowing his skiff, he had found equal pleasure in going over the slight rise of hill to Hoo church on a Thursday afternoon to hear the organist practising for the Sunday service : there he had discovered his love for music. The organist, at first surprised and then pleased to find the young boy always sitting quietly at the back of the church, had taught him to read music and, guessing he would go to sea as soon as he was old enough, suggested that the flute was the instrument for him to learn. They had discussed the violin – but varying climates

and long voyages, humidity and high temperatures would
warp the wood and snap the strings, and he would never
be able to carry enough as spares. The flute was small,
easily carried, durable and, more important, it made pleas-
ing music. So he had learned the flute and he had gone to
sea . . . and here he was standing on the quarterdeck of a
French bomb ketch, a commission officer by the age of
twenty-three.

More important was the fact that he was one of Captain Ramage's officers. Few captains had had more of their
actions described in the *London Gazette,* and in his imagination Martin saw himself back in the old house at Hoo,
his father listening to his exploits, and he would be able
to say casually, for the benefit of his brothers, and with
an airy wave of the hand: 'But you probably read about
that in the *Gazette* . . .'

Martin glanced round the *Brutus*'s deck and saw that
his half-dozen men had done everything possible to tidy
up the ketch, given that the first-lieutenant had forbidden
any scrubbing or polishing of the corroded brasswork
with brick dust. That was a clear indication that Captain
Ramage intended to scuttle or burn both ships, and although it was disappointing for a young lieutenant who
could reasonably have expected to be given the command
if the *Brutus* was being sent back to Gibraltar as a prize,
it made sense. There were so many French ships about
these days that they would be lucky to cover five hundred miles before being captured . . .

On the other side of the *Calypso,* whose gunport lids
were still closed and whose guns had their muzzles sealed
by tompions with canvas covers, or aprons, over the flint-
locks to keep out the damp of the night, the *Fructidor*
was a ship of frustration as far as Paolo Orsini, a midshipman in the Navy of His Britannic Majesty, was concerned.

His half-dozen men, working under Thomas Jackson, had
sluiced the decks with the only deckwash pump in the
ship, one whose leathers were shrunk and splitting from
disuse and needed wiping carefully with tallow before
they could be induced to suck, let alone pump. They had
coiled all the falls of the halyards, and then whipped some
ropes' ends. More tallow had been wiped into the pawls
of the windlass; a bored William Stafford had worked a
couple of Turk's heads on the tiller using line he had
found in the French bosun's store. That was all Mr Aitken
would allow; he said it was a waste of time and effort to
do anything else with the ships.

Paolo put down his telescope by the binnacle and
walked to the forward mortar. It was a strange weapon —
so stubby, like a cannon with most of the barrel sawn off,
and the trunnions at the breech. The inside of the barrel,
the bore (the first section in which the shell was slid), was
like the inside of a bottle with its bottom knocked off to
form the muzzle. The gunner said the gun was the equivalent of the British 10-inch sea service mortar, and certainly
with a muzzle ten inches in diameter it was a formidable-
looking weapon. He peered down the bore and could just
see where it narrowed into the chamber at the bottom, like
the neck of a bottle. That held the gunpowder charge
which would launch the mortar shell into the great parabola that should end on the enemy's head.

The whole mortar was fitted on to something that could
be mistaken for a solid cartwheel lying on its side. He
had been down below and seen how this great wheel – in
effect the base – was supported by under-deck stanchions
which spread the weight of the mortar and the shock of its
recoil over several extra floors and stringers, and the deck
beams were twice as thick as normal.

The 'cartwheel' had the mortar bed resting on it. This was a thick but flat rectangular wooden block with a hole in the middle of the underside. This fitted on to what would be the hub if the base had been a real wheel. A thick pintle or axle dropped down into a hole that went through the bed and into the base, so that the bed could revolve and the mortar be aimed.

The mortar was almost obscene, Paolo thought, like a fat and short pig that could only grunt. It was a stubby cast-iron pot with short, solid trunnions sticking out sideways at the bottom which acted as the axle when the gun was elevated. The trunnions were held down by metal clamps (called 'cap squares', although they were semi-circular) which stopped the mortar running wild when it fired.

The piece of timber which could slide back and forth in the slot under the mortar, and which had a saucer-like depression where the underside of the mortar barrel rested, was called the bed bolster. You levered up the muzzle with handspikes until it was at the right elevation, then you pulled on the two ropes and slid the bed bolster underneath until the barrel was supported. After that he was not sure what happened, so he had borrowed the gunner's notebook, although the handwriting was very difficult to read. He sat down on the mortar bed and concentrated.

He had not been reading for more than ten minutes when Thomas Jackson came along and inspected the gun.

'Looks as though it'd go right through the deck the first time you fired it,' the American commented. 'Still, there are three hundred shells for this one, and three hundred for the other – ' he gestured aft to the other mortar. 'The French presumably had faith in it.'

Paolo looked at the sandy-haired, thin-faced American,

and his jaw dropped with dismay. 'Do you mean you wouldn't want to fire this if the Captain gave you permission?'

'I'd sooner he gave me a direct order, sir,' Jackson grinned, teasing the boy. 'I've never had anything to do with these things. Always fired guns that shot horizontally. This is more like tossing a grenade over a wall and hoping to hit something you can't see.'

'*Exactly!*' Paolo exclaimed. 'You can't do *that* with an ordinary gun. If your enemy is behind the thick walls of a castle, or on the other side of the hill, you can't attack him with a cannon because it fires straight – more or less straight, anyway. With the mortar you can hurl shells down on him. *Explosive* shells.'

'Yes,' Jackson agreed as Stafford and Rossi walked up to listen to the conversation, 'but the fuse that makes the shell explode inside the enemy's walls might also make it burst inside the mortar before you can fire it.'

Paolo shrugged his shoulders with magnificent indifference. 'You might slip and fall from a topsail yard, you might get a hernia, a roundshot *might* knock your head off the next time we go into action . . .'

'Agreed, sir,' Jackson said amiably, 'but that's not to say I'm going to jump off a topsail yard deliberately, get a hernia, or stand and invite the enemy to knock my head off with a roundshot. When you play around with these mortars, though, you light the fuse in the shell, and if someone's made a mistake in the length or anything, it makes a big bang you never hear!'

'How heavy the shell?' Rossi enquired.

Paolo ran his finger down the page of the notebook, turned over the page and then said: 'The gunner says this is about the same as the British 10-inch. And . . .' The tip of his tongue was protruding with the concentration.

'. . . Ah, yes. "Weight of shell when fired" – *Mama mia!* It is ninety-three pounds – nearly a hundredweight! That's the hollow cast-iron ball and the powder inside.'

'How much powder in it?'

'Only seven pounds.'

'Seven?' exclaimed Rossi. 'Why, that is nothing!'

Jackson said : 'It doesn't need much to blast the shell casing into thousands of pieces. It's these splinters that do the damage.'

' 'Ow far will it toss a shell, then?' Stafford asked, peering down the bore like a farmer inspecting a horse's teeth.

'Wait,' Paolo said, consulting the notebook. 'It depends on the amount of powder in the charge. That's obvious, but as far as I can see, it's easier to use more or less powder than to change the elevation of the gun.'

Stafford slapped the side of the mortar. 'I should fink so; must weigh a ton!'

'One and a half,' Paolo said, having just found some details in a neatly-written table. 'Ah, here we are. First you must understand about the shell. It is round as you know, but it is cast so that it has the two carrying handles and the filling and fuse hole at the top.' He read on a moment and said : 'You might well ask why the shell falls the right way up – with the fuse at the top, because it might fall upside down and break off the fuse.'

'We might well ask, sir,' Rossi agreed politely. 'Why does it fall with the fuse upside down?'

'No, no,' Paolo said patiently. 'Why it falls with the fuse uppermost.'

'Yes,' Rossi said, having lost track of the conversation, 'that is most interesting, sir. But how lights the fuse, then?'

Paolo looked up in surprise and lost his place in the

notebook as Stafford and Jackson started laughing. 'Why the laughing?'

'We were waiting to hear why the shell falls the right way up after it's been fired, sir,' Jackson said.

'Ah, yes. Well, although the shell casing looks like a circular ball from the outside, in fact the bottom is much thicker, and therefore heavier, so it drops first.'

'Ah,' Rossi said. 'I was going to ask you about that, *signor*. But supposing you fire the shell and bang, it falls in the enemy fort with the fuse at the top and burning; what stops the enemy throwing a bucket of water at it and putting out the fuse?'

'Wait,' Paolo said, 'let me read more. There must be a reason why that will not work.'

'I can fink o' one good reason,' Stafford said emphatically. ''Oo'd be daft enough to walk up to a smoking shell with a bucket o' water? Not me! I'd duck down art of the way.'

There were two or three minutes' silence while Paolo read through the pages, occasionally grunting to indicate an interesting point, but saying nothing, obviously absorbed by the mental picture of a shell lying in the castle courtyard with smoking fuse.

'Here we are,' he exclaimed triumphantly. 'The fuse burns at the rate of an inch in four seconds and forty-eight parts.'

'Forty-eight parts of what?' Stafford asked.

Paolo looked appealingly at Jackson, who shrugged his shoulders. 'Of a second, sir? Most likely a second is divided into a hundred parts. It's the sort of thing they do,' he added darkly, knowing the unreliability of the Board of Ordnance.

'Well, it's not very long, is it . . . about half a second.

Anyway, you know how long the shell takes to land, so you cut the fuse to the . . .'

'How do you know how long it takes?' Rossi asked.

'*Accidente!* You have it here in the tables!' Paolo said crossly. 'Now just listen. Just suppose your target is 680 yards away. You elevate the mortar to forty-five degrees. Then you put in a charge of one pound of powder; then you cut the fuse to burst ten seconds after you fire the mortar.'

'Why ten seconds?' Rossi persisted.

'*Mama mia*, Rossi! Because it takes ten seconds for the shell to fly through the air and land on a target 680 yards away. That means it's no good having a bucket of water.'

'Who cuts the fuse?' Jackson asked.

Paolo had just reached the page giving details of the fuse. 'The fuse,' he said, like a priest reading a liturgy, 'is a conical tube made of beech, willow or some other dry wood. It is open at the top and at the pointed end. So it is filled with a mixture of sulphur, saltpetre and mealed powder – yes,' he said quickly, anticipating Rossi's question, 'obviously you keep a finger over the hole in the pointed end while you're doing it. Then each end – each hole, in other words – is covered with a composition of tallow and beeswax or pitch, to keep out the damp. When the fuse is put into the shell, the little end is cut off or opened, but the big end is left closed until just before firing.

'So, starting at the beginning, the shell itself is loaded with powder through the fuse hole in the casing. Then the fuse is inserted so that an inch and a half comes out beyond the fuse hole. Protrudes, it means,' he explained, proud of his English. 'You must make sure there is nothing to prevent the fire from the fuse exploding the powder in the shell – make sure the little end is clear, in other words.

'So there you are,' he said proudly, closing the note-book.

'Is all right if the enemy is 680 yards away,' Rossi grumbled. 'But suppose he is *più distante*? And the mortar, she is not even loaded yet.'

'Ah, yes,' Paolo said cheerfully, turning back to the middle pages of the notebook. 'Now, we know about the shell and the fuse. Now we have to hurl it at the enemy so that it bursts at his feet.' He waved a hand dramatically and slapped the wooden bed.

'*Their* feet,' Jackson said.

'Yes, *their* feet. First we put in the charge. Now,' he said hurriedly, to forestall Rossi, 'we will work on an elevation of forty-five degrees. Note that, forty-five degrees. Then we vary the charge to suit the range. The amount of powder can be critical – for example, one pound four ounces of powder gives us 892 yards and yet only another eight ounces gives us an extra 300 yards. I'll choose a straightforward one,' he said with a sharp look at Rossi. 'Here we are : three pounds of powder gives us a range of 1,945 yards and the time of flight – the time it takes the shell to land after it's been fired, Rossi – is twenty-one seconds and ten parts.'

'The fuse in the shell,' Rossi said casually, hoping he had now caught out the young midshipman, for a Genovese should always be able to get the better of a Tuscan. 'How long should that be so we burst at the enemy's feet?'

Paulo ran his finger across the table. 'Four inches and seventy parts.'

'Parts of what?'

'Seventy parts of a hundred parts of an inch,' Paolo said triumphantly.

'What is the maximum range?' Jackson asked.

'Well, the maximum given in another table for a 10-inch mortar with a different elevation is 3,821 yards, using a twelve-pound charge. The shell takes exactly half a minute to land . . .'

'I wonder if this bed –' Jackson pointed to the one on which the mortar was mounted ' – would take the recoil from a twelve-pound charge?'

'We do not have to worry about that,' Paolo said firmly. 'We are learning about mortars in general. So we have the shell filled and the fuse filled. Now we must load the mortar. First we put in the powder charge after carefully measuring it, and then a wad. We beat that down hard with the rammer – that is most important: it is under-lined here. Then we put in the shell, holding it with the two handles at the top – which of course means the fuse is uppermost.

'Now we are ready to fire. An officer points the mortar or gives the inclination. That means it is first trained and then elevated, using handspikes to lift it. The bed bolster is then slid in to keep the barrel at the correct angle. The top of the fuse is cut open – you remember it has a cover of beeswax and tallow – and the mortar is primed with the finest powder.

'Two seamen each take a slow match – these have been burning while hanging over water in the match tub, of course – and wind it round a linstock and stand ready. At the order, one seaman lights the fuse in the shell, and quickly gets clear while the other fires the mortar.'

'And away she goes,' Stafford commented. 'Our shell goes up high in the hair like a lark or a smokin' cabbage with the fuse fizzing away, and then it lands wiv a thump at the enemy's feet. A thump which puts out the fuse, sir!' he added as an afterthought.

'Oh no it doesn't,' Paolo said sternly. 'There's a note

here about that. The fuse burns in air, water or in the earth. No thump is going to put it out.'

'Supposing you don't want to fire an explosive shell?' Jackson said. 'Supposing you were on land and being attacked by a great mass of men? I've heard something about using shot.'

Paolo read through three more pages and then said triumphantly: 'Here it is, *pound* shot. Each shot weighs – well, of course, a pound. You use a two-and-a-half-pound charge of powder, and on top of that you put a wooden base. Then you put in one hundred of the pound shot. They're in a bag, I suppose – it doesn't say. Nor does it give maximum ranges. But just think, if the range was 2,000 yards. Imagine being hit with a shot weighing one pound which has just spent the last twenty seconds being hurled through the air. And for the last half,' he added with an authoritative note in his voice, 'with the force of gravity added . . .'

'Yes, there wouldn't be much velocity left from the charge,' Jackson said. 'In fact I should think it would be like being hit with a one-pound shot dropped on your head from a cliff a thousand yards high. Less, because you have to allow for the curve.'

'The parabola,' Paolo said. ' "Amplitude of the parabola" – that's what they call the range in these notes.'

'They would,' said Stafford sourly. 'Makes gunners sound more important and a mortar sound more dangerous to the enemy. But it still sounds to me like trying to kill your neighbour by 'eaving bricks over 'is wall – an' you don't even know if 'e's at 'ome.'

Rossi suddenly pointed up at the *Calypso*'s masts. 'They're hoisting a signal.'

CHAPTER FIVE

Ramage watched through the glass as the men in the *Calypso*'s red cutter heaved a cask overboard and half a dozen of them leapt into the surf to roll it up the beach. The big cask bobbed and spun in the waves, occasionally knocking a man over as it was pushed towards the line of surf where the sand started. The sun was glaring now, sparkling off the waves and almost blinding along the sand, which was nearly white along this stretch of the coast.

Fifty yards inland the juniper bushes began, then came the umbrella pines, a band of dark green, mushroom-topped trees forming a small elevated plateau. Even out here he could hear the whirring of the cicadas above the lapping of water against the hull, the faint whine of the wind in the rigging, and the slapping of the waves breaking on the beach. The smell of the pines was sharp and clean, the distant buzz of the cicadas continuous and punctuated by the occasional agitated squawking of the terns and the chattering of sandpipers striding along the water's edge like self-important midshipmen. He was once again back in Tuscany with Jackson and Stafford because charcoal was being made nearby, a heavier smell competing with the astringent pines. The *pinetas*, the charcoal smoke, the wash and gurgle of waves sluicing the sand . . .

He jerked back from his memories and looked through the telescope. The men from the red cutter had rolled their cask up the slope of the sand on to the level section beyond, halfway to the pines. Now they were levering it upright. He swung the telescope round to look beyond the *Fructidor*, where men from the green cutter were still struggling to get their cask up the sloping beach.

Each cask was exactly fifteen hundred yards away from its nearest ketch – or would be once it was set upright. Kenton had stood on the beach ahead of one ketch and paced out fifteen hundred yards, putting a marker in the sand, then he had done the same for the other. Now each ketch had a target 1,500 yards away, the one for the *Brutus* to larboard, the one for the *Fructidor* (he refused to use the whole name) to starboard. Fifteen hundred yards plus the extra two hundred yards or so distance from the ketches to the beach. Pythagoras.

In going over the loading, aiming and firing of mortars with Wagstaffe and Kenton, he had not reminded them of the two hundred yards. Both lieutenants had been given the gunner's notebook to make whatever notes they wanted from the range tables. Both had been told to use up to twelve shells, each charged with four pounds of powder. Ramage had emphasized that they were not to rush; the winner would be the ketch that smashed the cask with the fewest shells, not in the shortest time. From time to time Wagstaffe and Kenton were to go down below and inspect the under-deck stanchions and bracing supporting the mortar beds: he wanted no accidents. The French obviously had confidence in the way they had converted these galliots but . . . Still, Renouf had handed over his own list of ranges and charges which corresponded to those in the gunner's notes, and Renouf had been given the impression that he would be back on board his ketch, probably in irons, when the mortar was fired, so he would have been vociferous in expressing doubts if he had had them.

Ramage had, in effect, arranged a competition between

Wagstaffe and Kenton in which each had an assistant and team: Wagstaffe had the new fourth-lieutenant, William Martin, and his prize crew; Kenton would have Paolo, Jackson, Stafford, Rossi and three more seamen. Wagstaffe had gone over to the *Brutus* confident that he and Martin would easily beat Kenton – and an apprehensive Kenton had gone off to the *Fructidor* without realizing what allies he had waiting for him. Only Ramage knew that Paolo had been studying the gunner's notebook for a couple of hours that morning out of sheer curiosity, long before Ramage had decided on the shooting contest.

Predictably, there had been a great deal of grumbling among the rest of the men in the *Calypso* when they heard about the contest: they wanted Ramage to call for volunteers or, better still, put the opened pages of the muster book in front of a blindfolded man and let him use a sail needle to pick names – a modern version of the old 'pricking' as a way of choosing at random. Each mortar needed six men, so trying to choose a dozen from the *Calypso*'s two hundred was more unfair than saying arbitrarily that the two prize crews would also be the mortar crews.

Aitken had wanted to use both mortars in each ketch, but Ramage viewed the aftermost one with suspicion: if anything went wrong with the shell there was the risk that it would carry away the mainmast or mizenmast, whereas there was little chance of anything being carried away if a shell fired by the forward mortar ran wild like a winged partridge.

The green cutter's men had their cask at the mark left by Kenton and were levering it upright. They stood back to look at it as they slapped their hands against their thighs to get rid of the sand. Now they were running back into the sea and struggling out to the green cutter, whose crew were backing water as the coxswain shouted impatiently. One after another the cask men climbed on board and while the last one was being hauled up, the cutter started making its way back to *Fructidor*. Each ketch would have a cutter lying astern on a long painter, just in case of accidents.

Southwick came to join him, mopping his face with a large red handkerchief. 'Damned hot,' he grumbled. 'The temperature may be lower than the West Indies, but there's no trade wind to keep us cool.'

Ramage closed the telescope and turned to the master. 'You make the same complaint at the same time every day,' he said unsympathetically. 'You'll just have to remember you're back in the Mediterranean now. It has its compensations: there isn't a British admiral within a thousand miles, and we increase the distance every day. Nearly every day, anyway.'

The master grinned and waved vaguely towards the distant hills and mountains. 'I'm not complaining, sir. The nights are cooler, we'll dodge this year's hurricane season, and we've a better chance of seeing some action.'

'But we might face a Mediterranean winter – or even the Channel,' Ramage reminded him.

Southwick nodded and then looked first at one ketch and then the other. 'Which are you betting on, sir?'

'Neither,' Ramage said. 'I'm just putting up the prize guinea for the winning team.'

'I'm putting my money on the *Brutus*. Wagstaffe's a smart fellow, and this young Martin seems wide awake. I'm afraid Orsini's mathematics are so bad he won't be much help to Kenton, who's a long way from being a mathematical genius himself.'

'After the first shell, I should have thought a good eye for distance was more important,' Ramage said mildly.

Southwick shrugged his shoulders. 'Blessed if I know, sir,' he admitted. 'I've never served in a bomb ketch; never even seen one fire a round.'

'Nor me,' Ramage admitted. 'I spent three months in one as a midshipman, but we never fired the mortars. That's one of the reasons why I want to see what happens.'

Southwick looked at him knowingly from beneath bushy eyebrows. 'Aye,' he said enthusiastically, 'it's the kind of information that might come in useful one day.'

'One never knows,' Ramage said as he turned to the bosun and ordered: 'Hoist that signal now.'

He had been very careful in his instructions to the two lieutenants to ensure that they fired alternately, so that he could observe the fall of the shells. It was, as Southwick said, the kind of information that might come in useful one day – if you did everything wrong and Their Lordships put you in command of a bomb ketch . . . Officers did not have to accept such a command, but if the alternative, as it certainly would be, was to spend the rest of your life on the beach picking up seashells and looking longingly at the distant horizon . . .

Doing something wrong, being afraid to take a risk because of the doubtful wording of orders, being scared of doing something because you did not have written orders and thus allowing the enemy to escape: all these were the best argument for a captain having a private income. He need not be a rich man; just rich enough to avoid having to worry about the fate of a wife and children, if he had them. Then he could do what was best for the Service without worrying too much about the idiosyncrasy of an admiral. A nice payment of prize money was often just enough.

This was not to say that a rich captain could or should ignore or disobey proper orders or take needless risks.

Occasionally a situation arose which was not properly covered by written orders, however, and where the captain should use his own initiative, confident that his senior officer and the Admiralty would back him. In fact he could not always rely on such backing; in fact, too, he might do the wrong thing. Ramage remembered his father's advice – better to be blamed for doing *something* than for doing *nothing*. All too often doing nothing was a form of cowardice; the form that paralyses your brain in the wish to avoid being blamed. The clerk's creed, in other words: you could not be wrong if you never made a decision.

What the devil all that had to do with firing a couple of dozen shells from a pair of captured bomb ketches he did not know; nor, for that matter, did he know why the Navy always called them *bomb* ketches, abbreviated, oddly enough, as 'Bb', since what their mortars fired were called shells not bombs. When did a shell become a bomb? Grenadiers threw grenades – which were sometimes called bombs, but perhaps only loosely by people who did not know. Anyway, the Admiralty named most of their bomb ketches after volcanoes, several of which began with 'V', so in the Navy List there were, for example, '*Vesuvius* (*Bb*) . . . *Volcano* (*Bb*) . . . *Vulcan* (*Bb*)' although he could remember *Tartarus*, *Terror* and *Thunder*.

Southwick nudged him. 'Wagstaffe will be first,' he said. 'A couple of his men are already wrapping the slow matches round their linstocks.'

Ramage had a mental picture of young Paolo talking to Peter Kenton. He would have found out that there was no race against the watch; that it was the bomb ketch that blew up her cask with the fewest shells that won. Paolo was shrewd enough to know that the most vital shell of all would be the first one fired . . .

Over on the foredeck of the *Fructidor* the conversation

had already taken place, just as Ramage had imagined it. While the half a dozen seamen and two powder boys were collecting equipment from the ketch's magazine, Paolo had managed to persuade Kenton to walk aft with him. Twenty-three-year-old third-lieutenants, only two men removed from the Captain, treated midshipmen with disdain where service matters were concerned, and it was obvious to Kenton that Orsini had some idea he wanted to put forward. Orsini was a brave enough lad in action but had a little too much imagination at times . . .

'The first shot, sir,' Orsini said, taking great care that the 'sir' was clear and pitched at just the right level.

'What about it – are you afraid it'll push the mortar through the bottom of the ship?'

'No, sir. I was thinking about the second one, actually. Aiming it, I mean.'

'There's nothing difficult about that. We see where the first one lands, and that'll show us what correction we have to make for the second. It'll fall short, over, left or right . . . as simple as that. We then increase or decrease the charge, and train left or right.'

'Yes, sir, but I was thinking that Mr Wagstaffe might ₅ . .' He broke off, hoping Kenton would guess.

'Might what?' Kenton demanded. 'He's a very experienced officer.'

'But I don't think he has ever fired a mortar, sir. Which means – with respect – that he's likely to make mistakes in aiming. We might make the same mistakes, too.'

'What sort of mistakes?' Kenton asked sharply.

'Well, it might be a common error with the first shot for the shell to fall short . . . Or pitch well over.'

'It might,' Kenton agreed. 'But I don't see what we can do about it.'

'We could let Mr Wagstaffe fire first and see where his

shell lands . . .' Orsini murmured casually. 'And make appropriate corrections before *we* fire.'

Kenton stopped suddenly and stared at Orsini. 'Supposing we haven't made the same mistakes in aiming that Wagstaffe makes? What then?'

'Well, then, we'll be introducing errors,' Orsini said cheerfully. 'It's a gamble. Not much of one, though,' he added hurriedly. 'We're just gambling that we'd be likely to make the same sort of mistakes as Mr Wagstaffe and Mr Martin. None of us are used to elevating a mortar and using a plunge nob – '

'A plumb bob,' Kenton corrected. 'Sometimes called a plummet.'

'. . . yes, a plunge nob, so we have nothing to lose in seeing how Mr Wagstaffe's first shot falls? Sir,' he added uncertainly, because Kenton had taken off his hat and seemed curious about something that might be inside it.

Finally Kenton jammed the hat back on his head, pointed at the flags being hoisted in the *Calypso*, and said : 'All right, m'lad, we'll gamble. We'll look daft if Wagstaffe's had the same idea and waits for us to fire!'

'He won't,' Orsini said earnestly, only just stopping himself from adding that it took an Italian to think of such good plans. 'The men are waiting,' he added, gesturing to the mortar.

As soon as he reached the gun, Kenton showed he had not wasted the half an hour spent reading the gunner's notebook. 'Right, line up, you men. Jackson, you are number one. You should have the plumb bob. Who has it? Right, give it to Jackson. Now, Jackson, you command, point and serve the vent – under my direction, of course. Stafford, you'll be number two, so you're responsible for the cartridge cases and measures. And don't forget – you might be measuring in single ounces so don't be heavy

handed. You –' he pointed at the two boys ' – bring up
the powder from the magazine.

'Rossi, you'll be number three. You collect the fuses,
load, help lift in the shell, run out the mortar and train.'
He looked at the remaining three men. 'Gutteridge, you're
number four. You provide a funnel for the powder, sponge,
wipe the bottom of the shell to make sure there's no loose
powder on it, take the fuse from the box and put it in the
shell – don't forget one and a half inches must protrude.
Then you help number three run out. Number five – that'll
be you, Barnes. You bring up the shell with number six,
and the two of you lift it up while number three guides
it into the bore of the gun. Lower it gently. Then you help
run out, and then help number three to train. Then you
take a linstock and – when you get the order – light the
fuse. Number six – that's you, King. You help bring up
the shell, run out and train. Then you prime the vent. If
necessary you'll have helped number three guide the shell
into the bore.'

He made each man repeat his tasks and then said
briskly, 'There are only nine commands you are likely to
hear from me and they're fairly obvious: Run the mortar
up – Cross lift to the right (or to the left) – Muzzle to the
right (or the left) – Down (the bed bolster will be in place
by then) – Load – Prime – Fire!'

He made the men repeat the sequence and then said
suspiciously: 'You all seem to know your jobs and the
sequence of commands very well – why is that?'

Jackson looked at Orsini, who winked, so the American
said: 'Mr Orsini borrowed a notebook about this gun,
sir, so we all sat around this morning and went over it. We
were all curious, sir.'

'You didn't know the Captain was going to offer a
guinea prize for target practice?'

Jackson shook his head. 'No, sir,' he said ruefully, 'otherwise we might have paid more attention.'

Kenton grinned sympathetically. 'Very well, let's get started. The magazine is open, fearnought blankets unrolled? Right, I see the water tub is there and the match tub. Slow matches alight and – ' he looked carefully ' – burning steadily. Very well, wet the decks, and then we can load.'

The deckwash pump started wheezing and spitting fitfully as King began working the handle, and as soon as water came out of the nozzle two other seamen filled buckets and sluiced the deck. The sun had heated the planking and it took several buckets before the wood stayed wetted.

Finally Kenton gave the signal and four of the men and the two powder boys ran below.

Listening for the sound of the *Brutus*'s mortar firing, Kenton took out his watch and began timing. Finally Stafford arrived with his two wooden cartridge cases, cylindrical wooden boxes with lids that slid up and down on loops of line which also acted as carrying handles. He slid up one lid and began undoing the worsted bag, ready to measure out powder, while one powder boy held the second box, and the other waited to run for a third.

Barnes and King were now walking quickly towards the mortar with a wooden beam across their shoulders. Two thin ropes with hooks hung from the beam, the hooks going through the two carrying handles on the top of the black ball that was the shell. Until Kenton shouted at them to break step, they walked in time, cursing as the shell swung back and forth like a pendulum, catching them across the shins.

Jackson was walking round the mortar looking at the items the men had placed ready, and he named them out loud, as if checking a mental list. 'Plumb bob . . . two cartridge cases and measures . . . sponge . . . funnel for the powder . . . two linstocks . . . four handspikes . . . one priming wire . . . There's Rossi with the fuses, and I've got a knife and the tube box . . . Here comes the carrying beam and the shell. That's the lot . . .'

Kenton looked at his watch. Two minutes so far — appalling time, but this was the first occasion. Then he noticed that Jackson had been naming the pieces of equipment out loud so that Orsini could check them against a list he was holding in his hand.

After that the six men went to work as though they had spent the last few weeks doing nothing but fire mortars : Gutteridge held the funnel in the fuse hole of the shell while Stafford measured out four pounds. Rossi handed the cone-shaped wooden fuse to Kenton, who said : 'We'll wait a few moments before cutting it. For a nineteen-seconds flight it would be four inches and eighteen hundredths.'

He turned to Orsini. 'Stand by here. I'm going to the bow to watch where the *Brutus*'s — '

At that moment there was an explosion beyond the *Calypso* and Kenton ran to the bow, looking up at a small black ball still climbing into the sky at a steep angle. Then, as though rolling over the summit of a hill, it began dropping and Kenton lost sight of it but looked down at the cask. There was a flurry of sand well beyond it.

'A hundred yards over!' he exclaimed and suddenly realized that Orsini was beside him counting out the seconds.

'. . . twenty-three and four and five . . .'

'It's misfired,' Kenton muttered. 'It won't go off. The fuse is damaged.'

'. . . twenty-seven and eight . . .'

The explosion sent up a flock of birds which had been hidden in the pine trees, and along the beach the sandpipers which had stood fast for the mortar firing finally fled for the shell, skimming over the sand like tiny arrows to land again ahead of the *Fructidor.*

'Hmmm,' Kenton said, his voice sounding as judicial as possible. 'A good hundred yards over with the elevation, and more than six seconds too much fuse in the shell.'

'So much for Pythagoras,' Paolo said sourly, as though his suspicions of the untrustworthiness of both Greeks and mathematics were confirmed. 'Like us, the *Brutus* is two hundred yards from the shore; the cask is fifteen hundred yards along the beach. The range is the hypotenuse, which is 1,513 yards.'

Kenton took out the notes which he had stuffed in his pocket and smoothed flat the pages.

'Damnation, that range is within a dozen yards of the figure in the tables, with a two-pound-six-ounce charge. Wagstaffe must have gone for a much higher range – more than two thousand yards. Yet he wasn't five hundred yards over . . . I don't understand it. Anyway, we'll keep to our own figures.' He turned to walk aft to the mortar, calling to Stafford: 'Put in two pounds six ounces of powder as the charge.'

He turned to Orsini. 'I can't make out the twenty-eight seconds, though: the time of flight for the range Wagstaffe used should have been about nineteen seconds . . . The devil take it, I think he was unlucky and that fuse burned unevenly because of bad French powder. Cut ours to three and three-quarter inches – let's stop this "hundredths" business.'

Jackson handed the fuse and knife to Orsini and held

98

out a foot rule so that the boy could measure the cone. 'Keep the point upwards as you cut it, sir,' Jackson warned, 'just in case there's any loose powder.'

Kenton looked across at the *Calypso* and saw the Captain and the master both watching with telescopes. So were the first-lieutenant and, he realized, most of the ship's company, too.

Stafford finished measuring the powder charge into the mortar and Rossi put in a wad and rammed it down vigorously. Kenton told Jackson and Orsini to fit the fuse into the shell, which they did after opening the top, and then gestured to Barnes and King to lift with the beam to place the shell in the mortar.

A few moments later with the shell settled in the barrel, they were unhooking the lines and getting clear. The mortar was then trained round to the bearing that Kenton had already given to Jackson. The muzzle was lifted with handspikes and the bed bolster was slid underneath so that the mortar was inclined at the precise angle which a harried Kenton had worked out earlier, with a slight correction to allow for the *Brutus*'s overshooting.

Jackson reported to Kenton that the mortar was loaded and primed. Barnes, whose job it was to light the fuse of the shell, and Jackson, who would fire the mortar when Kenton gave the order, hurriedly wound slow match round linstocks, thin snakes round sticks each with a single red eye, where it burned.

Kenton nodded to Jackson, who signalled to Barnes. The seaman reached carefully into the bore with his linstock and warily held the glowing end of the slow match against the fuse. The moment it began to fizz, he jumped back and Jackson touched the vent with his slow match. The mortar gave a gigantic cough and suddenly the men

99

were standing in a cloud of smoke. Kenton and Orsini, both coughing, ran to the bow, looking up into the sky. Above them the shell curved up in the first part of its parabola, wobbling slightly.

On board the *Calypso*, Ramage watched the shell as Southwick said to Aitken: 'It'll land among the pine trees and start a big fire, you see.'

'Aye, if Wagstaffe was a hundred yards over, those two mathematical wizards in the *Fructidor* will be five hundred. The fuse must have been defective.'

'There are times when it's better to be lucky than good,' Ramage reminded them.

The three men watched the cask but suddenly it was obscured by a cloud of brownish, oily smoke.

'By Jove, and that's one of them,' Southwick said in an awed voice. 'Thirty yards short but the fuse burst it only four or five feet above the ground.'

Almost simultaneously there was a throaty explosion behind them as the *Brutus* fired again. They watched the shell, which exploded four seconds after it landed a good fifty yards beyond the cask.

'Both of them are training accurately,' Aitken commented. 'It's just the range that's bothering them. They've got to watch the amount of powder they use for the charge.'

'That French powder varies a lot,' Ramage said. 'The Board of Ordnance says that any captured should be used only in an emergency, and must never be mixed with ours.'

'But the powder in this ship is French,' Aitken protested, 'and it's never given us any trouble, sir.'

Ramage shook his head and Southwick laughed. 'It's British powder,' Ramage said. 'The French must have taken it from a prize they captured. They do, when they can. Southwick and the gunner checked it all as soon as we captured the ship and knew the admiral was going to buy her in.'

'The powder is *that* different?'

'Yes – the French is coarser for a start. But we tested it with paper.'

'Paper?' Aitken asked, obviously surprised.

'Yes – you put a clean piece of writing-paper down on the deck, make a small pile of powder (a drachm or so) in the middle, and then fire it. The best way is to use a length of wire heated until it's red-hot: slow match can leave some residue because the explosion usually blows the tip off.'

'But what does that tell you about the powder, sir?'

'Good powder gives a good flame and makes a crisp bang. More important, there is no residue, and no burn marks on the paper. If you find white specks left on the paper, or burn marks, you know it's inferior.'

He swung round as he spoke because the *Fructidor*'s shell was already in the air and he watched it land twenty yards beyond the little crater made by the first round. It sat there a moment, a grotesque black egg, and then vanished in smoke. Ramage waited for the smoke to clear and then inspected the cask with his telescope. It still stood four-square, but one of the staves had been pushed in just enough to make a shadow.

'Twice can still be luck,' Southwick said, his voice full of disbelief, as though he knew his eyes were playing him tricks but dare not admit it.

Ramage watched Kenton's crew reloading the mortar and was pleased at the smoothness with which they worked. He had already seen Wagstaffe's team at work and, as he had commented earlier to Aitken, they looked as though they had spent the last few weeks serving in a bomb ketch.

Suddenly he saw all the men serving the *Fructidor*'s mortar standing to attention behind the gun, with Kenton and Orsini standing in front. He pointed them out to Aitken and Southwick. 'They load faster, and they want to make sure we notice it!'

A full minute passed before the *Brutus*'s mortar fired. The shell landed only a yard or two beyond the water's edge and burst two seconds later, fifty yards short of the cask and spraying up sand and water in a muddy fan.

'Bit heavy-handed,' Southwick commented. 'Fifty yards over, and then fifty yards short . . . still, he's cutting the fuse to the right length.'

Kenton's fourth shell burst in almost the same place as the third, and when the smoke cleared Ramage saw that the shallow craters almost overlapped.

'That's the powder,' he commented to Aitken. 'Kenton must have made a correction in the charge, but the quality of the powder varies so much that it can trump the correction.'

Wagstaffe's fifth shell landed within ten yards of the cask and for a few breathless moments the three men watched, waiting to see if the fuse would fail. Ramage counted eight seconds and suddenly a cloud of smoke spurted outwards from the shell, swirling slightly in the breeze, and when it had cleared the cask had vanished. Ramage then saw a few pieces of wood scattered across the sand. He swung round to look at the *Fructidor* and realized that Kenton and Paolo were not bothering to look at the fall of the *Brutus*'s shells, so they did not know that Wagstaffe had won. Still, the *Fructidor* had her fifth shell to fire before the *Brutus* could claim the guinea.

Again the mortar grunted and spurted smoke, and Ramage, Aitken and Southwick watched the shell soaring up, the master cursing the sun, which had risen high enough to make a glare. They followed the black speck as it dropped towards the beach but before they could see where it had fallen a deep thud echoed back from the pines, with a pall of smoke, which the breeze quickly dispersed.

Ramage was just going to turn to the boatswain to tell him to hoist a signal when Aitken croaked, rather than spoke. 'A direct hit, sir! It must have exploded just as it landed right on the cask!'

Ramage stared unbelievingly through his telescope. The cask was gone; in its place was a large crater. He could just make out small pieces of wood, many yards away.

He glanced across at the *Fructidor*. Six seamen and two powder boys were lined up behind the gun. Orsini was standing to attention in front of it, but Kenton was at the bow, staring towards the shore. He was still looking for the cask, Ramage realized; his height of eye was much lower than those in the *Calypso* – a little more than level with the bank of sand on which the casks had been placed. Then suddenly he pointed doubtfully and Orsini suddenly ran forward to join him.

Southwick saw what was happening. 'It's cost you two guineas to find out that these old ketches are good for breaking up casks, sir. Can we change the prize crews round so that I can challenge the first-lieutenant?'

CHAPTER SIX

The reddish-gold reflection of the sunset came through the stern lights and both sides of the skylight and brought out the rich colour of the mahogany furniture in Ramage's cabin, deepening the tan of his face as he sat back comfortably in the armchair talking to Aitken.

'These sunsets,' the first-lieutenant said, 'the colours are quite fantastic. This one stretches across three-quarters of the sky. We take a pride in our sunsets in Scotland, but these . . .'

'You've never been along the Tuscan coast before?' Ramage said: 'Well, you commented this morning on the curious light. It has a strange clarity, inland as well as along the coast, particularly around Florence and Siena. In fact, you remember seeing paintings by Italian artists working in Tuscany?'

Aitken paused doubtfully, settling himself more comfortably on the settee, and then nodded. 'Yes. Religious pictures, and all painted in a kind of a *religious* light.'

'Not religious,' Ramage said, smiling at the staunch Protestant disapproval in Aitken's voice. 'That's Tuscan light. That's what you've been seeing all day.'

The first-lieutenant nodded slowly. 'Aye, I begin to understand now. Those artists weren't deliberately painting a special background – as though there was some holy light shining on the subject, and on the countryside round them . . .'

'No, they were just painting what they saw: that was, and is, the normal summer light in Tuscany, and their backgrounds were often Florentine. No one in Britain has ever seen such vivid light, and they just didn't believe it. They scoffed at the painters. It wasn't until people began visiting Italy in larger numbers that they realized that the painters were truly painting what they saw.'

'If one of them had been on the beach this morning he could have used those mortar shells bursting as a model for the entrance to Hell,' Aitken said. 'But even as a landscape painting, what a picture it would have made: the hills and mountains brown and bluish – grey in the distance; the pine forest a line of dark green, with the juniper bushes in front; then the dazzling sand. And the sea – from pale green to deep blue.'

'How does it all compare with those great beech trees turning coppery in the autumn at Dunkeld?' Ramage asked, curious to hear the Scotsman's reaction.

'When I look inland at the way the mountains start, I don't think it's so different from Dunkeld in summer, apart from the light. There are the pines, the grass here is more parched – they don't have enough rain in summer to produce rivers like the Tay . . . What I *have* noticed is the difference that's come over you, sir, and Southwick, and men like Jackson and Stafford: the minute the sun rose yesterday morning and you could see those Tuscan hills again, you all came alive! I don't mean,' he added hurriedly, 'that before then you'd been sleepy or anything like that. But you know how a man looks when he sees someone he loves after a long absence.'

Ramage did not answer and Aitken realized that the Captain had gone away with his thoughts to some private place – thinking of the Marchesa, no doubt. It was comfortable sitting here, knowing that a prize was anchored each side, and that thanks to the three French flags they would not be attacked. *Ruse de guerre,* a trick used by both sides with only one rule – that you could fly the enemy's colours, but had to drop them and hoist your own before opening fire.

'The Frenchman's orders,' Ramage said unexpectedly, coming back from wherever he had been. 'He was supposed to be taking these two bomb ketches to Crete.'

'Why Crete?' Aitken mused. 'What on earth can the French be planning against Crete? Surely they've occupied it anyway,' he added gloomily.

'I'm not at all sure,' Ramage admitted. 'I hope we aren't going that far. I've heard that the harbours aren't much use, but I don't think Crete was the bomb ketches' final destination. I'm sure they were going on to somewhere else. I have a feeling that the French are simply using Crete to assemble a powerful force – a fleet complete right down to bomb ketches, and transports, and an army to travel with it.'

'Where could they be planning to attack?'

'Another attempt at Egypt? A landing on the Levant in the hope of forcing a way through to India? With this madman Bonaparte one can never be sure.'

'Perhaps that's putting a lot of meaning into the orders for two bombs, sir,' Aitken commented cautiously. 'There might be some anchorage or harbour that the French are finding useful but which has no fort to protect it. Easier to anchor a couple of bombs there than build a fort . . .'

Ramage shrugged. 'There's no need to build a fort anyway – why not just construct a battery on a cliff? Some thick planks put down on levelled ground, a few baskets or bags of earth to make a parapet . . . No, Renouf received additional orders when he reached Toulon. Two frigates were to meet him at Porto Ercole on the thirteenth of this month. He was to water and provision there and be anchored outside by the time the frigates arrived to go in and embark cavalry and field guns. The frigates would then carry them to Crete, escorting the bombs at the same time.'

'*En flûte?*'

'Probably,' Ramage said, knowing that frigates carrying troops and stores usually had most of their maindeck guns removed to make more space and the port lids caulked, leaving the ships armed with only the guns on the fo'c'sle and quarterdeck. 'Using a couple of frigates *en flûte* makes sense here in the Mediterranean now; as far as the French are concerned, it's unlikely they'll meet any enemy ships of war. There may be occasional Algerine pirates – the Italians still call them *i Saraceni*, the Saracens – but nothing that two frigates couldn't drive off or sink.'

'I wonder what happens,' Aitken mused, 'when the frigates arrive at Porto Ercole on the thirteenth and the two bombs aren't anchored outside waiting for them?'

'I don't think you should worry yourself with questions like that.'

'I beg your pardon, sir,' Aitken said hastily. 'I didn't mean to –'

'No, always make your views clear. All I meant was that I can see no reason why the bomb ketches shouldn't be anchored outside Porto Ercole waiting for them.'

Aitken sat bolt upright, his eyes bright. 'What a trap!'

'It can be a trap only if it was good shooting and not luck that blew up those casks this morning.'

'I had a talk with Wagstaffe and Kenton because I was curious too,' the first-lieutenant said. 'It was good shooting. They both complained that the French powder is so bad that every round fell differently. If they realized that, then they must have been confident. Both reckoned that with our own powder they'd have hit the casks with the third shell. Each of them told me that before he had had a chance to compare notes with the other.'

Ramage nodded and stood up to take a rolled-up chart from the rack above him. As he opened it on his desk, using paperweights to prevent it rolling up again, he said: 'You might wonder why the French chose Porto Ercole. Look, here you can see Argentario. It is almost an island a mile or so from the coast, and I always think it looks like a bat hanging from a beam, with each leg a causeway. Here,' he ran a finger from the island to the mainland, 'you can see the northern one is the Pineta di Gianella, and the southern, which is wider and almost touches Porto Ercole, is the Pineta di Feniglia.

'The Feniglia is covered with pines but there's a track cut through it, which is the route to Porto Ercole from the mainland. Between the two causeways is a large lake. Shallow, of course. And here, sticking down like a stubby finger between the two causeways, and pointing at Argentario, is a peninsula with the town of Orbetello on the end, almost surrounded by water.'

'Why did the French choose this place to embark troops?'

'I've been thinking about that. This road here on the mainland, running parallel with the sea, is the via Aurelia, one of the great Roman roads leading to Rome. If you want to embark troops and cavalry along this coast you can use Leghorn, way up here, a hundred miles to the north, or Civita Vecchia, forty miles to the south. I assume these particular French troops are stationed closer to Porto Ercole than either of the other two points. Probably at Grosseto, the nearest big town.'

He picked up a magnifying glass. 'Hmm . . . three and four fathoms inside this little bay that forms Porto Ercole; ten to fifteen fathoms outside. The French frigates can get in – the point is, will they? They might decide it is too shallow.'

'The alternative is loading guns and horses, using their own boats. Hoisting frightened and kicking horses on board using slings under their bellies . . .' Aitken muttered, clearly talking to himself, seeing the problem through the eyes of a first-lieutenant, upon whom the responsibility for the task would fall. 'I doubt if there'll be any lighters or barges in a place like Porto Ercole: it's simply a fishing village. Those forts,' he said, 'I hope they're not manned . . .'

'I don't know,' Ramage admitted. 'But I doubt it. There are two of them – Santa Catarina, the star-shaped and small one low down on the headland on the north side, and Filippo, which is on the top of a big hill overlooking the whole port. Both are Spanish. Probably built by Philip II – he seems to have spent his time and money building forts on the coasts of the West Indies and Europe when he wasn't sending an Armada against us. You see that Porto Ercole is one side of the little bay and Le Grotte is the village at the other.'

Aitken pointed to the jetty, which formed the western side of the small bay. 'The frigates can't get alongside because it's too shallow. I think I'd get in as close as possible, securing stern to the jetty, and use fishing-boats as ferries. Even use 'em as a bridge of boats, planks lashed across them, if I could get in far enough.'

'Let the French worry about that,' Ramage said, lifting the weights and letting the chart roll up. 'I'm sure they'll anchor inside. The bomb ketches can anchor wherever they want, and because they have the advantage in range they might as well choose a place beyond the reach of any guns there might be in the forts.'

'The gunner's tables give a maximum of 4,000 yards for

a 10-inch mortar,' Aitken said. 'That's with a 12-pound charge.'

Ramage shook his head doubtfully. 'That might be all right for a properly designed and constructed bomb ketch, but a 12-pound charge sounds too much for converted galliots. I'd expect the recoil to drive the mortar through the bottom!'

'Aye, I wasn't suggesting we tried 'em at that, sir,' Aitken said hastily, thumbing through the gunner's text-book. 'Here we are – this seems the most likely. It's a table of ranges using a 92-pound shell and with the mortar set at an elevation of forty-five degrees. A three-pound charge gives a range of 1,945 yards, which is 900 more than the French frigates are likely to reach if they're only armed *en flûte*. And even if they're not,' he added with a grin, 'they'll hardly be expecting visitors. If they moor stern to the jetty their guns won't bear round to cover the entrance anyway.'

Ramage unrolled the chart again and weighted it down. He took a pair of dividers from a rack and set them to a mile on the latitude scale. Then with one point stuck on the jetty of Porto Ercole he swung the other in an arc covering the outside of the port. 'We'll be able to get the exact range from the heights of the frigates' masts, but as I shall wait two or three days before we go down to Porto Ercole, we'll have the bomb ketches practising on targets along the beach at 2,000 yards. We might even experiment and increase the charge half a pound at a time and see what we consider a safe maximum range.'

'That French captain,' Aitken said. 'He might have . . .'

'Yes, I'm going to have a chat with him. Fortunately he's expecting to be returned to the *Fructidor*, so he knows it's in his interest to give us accurate information, otherwise he might find one of the mortars crashing down on his head.'

Ramage put the chart back in the rack. 'We must keep a sharp lookout for any French cavalry riding along the beach and wanting to pay us a social call: their commanding officer might take it into his head to try to invite himself to dinner.'

'Then what do we do, sir?'

'Ignore shouts from the beach and call me. Always be ready to resume mortar practice at short notice: a mortar shell exploding on the beach will panic horses. You'd better work out some system of signals between us and the bomb ketches so that we don't have to hail in English.'

'Wooding, sir. Can I send some wooding parties on shore? There's no fresh water around according to the chart. No streams or anything.'

Wooding and watering: tasks which were a recurring problem in the course of a cruise: the cook always needed wood to fuel the galley fire under the water in the coppers in which most of the ship's food was cooked, and a sensible captain grabbed every opportunity to fill casks with fresh water because that was almost the only thing that limited the range of a cruise. But as Aitken had commented, the chart showed no streams running into the sea for several miles, apart from one which came out of the pine trees to reach the sea just ahead of the *Calypso* as a stony sunken track, laced with tree branches washed down in the winter and now stripped of bark and bleached by the scorching sun. There had been no rain for many days and summer had parched the area. Was it worth the risk of having a party of seamen cutting or picking up wood being surprised by a French patrol? A few cords of wood in return

111

for risking the whole operation with the bomb ketches? Ramage shook his head. 'We're not desperately short of wood. And we can always stretch over to the Corsican or Sardinian coasts afterwards for both wood and water.'

Later that evening Ramage gave his orders to Wagstaffe and Kenton: they would each send a party on shore next morning to place casks at 2,000 yards and 3,000 yards. Each would fire a dozen shells at the 2,000-yard target, and then increase the range by increasing the powder charge, using the 3,000-yard cask to help estimate distances. But, he emphasized, they were to watch the mortar bed; they must not risk damaging their ships.

Ramage did not tell them that Renouf, who was genuinely fascinated by bomb ketches and very proud of his mortars, regarded 4,000 yards as an acceptable range: the master armourer at Brest had tried out all four mortars at the sea range off Camaret, firing five rounds from each, with the master shipwright in attendance, and going down and inspecting the under-deck stanchions and the stringers after each round was fired.

Almost more important as far as the two lieutenants were concerned was Ramage's agreement that they could take a barrel of powder with them. With powder made by the British Powder Factory, they said, they would guarantee better shooting. The French powder should be fed to pigs; it would produce streaky bacon of a high quality.

CHAPTER SEVEN

'Haystacks,' Southwick growled, giving one of his sniffs that expressed contempt without wasting words or breath. 'A soldier's wind – and it'd have to be a gale – is the only thing that'll get them going.'

'At least they can lay the course,' Ramage said mildly, 'and it's a nice sunny day.'

'Aye, but it'll be winter and blowing a maestrale before we get to Porto Ercole,' Southwick said. 'Or a sirocco – we just need a few days of strong south winds; then these dam' bombs would end up aground at Genoa.'

The *Calypso* was gliding along in an almost flat sea under only a maintopsail; the foretopsail had been furled half an hour ago, 'Otherwise we'll dishearten those two lads,' Ramage had told Aitken, gesturing at the *Brutus* and the *Fructidor*. They were once again abeam, with every square foot of working canvas set and, in the case of the *Fructidor*, an awning or a large tarpaulin hoisted out on a boom as a rudimentary stunsail in the hope of coaxing a little more speed from a hull designed to carry cargo.

Southwick had given yet another sniff, this time one which Ramage recognized as indicating either disapproval or disagreement. He raised an eyebrow and looked round at the master, who said: 'I doubt if those dam' bomb ketches have ever before been sailed so fast in a wind like this: but for all that, if Wagstaffe and Kenton think they'll get a broadside from you if they're left behind, I guarantee they'd find another half a knot from somewhere.'

It was then that Ramage noticed both ships were trimmed down by the bow. He had seen their waterlines when they were at anchor – the bow high because one of the anchors was on the sea bottom. He had forgotten to look again when they weighed anchor, adding the weight of the anchor, and perhaps the cable too, if it was stowed well forward which it probably was, to leave as much space as possible for the original task of carrying cargo.

'Let's pass within hail,' Ramage said sourly, irritated with himself. 'I'll give them an extra half a knot with only one shout.'

While a puzzled Southwick gave the orders to the quartermaster, Ramage looked round. Along the whole larboard side, from north to south, stretched the mainland of Italy, with Punta Ala now on the *Calypso*'s quarter. Argentario was jutting out like a mountain which, complete with its surrounding foothills, had been pushed out into the sea. It was fine on the larboard bow, seven or eight miles away, just too far for the long and sandy causeways joining it to the mainland to be visible to the naked eye. Because the nearest one was still below the curve of the horizon only the tips of the pine trees could be seen; the sand in which they grew was out of sight.

The small island topped by a fortress and now on the starboard bow was Giglio. He remembered once trying to teach Stafford how to pronounce the name. He had been the junior lieutenant of a frigate at the time, so it seemed like a century ago. It was impossible to teach the Cockney to say the soft liquid 'g' which was spoken with the teeth almost together. He had finally compromised with the first 'g' sounding like the 'j' in 'jelly' so that Stafford had produced 'jeel-yoh!', which was certainly an improvement on Giggly-oh. Now Giglio was on the starboard bow, the

114

even tinier island of Giannutri beyond, fine on the starboard bow.

On Argentario was the little town and port at the northern end, Santo Stefano, which would be hidden from sight until the last moment and protected from attackers by the great fortress built on a hill overlooking it.

The first time he had seen it he had been the fifth-lieutenant of a frigate which had just been sunk by a French ship of the line. Now he had more experience and certainly he was a post captain, but somehow, apart from the different uniform he now wore (with the single epaulet showing he was a post captain with less than three years' seniority) and the fact that he commanded this frigate, did he really feel any different?

He thought about it and decided that the difference was slight. Perhaps there was a sameness (despite the passing of the years) because still serving with him were some of the men who had shared those few desperate hours spent rescuing Gianna. A young lieutenant, a few seamen and an open boat to do the job for which the admiral had originally sent a frigate ... And most of those seamen were at this very moment over in the *Fructidor* serving with her nephew. 'Yes, Mr Orsini,' they all said respectfully, as the law and custom of the Navy required, but there must be many times when they thought not of the fourteen-year-old boy but of his twenty-four-year-old aunt. None of them had ever seen her kingdom of Volterra, but they knew it was not far to the north-east, just over a few hills and now ruled by the French. But they all knew its heir at present was Paolo, and it must cross their minds that many young men heir to such a kingdom would take good care to stay alive, living comfortably, luxuriously, in some place like London, certainly not serving in a British frigate and always finding his way into any boarding-party that seemed likely to cross swords with the French.

'Speaking-trumpet, sir,' Southwick said, and Ramage saw that the master had brought the *Calypso* close along the lee side of the *Fructidor* and, like starlings on the bough of a tree, Kenton, Paolo and several others were lining the bulwark and looking up at him as he stood at the quarterdeck rail. Ramage remembered his days as a young lieutenant. No doubt they were very worried: usually when a senior officer brought his frigate close alongside in circumstances like these it meant trouble.

He lifted the speaking-trumpet to his lips, hating the smell of the brass, polished that morning with brick dust but already corroding again from the salt air. Why the makers did not japan the whole trumpet, mouthpiece as well as the bell, he would never know.

'Kenton – ahoy there, Kenton!'

'Sir?'

'You're trimmed down by the bow – at least a foot. Shift some weight right aft. Have some men carry shells from the forward locker and stow 'em aft.' An empty shell weighed about eighty-five pounds. 'Try a dozen and see if you increase speed. If you don't, try half a dozen more. Is she griping?'

'Yes, sir. We've been trying to trim the sails to check it.'

'Well, it's probably because you're down by the head. Check the helm now and then again later to see if it improves.'

'Aye aye, sir.'

Ramage nodded towards Southwick. 'Let's give the glad news to the *Brutus*, although Wagstaffe should have worked it out for himself. It's obvious he didn't check the draught forward and after before he weighed this morning and enter it in the log.'

'I should have thought of it myself,' Southwick said ruefully.

'Me, too,' Aitken added as the master called a new course to the quartermaster.

Fifteen minutes later Wagstaffe listened as his captain's voice came across the water, distorted by the speaking-trumpet, but hitting him like ricocheting musket shot. He waved shamefacedly and shouted back, 'Aye aye, sir.' Cursing under his breath, he turned to Martin. 'She's grip-ing, she sails like a haystack, we can't get the sails settling to balance her properly . . . And we never thought we might be trimmed down by the bow! It's so obvious now. You take the helm so that we can be sure whether or not shifting those shells aft helps us. We'll start off with a cast of the log to see our present speed.'

Over in the *Fructidor* pairs of seamen with carrying-bars resting across their shoulders staggered aft with shells knee-high, hooked on to the ropes. Weighing less than a hundredweight, an empty shell was not heavy for two men to carry with a bar, but it was awkward: as they walked it swung like a pendulum because the ketch was rolling slightly with the following wind, and while one man was looking at the shell, trying to avoid it swinging into the back of his knees, he would stub his toe on a ringbolt or walk into a cask or a hencoop lashed down on the deck, stumbling and causing the shell to hit his mate.

Jackson and Stafford stood by the taffrail with a long rope, one end of which they had already secured to an eye-bolt on one side of the ship. As the carriers, perspiring and cursing, arrived with a shell, Stafford lifted it while Jackson unhitched the two hooks from the carrying handles on each side of the fuse hole and together they swung it over to the pile they were building. As Stafford steadied

117

it, Jackson threaded the line through both handles and they waited for the next shell to arrive.

Rossi and Gutteridge staggered over. 'You look like a couple of drunken milkmaids carrying a pail of curdled milk,' Stafford jeered.

Both men twisted the beam so that the shell swung at Stafford, who had to leap back a couple of paces to avoid it cracking him across the shins. They had to wait a few moments for it to stop swinging, so that Stafford could lift it and enable Jackson to release the hooks.

Kenton was sitting astride the bulwark on the larboard side abreast the mainmast, staring down into the water. 'How many is that?' he shouted to Jackson.

'Eight, sir.' Then, knowing that Kenton was concentrating on the water surging by so that he could estimate if the ship was sailing any faster, he added: ' 'Bout 650 pounds, sir, nearly a third of a ton.'

Kenton watched the water passing the ship like a millrace. A third of a ton taken from forward and put aft. That made a difference of two-thirds of a ton in the trim – didn't it? He was never very good at these sorts of calculations, and tried to picture the ship: right, there's a third of a ton up there in the bow. I pick it up. The bow is now a third of a ton lighter. I put it down on the stern – and the stern is a third of a ton heavier. So the total effect is that the bow has a third less and the stern a third more, which makes two-thirds. It sounds right, but it's too easy. To change the trim by two-thirds of a ton by carrying only one-third?

'Well, helmsman?'

'She's a lot easier already, sir,' the seaman replied. 'She b'aint be griping now. Afore we shifted them shells aft her bow was wandering like a sheep trying to find which 'ole in the 'edge she strayed through.'

By now Kenton was sure the ship was sailing faster. She was forging ahead of the *Brutus*, and from the way the other bomb's sails were filled it was not just a lucky fluke of the wind. He swung his leg back over the bulwark and picked up his telescope to examine the *Brutus*.

Wagstaffe's men were just reeling in the line after taking a cast of the log. There was the first pair of men carrying a shell, with four others – six or eight, in fact – waiting impatiently for more to be handed up from the shot-locker. The *Fructidor* had put on perhaps a knot by just doing as Mr Ramage said.

'A pity, sir,' Paolo said, shaking his head with a sadness more befitting a priest talking to his errant flock, 'a pity we didn't think of it ourselves, then we would have gone ahead of the *Brutus* without Mr Wagstaffe realizing what was happening. Now he does it and he'll catch up.'

'Well, we *didn't* think of it, and we *are* going faster,' Kenton said crossly, annoyed with himself. 'And you can practise your navigation. Get out your quadrant and put our position on the chart. You can fix it in two different ways – vertical sextant angles and bearings on the highest peak of Monte Argentario, and the mountain on Elba – you can just see it, but don't place too much reliance on it because of the distance – and the one on Giglio. Then horizontal angles of each end of Giglio and the westernmost edge of Argentario.'

Paolo groaned and then brightened up. 'I haven't the heights of the peaks, sir.'

'I've written them in on the chart,' Kenton said coldly, remembering his own ingenuity with excuses when he had been a midshipman not so long ago. 'Argentario's 2,000 feet, Giglio's 1,600 and the highest peak on Elba is 3,300. All nice round numbers. You didn't leave your quadrant on board the *Calypso*, did you?' he asked suspiciously.

'No, sir,' Paolo said miserably.

Kenton stopped, wondering if the boy was depressed at the thought that Volterra was only fifteen miles away to the north of them, halfway between Siena and the sea. It must be strange for a boy to think that so close was not only his home but the kingdom he might eventually rule if the Marchesa never had a son and if Paolo survived, though this seemed unlikely the way the lad pitched into action. Still, Volterra might be only fifty miles from the *Fructidor* but, Kenton began to suspect, the only thing making the boy unhappy at the moment was the prospect of working out some vertical sextant angles. They would be passing Argentario and preparing to round up for Porto Ercole before he had finished . . . Hmm, at last he was coming up on deck with his quadrant, slate and piece of chalk.

As Stafford held the twelfth shell and Jackson slipped the line through the handles he said: 'Wiv a bit o' luck we'll use these termorrer, so we'd 'ave 'ad ter carry 'em up anyway.'

'We haven't carried them at all, and we'll probably use the forward mortar anyway if we do open fire,' Jackson said, 'so you may get landed with carrying them forward.'

'That'll be the day,' Stafford muttered. 'I didn't get landed with it this time, no more did you.'

Stafford suddenly nudged Jackson and whispered: 'Just watch Mr Orsini. 'E's gettin' in such a muddle 'e'll soon be trying to take a sight wiv the slate and chewing the chalk . . .'

'He's covered the slate with figures. He'll soon have to start using the other side.'

The two men then saw that the third-lieutenant was watching the *Brutus* with his telescope and the other bomb was no longer falling astern. Stafford nudged Jackson again and murmured: 'I think Mr Wagstaffe's now got 'is dozen shells stowed aft . . .'

At that moment the lookout aloft hailed excitedly: 'Deck there!' and when Kenton answered he called down: 'There's a sail just coming clear of Giggley-oh, sir. Looks like a frigate. Ooh! There's another . . . and another!'

Kenton waited but the lookout finally concluded: 'That's the lot, sir: three frigates.'

Kenton could just make out three specks on the horizon, but the hulls of the ships were still hidden below the curvature of the earth, although just visible to the lookout aloft. He lifted his speaking-trumpet.

'What course? Report the course, blast you, without me having to ask!'

'Sorry, sir: I think they're steering for the south end of this Mount Argent place.'

Kenton called to Paolo. 'Here's the French signal book. Find the signals for sighting three strange sail, and steering south, and then make both to the *Calypso,* using the French flags, since we don't have a set of British.'

CHAPTER EIGHT

On board the *Calypso,* Ramage was already listening to a slightly breathless report from Aitken, who when the lookout hailed had run aloft with a telescope, examined the ships and then come down again to give Ramage a fuller report.

'They're frigates all right, sir, and they look a similar design to us. And they're steering for the south end of Argentario with a quartering wind.'

'They look like us, eh? You're sure of that?'

'Built from the same draught, I'm sure,' Aitken said confidently. 'Sister ships.'

'Three of them, though,' Southwick grumbled. 'There's only supposed to be two.'

'Don't complain,' Ramage said, 'because it means that some French admiral has changed his mind.'

'I don't see how that helps *us*, sir.'

Ramage shook his head sadly. There were times when Southwick was remarkably obtuse. 'The senior officer of those three French frigates knows the two bombs are expecting to meet only *two* frigates in Porto Ercole, so he knows that the bomb captains – Renouf anyway – will be surprised to see three. Very well, when he sights the two bombs in company with yet *another* French frigate – and don't forget we are French built and rigged – he's going to assume the admiral has changed his mind yet again or, more likely, forgotten to tell him an extra frigate has already joined the bombs. Or,' he shrugged his shoulders, 'we could just be passing them at this very moment . . .'

The explanation seemed to satisfy both Aitken and Southwick, and Ramage listened as the lookout at the mainmasthead shouted down that the *Fructidor* had hoisted a signal.

Ramage reached for the French signal book, looked up the signal for sighting a strange sail, with the additions indicating the bearing and how many ships there were. Taking the speaking-trumpet from Southwick, he called up to the lookout, asking him to describe the flags.

The signals were correct and Ramage ordered the French answering pendant to be hoisted.

'Remind me to tell Kenton to commend that lookout, because the *Fructidor*'s masthead is so low,' Ramage told Aitken. 'The *Brutus* should have seen them.'

He turned away and began pacing the windward side of the quarterdeck. Aitken, Southwick, the quartermaster and the two seamen moved to leeward to leave him a clear space between the breeches of the guns and the skylight and companionway.

If the three frigates continued making for the south end of Argentario and rounded it, then they could only be making for Porto Ercole to pick up the troops, cavalry and artillery. They would have seen the bomb ketches coming down from the north and noted that they were well ahead of schedule, which was probably a fairly unusual situation for the French to meet. Would they go in to port and pick up the troops and artillery, or anchor and wait for the bombs to provision and water first, as originally ordered?

Three frigates instead of two . . . that probably meant that the French were sending more troops and artillery to wherever it was with the bomb ketches than they had first intended. Porto Ercole was small, so would all three frigates try to berth in the harbour together? It should not be impossible if they used their boats to tow.

He pictured the chart with the harbour showing very small. Three frigates with anchors out ahead could lie with sterns to the quay. Their bows would be to the east, which meant that with the wind from the north, west or south they could get out again just by making sail: they would not have to be towed out. If the wind was east, from ahead, it would depend on the strength. If it was light, their boats could tow out the frigates one at a time just far enough so that as they let fall their sails, each would clear the headland forming the southern entrance and then the tiny island just south of it – little more than a huge rock called Isolotto – as they tacked. If the wind had

123

any strength, then the frigates would be trapped in Porto Ercole until it changed, and it would have to be a change of several points.

Was there any chance that this present northerly breeze would freshen and veer to, say, east-north-east, even if it would not veer the whole eight points and set in from the east? Forecasting the weather in the Mediterranean was only slightly easier than in the West Indies, and less certain than throwing dice. There was a chance – but no more than that.

At the present rate of progress the galliots, bomb ketches, call 'em what you will, would not get to Argentario until after nightfall, and then only abreast the northern end. They would have to go almost three-quarters of the way round the coast before arriving at Porto Ercole – by then it would be almost dawn. The French in the frigates would have had a good night's sleep; the men in the bombs and the *Calypso* would have spent a restless night trying to catch every whiffle and back eddy of wind to get round Argentario. Spaccabellezze, Spadino, Vongher, Bocca d'Inferno, Argentario itself – the names of the peaks came back to him without any effort, and each of them would affect the wind. If the wind was light north or east, those peaks cast a windless shadow well ashore. With luck there would be an offshore wind for the night, enough to let them creep round. Apart from hitting the cliffs themselves, at least there was nothing to run into : just the rock of Argentarola sticking up like a tooth beyond Cala Grande, but they would not be that close inshore.

Three fully-manned French frigates versus two tiny bomb ketches and a single frigate, her ship's company depleted by two prize crews and the Marines needed to guard forty prisoners. Their Lordships at the Admiralty would regard the odds as about even . . . Given surprise as an ally, this was probably true. Surprise. You suddenly leapt out of the hedge and said 'Boh!' Or you surfaced from the deep like a whale and blew a great fountain of water.

He did not turn at the next walk forward; instead he went to the quarterdeck rail and looked ahead at the two bomb ketches rolling along like plump wives on their way to the market, and at Argentario beyond, a mountainous, sprawling island with rounded peaks and laced with narrow valleys still in shadow, although it was nearly noon. In the West Indies one could stand upright and throw no shadow because the sun was directly overhead, but Italy was too far north for that, and the shadows of trees and valleys gave more emphasis to the landscape. He broke his own rule and leaned his elbows on the rail, but resting your head on your hands really did not help concentration – at least it seemed silly to think it did.

It was all a gamble, a double gamble rather, or it would be if he tried it. He had to gamble everything, first on the wind not dropping away any more, and then on it not turning south – a head wind would stop everything. He did not have to gamble that the wind would turn east, although it would help if it did. Surprise, he also had to stake everything on surprise . . .

He turned to the quartermaster. 'Pass the word for my steward, please.'

The sound of his voice seemed to break a spell: Southwick swung round to face him from his position by the binnacle; Aitken, just about to go down the ladder to the main deck, stopped expectantly. He turned and walked back to Ramage who said: 'I need a dozen steady men. Not topmen. Six for the *Brutus* and six for the *Fructidor*.

'We'll put them on board just before sunset. Tell the gunner to give them an hour or two of instruction about mortars. I know they've probably never seen one, but he can explain the theory, and take them through the loading procedure.'

Aitken hesitated a moment and Ramage guessed that, like Southwick, the first-lieutenant was curious why the Captain had passed the word for his steward. They probably assumed that whatever the reason it was part of putting more men on board the bombs. Well, the pair of them were going to be disappointed.

He looked up and found Silkin waiting. His steward could be profoundly irritating, but he did his job well. Too well, which was why he was irritating: half the time he verged on fussiness.

Ramage shook his head. 'Belay that call, Silkin,' he said. 'I've changed my mind.'

Southwick looked at Aitken with raised eyebrows. The Scotsman began to go down the ladder, deliberately not walking quietly. There's plenty of time, Ramage thought; if I explain everything now, I might have to change it all later on because something else unexpected occurs – like the three frigates.

An hour later, as Ramage watched over the larboard side, making a mental journey through the Tuscan countryside, spotting and identifying various hill towns as the *Calypso* sailed southwards like a great sheepdog patiently driving two tiny, fat and very slow lambs, a question came to his mind. At first it was like a small patch of mist forming on an autumn evening in a little valley. Then it thickened and expanded to the size of a fog bank.

The question was obvious and simple. So obvious and so simple that he had completely overlooked it. He had walked right up to it and still not seen it. He had discovered that two French frigates were due in Porto Ercole to embark cavalry, foot soldiers and artillery, and then escort the two bomb ketches to Crete. He had been bright enough thus far to wonder why the French thought it necessary to escort the bomb ketches when they knew that the Royal Navy had long since been forced out of the Mediterranean. He had even speculated that the French were frightened that the bomb ketches might be attacked by the Algerine pirates, still occasionally raiding the Italian coasts. He had even – at this point he cursed his own stupidity – wondered if the two bomb ketches were going to Crete to serve as the defences of an anchorage, to save the French building a fort. Then three frigates had come in sight, not two, and he had become absorbed with wondering why there was the extra one.

No, he told himself bitterly, there was not even that excuse. He was lying to himself, like an errant schoolboy trying to avoid half a dozen with the birch by telling a string of lies. There was no excuse. Within moments of reading Renouf's orders telling him to make for Crete he had wondered if the bomb ketches were intended to join a French fleet assembling there. He had even speculated to Southwick that the French fleet and troops might be preparing for a new attack somewhere; a piece of speculation which had drawn from Southwick the sour memory that they had missed the Battle of Aboukir Bay, when Nelson had smashed a French fleet and wrecked Bonaparte's first attack on Egypt.

There he had left it: he had not taken the obvious extra step; the one that would have led him to the next question – the final, main, obvious and vital question which the Admiralty must have answered as soon as possible: exactly where *is* the French fleet bound?

If they intended an invasion of the Morea, Egypt or the eastern end of the Mediterranean, then Britain was going to have to scrape together a fleet from somewhere, and an army, to drive them out again.

That was the question. What about the answer? It could be anything. The French might be doing just what he had thought of first – using the bomb ketches as defences for an anchorage. The transfer of the bomb ketches might be some whim of a Minister of Marine, and the cavalry and troops being carried by the once two, now probably three frigates, might be a routine replacement. The lack of British ships of war made supplying garrisons by sea easy for the French. Troops died of diseases, and so did horses. The transfer of artillery might also be routine; the garrison did not have any guns, and the lack might now be being made up. Finally the frigates, bombs and troops might be part of some massive operation planned by Bonaparte in complete secrecy.

Ramage had a simple choice: he could act on the assumption that it was a normal change-of-garrison operation, and proceed to do what he could to destroy or capture the frigates. That was just the sort of thing his orders expected him to do. Or he could try to find out whether they were joining a fleet, and its destination, and then sink or capture the frigates.

Renouf knew nothing more than that he was to go to Crete; Ramage was sure of that. If he knew nothing more, then that drunken sot who had been commanding the *Brutus* would be equally ignorant. It was clear that when the original orders were drawn up for the two bomb ketches while they were still in Brest, it was intended that they should go up to Toulon to get more provisions and water.

That was odd, he thought suddenly, because it added many hundreds of miles to the voyage when they were in fact passing large Spanish naval bases like Cartagena, where they could water and provision. Perhaps the French guessed that the Spanish were so short of everything that a couple of French bomb ketches would get little more than derisory remarks about their odd rig if they visited a Spanish port and asked for stores.

By the time the bombs arrived in Toulon something had happened to make it necessary to give them an escort – not all the way from Toulon to Crete; only from just north of Rome. Was that significant? Probably not; the troops, cavalry and artillery the frigates were to carry to Crete were probably doing garrison duty in Tuscany preventing the sporadic attacks by Italian partisans, and it had dawned on the French that they were not vitally needed in Italy. Perhaps France was so short of men that, for a great operation to be mounted from Crete, soldiers had to be collected from every possible place.

Whichever it was, it fitted – either harbour defence by the bomb ketches and garrison replacement by the troops sailing in the frigates, or preparations for a great invasion, using Crete as the assembly point.

For all that, 'either, or' still brought the *Fructidor* and the *Brutus* to anchor off Porto Ercole with three frigates moored stern to the jetty inside the harbour embarking soldiers, frightened horses and field guns. The final question was how could Ramage discover the ultimate destination of the troops and bomb ketches?

Within reach, there were just two people likely to be able to answer the questions: the senior of the French frigate captains, or the senior of the army officers who would be embarking. Even they might not know; in the interests of secrecy, the Ministries of Marine and of War in Paris might only have told them to go to Crete, where the general and admiral commanding the expedition would give them fresh and final orders ...

There was just a hope that at Porto Ercole the senior

navy and army officers would know that Crete was in fact their final destination and that all this was a perfectly normal operation, a rotation of the regular garrison and strengthening of the usual defences.

Ramage eyed the mountains far inland that formed the spine of the Italian peninsula. He needed a group of men who spoke fluent Italian so that they could wander round Argentario without being bothered by the Italians, and fluent enough in French to be able to chat with senior French army or navy officers . . .

Apart from himself, only young Paolo and the seaman Rossi spoke Italian. Rossi's native Genoa was now a French republic, so he would be shot as a traitor if he was caught. That left Ramage and Paolo. Yet the French would strap Paolo to the guillotine the moment they found they had caught not just an aristo but the heir to the kingdom of Volterra.

A strange, high-pitched noise, musical and reedy, was coming from the *Brutus*; young Martin was playing his flute. It was a more musical version of the kind of flute often played by Italian shepherds. He could remember from the days when he had lived there as a boy how often, when riding across the Tuscan hills, he would gradually become aware that in the distance someone was playing what could well be Pan pipes. The music would begin almost imperceptibly, like warmth from a rising sun. Usually it turned out to be a young boy sitting in the shade of a wild olive tree, playing to himself as he kept an eye on a dozen goats and twice as many kids which played like children, chasing each other – most of them seemed to be twins: did goats never have single kids? He remembered the kids jumping into the air, all four legs stiff, and then running to their mothers and butting against the teats. It was a scene going back to

Biblical times and earlier . . . 'Blower' Martin, fourth-lieutenant, playing his flute with an audience of tanned and
tough seamen on board a French prize was neither historic
nor romantic; simply unusual. Someone ought to pass
round Martin's hat to see how much money they could
collect.

He stopped at the quarterdeck rail and held the woodwork, his body rigid. Southwick looked at him in alarm
but then did not move because over the years he had seen
it happen several times: that was how ideas hit the Captain. After a minute Ramage turned to him and said:
'Make the signal for captains to come on board: I want to
talk to Wagstaffe and Aitken.'

CHAPTER NINE

There was a faint hiss and a gentle splash as a tiny wave
broke on the beach, then the cutter's keel grated on the
sand. A moment later several seamen jumped over to
hold the boat so that it would not broach. Ramage leapt
out in the darkness to land on the dry sand, followed by
Paolo Orsini and finally Martin.

Southwick, who had just told Ramage: 'First time
you've had to avoid getting your feet wet, sir!', now said in
a low voice: 'We'll be waiting to hear from you,' and then
gave the order for the men to push off the cutter and start
rowing back to the *Calypso* frigate.

While coming out and heading for the causeway, the
old master had not been sure he approved of the Captain's
latest plan. As the cutter sped back towards the black
shape of the *Calypso*, anchored in the middle of the bay

formed by the mainland and the northernmost of the two causeways to Argentario, he decided it was madness.

All three of them were bound to be caught and guillotined or shot. No one could blame the French because they were in disguise and so were acting as spies. The three of them, helped by Jackson and Aitken, had spent the last two hours making themselves look like wandering gipsies, with young Paolo laying down the law about exactly how *zingari* should appear. *Zingari*: it sounded a silly word, and it described the whole business.

The Captain's hair had been ruffled until it looked like a mop, then it had been made greasy and he had put on a tattered shirt belonging to one of the seamen and then something that was halfway between a kilt and breeches, a short skirt with a few odd stitches turning it into a rude apology for trousers.

Young Orsini had made up his own disguise and Southwick had to admit the boy did look just like one of the young scoundrels who, in any Latin seaport, marched up barefaced and demanded 'baksheesh' or sidled up with some vile proposition. He had not even recognized young Martin by the time Orsini and Jackson had finished with him: the *Calypso*'s fourth-lieutenant had been transformed into any village's idiot, complete with a line round his waist that Mr Ramage intended to hold, so that Martin, in his role of a fool who could play a flute, could not escape.

It was a clever idea, though, because it got over the difficulty that Martin did not speak a word of Italian: it was not unusual for an idiot to be dumb. Natural enough, too, for a gipsy idiot to be dressed absurdly, with two or three brightly-coloured shirts, tattered and torn and worn one on top of the other, and trousers so big that they were baggy round the waist and hips, making Martin look like a shapeless sack of potatoes. No one would think of searching him – which was just as well, because in a specially-made belt that the sailmaker had completed only just in time were three pistols, spare powder and shot, and three knives, their blades thinned down and sharpened on the grindstone so that, by any honest man's standards, they were daggers of the type favoured by footpads and assassins.

Both Mr Ramage and Orsini had watched carefully while those knives were being ground down; they had balanced them on their fingers and it had been some time before Southwick realized that they were testing them for the distribution of weight, to make sure that they could be thrown properly. Then Southwick remembered Mr Ramage's skill at knife-throwing – a skill picked up during a childhood spent in Italy before the war. Southwick had not bothered to ask where Orsini had learned; it was obviously an aptitude that prudent Italians picked up at an early age.

What could a trio of gipsies find out about the final destinations of these French frigates, troops and bomb ketches? Mr Ramage seemed confident enough. Certainly his Italian was fluent; Mr Orsini had told Jackson some time ago that Mr Ramage could pass for someone born in Volterra or anywhere in Tuscany, and he could imitate the accents of other states. Naples was one of the most difficult, apparently; it was the Italian equivalent of real Cockney, and they pronounced only the first half of a word.

Something else worried Southwick: what would the senior officer of the French frigate squadron now in Porto Ercole think when he found that the two bomb ketches which should be anchored close to him at Porto Ercole were in fact on the opposite side of Argentario, off Santo

Stefano? When Southwick raised the point, Mr Ramage had said he would think either that the current and light wind had prevented the unwieldy vessels from getting round Argentario, which was quite likely because the mountains made wind shadows, or that Renouf had made a mistake and gone to Santo Stefano instead of Porto Ercole. Again, a likely sort of mistake for these damned Frenchmen.

There was another possibility – that Renouf, seeing the frigates arriving early, had very sensibly gone into Santo Stefano to water and provision, leaving Porto Ercole free for the frigates and thus saving time. Actually that sounded the most likely as far as Southwick was concerned; it was a seamanlike thing to do, and there was the added advantage that even if the senior officer of the frigate squadron did not credit Renouf with that much intelligence, he might well think that the captain of the frigate with the bomb ketches would have given the order. He might even speculate, Southwick realized as the cutter was hailed from the *Calypso*, that the frigate also wanted water and provisions.

The Captain had merely shrugged when Aitken asked what was to be done if the French sent out an officer in a boat to ask questions. 'Keep a sharp lookout, and the moment you see any signs of a boat coming out, get under way ... If you happen to run down the boat in the process, make a note in the log ...'

Southwick had admitted that he had no right to ask the Captain why he was risking his life and future, the life and future of the fourth-lieutenant, and the life and future of the Marchesa's nephew (he thought it a cunning touch to bring in the family relationship), quite apart from leaving his ship under the command of her first-lieutenant.

Mr Ramage had just grinned and said that only yesterday the master had complained of missing Nelson's great victory at Aboukir Bay, and they would all look dam' fools if they missed the chance of having their own Aboukir Bay in a month or so's time.

Southwick climbed up the side of the frigate to be met by Aitken, who immediately asked: 'They landed safely?'

Anyone would think it was ten miles to the beach and they were under heavy fire. 'Yes, of course.'

'Very well, tell Jackson to make up the cutter astern; we might need it in a hurry.'

Southwick turned to call down to the boat, and at that moment he remembered that the man at the tiller coming back had not been Jackson, who as coxswain had steered the boat to the beach.

'Jackson – ahoy there, Jackson!'

There was a curious silence. Men who had been stowing the oars along the edges of the thwarts seemed to redouble their efforts and make more noise.

'Stafford?'

'Aye aye, sir?'

'Where's Jackson?'

'Dunno, sir; 'e ain't 'ere.'

'When did you see him last?'

'Well, sir, it's dark and . . .'

'He was at the tiller when we landed at the beach, wasn't he?'

'I think so, sir.'

'But not when we shoved off?'

'I couldn't rightly say, sir,' the Cockney seaman answered, obviously being evasive.

Southwick thought for a moment and then snapped: 'Is Rossi down there?'

For a few moments half a dozen voices enquired: 'Is Rossi here?', all of them with the assumed innocence of choirboys.

Aitken tugged Southwick's sleeve, pulling him away from the bulwarks.

'Jackson and Rossi must have gone after the Captain. I saw them talking this afternoon. What the devil they think they can do, just the two of them, I don't know. I can only hope they don't do anything silly and get the Captain caught.'

Southwick sniffed his disapproval of the whole thing. 'I proposed to the Captain this afternoon that he took Rossi with him. Rossi is not only Italian but he has his wits about him: Mr Ramage refused. He said that Martin and Orsini were just right. He'll be furious when he knows he has Jackson and Rossi as well.'

'Well, there's nothing we can do about it now,' Aitken said. 'If the Captain had wanted them with him he'd have told them. He'll probably make them sit among the juniper bushes until he's ready to come back. The mosquitoes will make them look like prickly pears ...'

After leaping from the bow of the cutter, Ramage, Martin and Paolo ran up the thirty yards of sloping sand until they reached the first of the juniper bushes and then threaded their way towards the pines, their feet slipping and sliding, their balance uncertain after more than a year at sea without going on shore for more than an hour at a time.

The pine forest which ran the length of the causeway, from the mainland to Argentario, suddenly loomed up, a black wall of sound ticking and buzzing with the noise of insects and punctuated by the occasional grunts of wild pigs snuffling among the pine cones. All we need now, Ramage thought to himself, is to be charged by a wild boar and get cut to pieces by those sharp tusks.

The keen smell of the pine leaves, the way the pine needles thick on the ground were holding the sand together and stopping it squeaking underfoot, the spreading carpet of long green fingers of the *fico degli Ottentoti* plant, trying to hook round ankles and bring a running man sprawling on his face . . . Ramage remembered it all. The damp heat, the feeling that heat from the day's sun was being stored for the night among the pines, making the air seem almost solid, whereas out at the ship it was fresh, with even a slight chill . . .

Once they were inside the first of the pines, as though they had penetrated the outer wall of a maze, Ramage called: 'Right, stop here.' The three stood panting, all of them surprised at the way the muscles in their shins pulled, showing how little actual walking they did in the *Calypso*.

'From what I could see from the cutter, the mainland is only fifty yards or so along this way,' Ramage said, pointing to the north-east. 'Then we have a few hundred yards to walk along the via Aurelia and we should find Orbetello on our right. The causeway to Porto Ercole will be farther along, also on the right.'

Martin said: 'Where do you expect to find the French army officers, sir?'

Ramage felt a sudden irritation that the fourth-lieutenant should now casually ask a question which he had himself been trying to answer for most of the afternoon and all the evening. Paolo had obviously considered it too. 'Boh!' he said, in that Italian expression which has a thousand meanings. Ramage was interested to hear what young Paolo had to say: he was Italian and he was shrewd and far more likely to understand the Latin mind than Ramage.

'Well, Orsini, where will I find 'em?'

'Orbetello,' Orsini said promptly. 'The town is fortified and will have inns. French officers do not like tents. I doubt if Porto Ercole has more than a tavern. Probably only a cantina, where the soldiery can get drunk and buy wine in jugs. The officers will stay in Orbetello until it is time to board the frigates. With their women, no doubt,' he added bitterly, knowing that the women were likely to be Italian and therefore, in his straightforward code of conduct, traitors. 'The troops will be in tents near the main road.'

Just as Ramage thought he heard the squeaking of sand, a twig snapped loudly. The three of them stood silently, Martin expecting French soldiers while Ramage and Orsini listened for the grunting and snuffling of a wild boar. Instead they heard Rossi whispering hoarsely: 'Shall we give a hail, Jacko? Just a –'

'No!' Ramage's voice cut through the darkness, and he almost laughed aloud as the sound of more breaking twigs showed that both Rossi and Jackson were startled enough to take at least one step backwards.

He nearly laughed, but it would have been a humourless laugh. The night turned cold as he considered that, instead of three gipsies, of whom one was a dumb half-wit and the others spoke perfect Italian, he was now in effect at the head of a boarding-party: five men would not be able to move where three gipsies could walk openly, drawing attention to themselves with a flute and collecting money and listening to gossip.

'Jackson, Rossi, come over here. Quietly.' He heard a few more twigs breaking, some muffled cursing from

Rossi, and then silence. Then Jackson whispered, and Ramage could picture his shamefaced look.

'Where are you, sir?'

'Here,' Ramage said quietly.

A few more twigs snapped and Ramage thought he could hear the carpet of pine bristles creaking, but he was determined not to make it easy for two men who had not only disobeyed orders but simply ignored their duty, which was to return to the *Calypso* in the cutter.

'Here,' Ramage repeated sarcastically. 'You sound like a herd of water-buffalo.'

Then the two men were facing him in the darkness and Ramage could just distinguish the plump Rossi from the lean Jackson. 'Well?' he said to Jackson with deliberate cruelty, 'decided to "run" after all these years, eh? And you, Rossi?'

The sudden accusation of desertion left Jackson speechless. There were only three ways of leaving one of the King's ships in wartime, and they were marked down in the muster book with one of three abbreviations – 'D', for discharged to another ship which was usually named; 'D.D.', for discharged dead, normally noted down without any explanation although the cause of death could range from yellow fever to a fatal fall from one of the yards; or 'R', for 'run', or deserted, and the penalty for which was anything from several hundred lashes with a cat-o'-nine-tails to being hanged. In wartime the Navy was always so short of men that deserters were rarely hanged if they were caught.

Rossi, waiting impatiently for Jackson to explain but finding him staying silent, said hurriedly: 'We came to help you, sir. You see, we –'

'Help?' Ramage interrupted angrily. 'If I thought I needed you I'd have given you orders. What am I supposed to do now you're here? Hold your hands as though you were two little boys caught stealing grapes?'

'Well, sir,' Jackson muttered, finally realizing that what had seemed a good idea on board *Calypso* was completely impractical now they had actually landed, 'we thought you needed some protection, and with Rossi to do any talking . . .'

'Protection!' Ramage exclaimed. 'You come blundering through the trees making enough noise to rouse the whole French army, and then have the infernal impudence to suggest that *you* are going to protect *me*?'

Even as he spoke he could feel the mosquitoes whining round his ears and settling on his face and neck. He shook his head and realized that his hair, hanging loose, acted as an effective fly whisk – for a few moments, anyway. What was he to do with these two idiots? The whole gipsy business, which was by far the best role for him, would be endangered if these two were within hailing distance. Since he could not send them back to the ship – the *Calypso* and the two bombs were anchored much too far out to hear a hail – they must stay somewhere out of the way.

He thought for a few moments. Rossi was shrewd; there was little doubt that he had a criminal past, and this was his own country. Jackson was American, and if he had brought his Protection with him he could always try to persuade the French to release him because he was, strictly speaking, a neutral, and could claim he had been pressed by the British and forced to serve. Rossi might manage to find out something from the people drinking in the cantina in Porto Ercole.

The alternative was to leave the pair of them hiding in the pine forest, trying to find fresh water to drink and something to eat. Given that they had landed at all, they would be more useful listening in a cantina – not that either of them spoke French – than cowering among the junipers.

'Listen,' he said, trying to keep the anger from his voice, 'you both go to Porto Ercole as fast as you can. Pretend you're seamen looking for a berth. Rossi, you do the talking. Think of a story in case French patrols stop the pair of you. Your ship arrived in Leghorn. The captain sent you both on shore to do some errands but while you were away the ship sailed. And you're owed a year's pay. Calculate how much. You've been making your way down to Civita Vecchia, hoping to find a ship there. You came over to Porto Ercole because you saw some French ships coming in and you hoped there was a convoy forming – something on those lines. Mind the French don't press you into their service.

'Now, listen closely. In Porto Ercole, go to one of the bars and listen. I know neither of you speak French but you, Rossi, must arrange something with an Italian who does. Jackson, you'd better pretend to be drunk. What I'm trying to find out is where the troops boarding these frigates are really heading for. They might be going to Crete for ordinary garrison duty; but they could be going there to join a much larger army which will go on to attack somewhere like Egypt, just as the French did recently.

'Bear two things in mind,' he emphasized. 'I don't want to hear a lot of barrack room gossip, so I want to know the rank of any man who says anything interesting, and you must not show undue interest so that the French get suspicious. Tease them and tell them Crete – if that's where they say they are going – is full of poisonous snakes, or mermaids, or the wine tastes like twice-boiled pine needles.'

Both men murmured that they understood, then Ramage

remembered something. 'Are you armed?'

'Yes, sir, pistol and knife,' Jackson said. 'And Rossi has his knife, too.'

'What are you wearing?'

Ramage could just make out Jackson's hands in the darkness pulling at his collar. 'Usual seamen's clothes, sir. Just the same as an Italian would wear. Rossi checked it all.'

By now Ramage was beginning to relent. His initial apprehension that the pair might spoil his plan still remained, but he realized that they were not being deliberately reckless; they genuinely wanted to help protect him and Paolo. Still, he had to be ruthless with them because their presence would wreck the wandering gipsies' act, and perhaps they might find out something in Porto Ercole.

'Very well, off you go. Don't stray far from the bars because we'll be arriving there tomorrow evening. If we are not there by midnight, you'd better look around for a boat to steal to row yourself out to the bomb ketches — if they ever arrive.'

With that the two men disappeared into the darkness, and as the sound of snapping twigs faded in the distance Paolo muttered, as though to himself but obviously intending Ramage to hear: 'They were only trying to help.'

'Yes, they were,' Ramage snapped. 'If they get us captured, it'll be small consolation as the French strap you down on the guillotine that you were caught only because of the stupidity of two men who were trying to help.'

CHAPTER TEN

An hour later Ramage arrived in the piazza at Orbetello, walking with the smooth furtiveness that he always associated with Italian gipsies and followed by Paolo, who was holding the line which was tied round Martin's waist, leading him like a performing bear.

The town, jutting out into the lake formed by the causeways, was surrounded by a thick, defensive wall. The narrow road from the via Aurelia came in to one side of the roughly cobbled, rectangular piazza. The *municipio*, Orbetello's town hall, was in the middle of a long side with a circular balcony, like a church pulpit, jutting out from one wall so that the mayor, or garrison commander, could woo or harangue his people when he felt the need, looking down on them as he gave them good news or bad.

Ramage saw that just beyond, its tables lit by lanterns, was either an inn or a cantina crowded with customers: customers wearing bright clothes, the well-cut uniforms of officers. Occasionally there was glinting as the badge on a shako or a sword hilt or scabbard flashed in the lantern light where they were lying on the tables among bottles, carafes and glasses.

Then Ramage saw two things that for a long time now had been familiar sights in most Italian towns occupied by the French. The first, standing just to the right of the big double doors of the *municipio*, was the Tree of Liberty, a metal skeleton that owed its likeness to a tree to the skill of a blacksmith who made it out of narrow iron strips. The second was across the piazza: a small platform with a wooden structure rising vertically at one end, like a tall and narrow but empty picture frame, with a low bench in front of it – the guillotine. The blade had been removed; that would be cared for by the executioner, who would keep it sharp and well-greased so that it did not rust.

Curious that the French could see no contradiction in the two objects, Ramage thought; the dreadful irony that a Tree of Liberty stood in the shade of a guillotine.

There were no horses tethered to the trees growing round the sides of the piazza, so the French officers had not ridden in for a night's carousing: they must be staying at an inn close by; perhaps even this one, next to the *municipio*. Just as Paolo had forecast, they were not sleeping out under canvas, and he wondered idly where the troops were bivouacked.

Most of the officers seemed to be drunk. Some were trying to sing and several were bellowing in French for waiters to bring more wine. Ramage muttered in Italian to Paolo, who gave a double tug on the line. Martin, putting on a good act as a half-wit (helped by the fact that he could understand nothing that was being said), scrabbled about among his ragged clothes and fetched out his flute. As Ramage bellowed *'Viva!'*, Martin began playing *'Ça Ira!'*

It was sudden and it was unexpected at the inn, and the shape of the piazza meant the walls acted like a concert hall, giving more body to the reedy notes. The French officers were drunk enough to leap to their feet to cheer the three shadowy figures shambling towards them across the piazza, joining in the words of the most famous of the Revolutionary songs. Martin had not in fact heard it until that afternoon and had been practising, with a few other tunes, under Paolo's watchful eye and ear until the cutter had been ready to leave the *Calypso*.

Ramage stopped five yards from the tables and turned round to conduct Martin's playing with all the flourishes of a maestro commanding a huge orchestra. Paolo stood at what a gipsy boy would regard as attention and saluted. The absurd sight of the motley trio made the officers sing even louder, a few of them redoubling their shouts of wine for the *tziganes* and, as Martin rounded off the last notes, calling out the names of more tunes they wanted to hear.

Ramage turned back to the tables, swept his hand down and outwards in an exaggerated bow, and noted that the arrival of a gipsy flautist was a welcome interlude for the officers and, judging from the way he was hurrying his waiters, no less welcome to the innkeeper. Every glass of wine he could get poured down a French throat meant good money poured into his own pocket.

Ramage turned back to point at Martin, an offhand gesture that a conceited maestro would make to a nervous soloist, but also one that a flamboyant gipsy father would use to draw the attention of a half-witted son. Obediently Martin began to play a sentimental, languorous Italian tune, one from Naples, which Paolo and Ramage had decided would bring just the right amount of nostalgia to the officers. Then there came a lively tarantella, which quickly had the officers banging their hands on the table tops in time with the rhythm and demanding an encore.

By the time Martin finished that and two more tunes, the French officers were shouting for the *tziganes* to come and drink, and Ramage and Paolo adopted a pose of nervous shyness so that the officers shouted even louder and the innkeeper, worried at losing trade if the *zingari* went to the tavern round the corner, overlooking the lagoon formed by the causeways, hurried across the cobbles to lead Ramage in by the arm, thanking him in Italian and congratulating him on the playing.

Ramage paused for a moment, indicating that he wanted to whisper something to the innkeeper, and when the man stopped Ramage mumbled: 'The boy – a cretin, you understand. The flute is all he knows. He cannot even talk – except with his flute.'

'*Mama mia*,' exclaimed the innkeeper, who had a normal Italian's love of music, 'he may not be able to talk, but he makes that flute *sing*.'

'Any scraps from the kitchen,' Ramage murmured as he let himself be led to the tables, 'would be very welcome; we are very hungry and have walked a long way today.'

'Of course, of course.' The innkeeper saw one of the officers beckoning and pointing at Ramage. 'Quick, the colonel wants us. Your name?'

'My name?' Ramage repeated stupidly. 'Why, we all have the same name!'

'I know, I know! But what is it?'

'Buffarelli. From Saturnia.'

'I thought as much,' the innkeeper growled, pushing Ramage forward towards the portly colonel sitting at the table, his chubby face streaming with perspiration reflecting in the lantern. 'I can smell the sulphur.'

The innkeeper has a vivid imagination, Ramage thought. Saturnia, several miles inland and halfway to Monte Amiata, was now just a small village beside a great stone wall, built round the hot sulphur springs which had made it a favourite spot for the Romans, who celebrated the feast of Saturnalia there. A swim in the hot springs with the water so thick that it was impossible to sink, left you reeking of sulphur for days. Obviously the word Saturnalia came from the place, or was the place named after the rites? Ramage was far from sure.

'Sulphur!' he said petulantly, then repeated it several

times with a whimper in his voice as he followed the innkeeper among the tables. The innkeeper glanced over his shoulder and Ramage seized the opportunity of almost shouting, 'Sulphur, eh? I'll give you sulphur! Just because we are *zingari* you insult us, but be careful, we are Buffarelli, too!'

Ramage managed to time it so that his outburst ended just as they arrived at the colonel's table, leaving the innkeeper at a disadvantage and needing to translate an explanation to the colonel. This allowed Ramage to be sulky, so that both the colonel and the innkeeper would have to try to make amends if they wanted any more music. Ramage hoped it would lead the colonel to invite this wild-looking gipsy to sit down at his table, if only to emphasize that the last two of the three words of the Republic's slogan really were *Fraternité* and *Egalité*.

In contrast to Ramage, who was trying to look both furtive and indignant, the innkeeper was ingratiating. He spoke good French and interspersed almost every word with '*mon colonel*' while he explained that the *tziganes* had just arrived in Orbetello from Saturnia, a village many miles inland, and that the unfortunate *flûtiste*, who was dumb and not quite possessed of all his senses, had been practising French patriotic tunes for many days in the hope that he would be allowed to play them to the officers of the 156th Artillery Regiment as a farewell to Italy and a token of Tuscany's best wishes for their long voyage.

The colonel nodded, as though accepting on behalf of the regiment, if not the commanding general, these routine greetings.

'The *flûtiste* is this man's son?'

The innkeeper looked questioningly at Ramage, who just managed to avoid answering in French and said instead: 'I do not understand?'

When the innkeeper translated, Ramage shook his head. 'Brother. The other one is my son. Everybody is dead,' he added vaguely. 'I feed them both. Very hungry we are, too; it has been a long walk.'

The innkeeper understood his customer better than Ramage, and in translating Ramage's explanation into French made it such a heart-rending story that the colonel first began to sit upright, instead of lolling back in the chair, then topped his glass from a carafe, and then held up a hand to silence the innkeeper.

'A meal!' he said in a voice which would have carried well down the aisle of a great cathedral. 'For the three of them. Here, at my table – I have never before spoken to Italian *tziganes.* But until the meal is ready, the *flûtiste* shall give us his music – music to pay for their supper, eh?'

Several officers applauded their colonel as the innkeeper gave Ramage a rapid translation before disappearing in the direction of the kitchen. Ramage gave a brief whistle to Paolo, indicating Martin as well, and the midshipman gave the line a tug and the two of them came over to the colonel's table. Ramage went through the ritual of introducing them and, although the Frenchman obviously did not understand a word of Italian, he smiled benevolently at Paolo's carefully ill-contrived salute and at Martin's vacant grin as he placed his flute on his shoulder as though it was a musket.

The other officers clapped and one of them cleared a nearby table, with a sweep of his arm that sent the bottles and glasses crashing to the ground, then indicated that Martin should stand up on the table and play. The young lieutenant gave an idiotic grin and climbed up, immediately beginning a popular French tune that Paolo had taught him.

In the meantime a waiter set down more glasses and a bottle in front of the colonel, who indicated that he should fill all three. The colonel then snapped his fingers at Ramage and pointed to two of the glasses. Ramage picked up one with carefully assumed nervousness and sipped, and then signalled to Paolo, and clumsily raised his glass to the colonel.

He wanted to avoid having to sit alone with the colonel. If he did there would be no conversation, because the colonel assumed he spoke no French. He dared not admit otherwise because a gipsy in Orbetello speaking French would arouse suspicions. He wanted a couple of other officers to come to the table; then they would gossip with the colonel and, with luck, reveal scraps of information.

'The colonel enjoys the music,' a voice said in French-accented Italian, and Ramage looked round to find a young officer standing there, smiling – at the colonel, rather than Ramage, and explaining to the colonel in French what he had just said. He was obviously the colonel's aide, and he listened as the colonel explained that the *tziganes* had learned French tunes and come in from the hills to play a farewell.

'Farewell, sir?' the young captain asked sharply. 'How did they know we were going anywhere?'

'Ask him,' the colonel said, obviously too tipsy to care very much.

'You have come to say goodbye to us,' the young captain said to Ramage amiably. 'We appreciate it.'

'Goodbye?' Ramage repeated, trying to look owlish. 'But we have come to say hello. We practise the French tunes. They tell us there are French officers in Orbetello, so we come here – a long way,' he added plaintively. 'Too far to come to say goodbye. Why? Are you going home?'

'Not home,' the captain said with a relieved grin, and

149

turned to the colonel.

'They had no idea we were going anywhere, sir,' he said. 'I expect that innkeeper added to the story to get them a bigger tip – you know how these Italians work together. They learned the French tunes to come to play – I have the impression that they think we're stationed here, so they can play to us for a few weeks.'

'We might wish we had them to cheer us up, considering where we *are* going,' the colonel said bitterly. 'Still, no need for alarm, eh? You're always seeing spies under the bed, Jean-Paul. Sit down and have a drink. Where's the major?'

His voice was becoming querulous and obviously his aide recognized the symptoms. He called to a thin-faced officer sitting at the far side of the bar, a sad-looking man with inordinately long moustaches that hung down from his upper lip like curtains pulled away from a window. He picked up his shako and, with obvious reluctance, made his way over to the colonel's table.

'You wanted me, sir?'

'Sit down,' the colonel said in what obviously passed for his friendly manner. 'Pour yourself a drink. This local wine is good. From Argentario, over there. Not really white and certainly not red. Deep gold . . .' He held up the glass against the light of a candle in a lantern. 'Just look at it. They say it turns to vinegar if you move it. Pity, I'd like to take a few casks with us. That Cretan wine – *mon Dieu*, they use resin to flavour it. They'll try to persuade us to buy some casks when we get to Candia, but where we're going to it is hot enough without having to soak up resin.'

Ramage waited anxiously: one grunted word from the major would reveal the precise destination. But the major said nothing: he reached for the carafe, saw there was no glass and took the one that Ramage had just set down on the table.

The colonel noticed immediately. 'That is the glass of the *tzigane*,' he snapped. 'Get another one for yourself.'

The major put the glass down, glowered at Ramage and walked to the next table, taking the glass from a young lieutenant, swilling the wine round and then emptying it on the floor, and returning to the table to refill it.

'We leave for Porto Ercole in the morning two hours later than arranged,' the colonel said suddenly, his voice slurred.

'But, sir, all the movement orders are . . .'

The colonel glowered at the major, his podgy face growing even redder, as though he was holding his breath. 'I ride at the head of the regiment, and I shall not be ready in time,' he announced. 'I intend to listen to this *flûtiste* for at least another hour, and by that time I shall be drunk and sad, and when I go to bed drunk and sad,' he said with the honesty of someone already drunk, 'I wake up next morning with a bad liver, a bad head and a bad temper. With me in that state you expect me to sit on a damnable horse and be shaken up violently for an hour while we drag those thrice-damned guns over cart tracks to Porto Ercole. And then – *then*,' he half-shouted, the thought of it clearly making him lose his temper, 'we have to get the guns and the horses on board those ships! Have you ever seen the way the navy goes about its business?'

He glared at the major and clearly expected an answer.
'Well, sir, not really, but – '

'Heh, then you have a treat in store. Slings under the bellies of the horses, and the first ones hoisted make such

151

a squealing that the rest of them try to bolt. Guns the same. They try to lift them off the carriages and forget to undo the cap squares so that, instead of the gun being lifted, the whole damned carriage goes up like a rocket, and the sailors panic and drop it again, smashing the carriage, killing a couple of people, and making more horses bolt, probably with men on their backs. Oh, major, embarking a battery of field guns, with men and horses, is an experience. When you add to it our destination,' he added balefully, 'you realize why I wish those fools in Paris had never heard of me or my battery. I tell you,' he snarled, his voice dropping, 'if you think trying to shift those guns across the sands of that causeway to Porto Ercole is hard work, then you can think again: that sand is only a few inches thick, spread on rock. Where we are going, my man, the sand just goes down and down, bottomless like the ocean. When the wheels of a gun carriage sink into it, your heart sinks with them . . .'

The rest of the sentence was drowned by the officers clapping as Martin finished a tune and Ramage turned, gave a dramatic wave and pointed upwards, signalling to the young lieutenant to go on playing. He just had time to hear the colonel continuing.

'. . . so you talk too much, major, and I can't hear the music. Sand! In your mouth, in your food, in your wine, in your boots, in your eyes . . . It makes the axles of the gun carriages run hot, blocks the barrels of muskets and the touchholes, even gets into the scabbard of your sword so that you can't draw in a hurry . . . And you want *me* to hurry towards it! No, major, I just want you to be silent now so that I can hear the music!'

With that the colonel's head slowly drooped forward and he began to snore as the outraged major, so far unable to say a word in his own defence, drained his glass and filled it again with a savage movement that slopped wine across the table.

Ramage saw the innkeeper and two waiters coming out of the kitchen with a large plate heaped with steaming spaghetti. 'Food for the *tziganes*!' he shouted as he zig-zagged between the tables.

Martin had just come to the end of another tune and two of the cheering officers repeated the innkeeper's words in a drunken chorus, pulling at Martin's arm to attract his attention. The lieutenant, grasping his flute, looked down at them, not understanding what they were shouting and feeling the table beginning to rock as they pulled him. A moment later he toppled over as a leg of the table gave way and in falling he grabbed one of the officers in a futile attempt to keep his balance. He and the other man hit the floor together, there was a metallic thud, and Ramage just caught sight of a shiny object sliding across the floor and coming to rest almost at the major's feet.

The major bent down and picked it up. It was a pistol, the brass polished and the wood newly-oiled. He examined it curiously, noting that it was loaded. Suddenly he cocked it and pointed it at Ramage as he stood up.

'Who are you?' he demanded in French. 'This is a British pistol!'

CHAPTER ELEVEN

Orbetello's jail was next to the town hall, on the other side from the inn, and was simply a large room at one end of the cellar. Because the town was built out on the peninsula the defensive walls were on the water's edge. Indeed, Ramage thought, it was too much like Venice to be comfortable; the foundations of most of the town were below the water level so that the walls of the cellar were sodden with damp. The cellars of most of the houses must have a foot or two of water in them and the cell was either pumped out regularly or the floor had been raised.

The major was a remarkably patient man, even though he was almost cross-eyed from weariness. He had Ramage, Martin and Orsini tied securely to three chairs placed side by side in front of him with two sentries behind them. He had a chair and table brought down and he sat there, a lantern on the table so turned that the light from its window lit the three prisoners, leaving him in shadow.

With only a rudimentary knowledge of English, the major was trying to interrogate Martin and Orsini. He had established that Ramage spoke a little Italian. Ramage had had to admit to that, having been heard speaking to the innkeeper. The other two had been quick enough to insist that they spoke only English – a statement of fact in the case of Martin. Ramage was thankful that the major either disliked the colonel's aide or did not know he spoke Italian.

The major had also been so absorbed with Martin's

Sea Service pistol, with its belt hook and the word 'Tower' and a crown engraved on the lock, that it never occurred to him that Martin might have more weapons hidden under his layers of shirts. Other officers had seized Ramage and Orsini and quickly searched them but found no weapons. Obviously Martin was the only man carrying a pistol, and they had not noticed the canvas belt round his chest even when they stuck the flute down the front of his clothing, a chivalrous gesture which none of the British had expected.

Ramage felt a curious sympathy for the major: his colonel had eventually slid to the floor, dislodged in the struggle and blissfully unconscious from too much wine. The battery was due to move off to Porto Ercole next morning – this morning, Ramage corrected himself; it was now well past midnight – and suddenly he had discovered three British spies in his midst. Spies who came from nowhere, apparently, because they had not been recognized as naval officers. His commanding officer was beyond reach, thanks to the wine, and he did not know how much of the colonel's diatribe the Englishman had heard and understood.

Indeed, as he questioned the three men, the major tried to remember exactly what the colonel *had* said. The old man had insisted that the battery's departure be delayed by two hours, to allow him to get sober. Then he had gone on about the sandy track to Porto Ercole. Then he had grumbled about sand getting into everything – but had he mentioned the name of their final destination? The major finally decided that the colonel had not; the diatribe was against sand and its problems; there had been no reason to mention the country's name.

If he had mentioned the name, would this damned Englishman have understood? He admitted to speaking some Italian (with an atrocious accent), but apparently no French. The major had tried to trap him, suddenly giving orders or asking questions in French, but there had been no indication that the man understood. So the colonel was unlikely to have given away any secrets, although the major had no idea what had been said before the colonel called him to the table, except that the colonel's aide, a fop if there ever was one, had sworn that nothing had been said, apart from the innkeeper's remarks about the so-called *tziganes* coming down from the hills to play for the French soldiers.

It was cunningly contrived, the major admitted. A *flûtiste* pretending to be a gipsy and acting like a half-wit, his brother, and his nephew leading him on a piece of string . . . And they were only caught by a plate of spaghetti: the major felt himself grow cold at the thought of what might have happened had not the two drunken ensigns from 'B' battery tugged the *flûtiste* so that he toppled from the table and dislodged the pistol.

In fact it did not matter what the British had heard and understood, because they could not now pass any information on to anyone else: they were locked in here, and in a few hours they would be slung in the baggage train, securely bound and heavily guarded, and taken on board the frigates. There the colonel could bring them to trial as spies, and then they could be shot, or hanged, if the navy preferred.

The major sighed with relief. He should have thought of that earlier: the three men could have all the secrets in the world and it would not matter because they could not pass them on to their own people. Quite a problem for a spy, he realized: information was only of use, of value if one was spying for money, when it was passed to a person or country that could take advantage of it.

But what were British spies doing here in Orbetello? By adopting the disguise of *tziganes* they could, of course, travel easily; no one expected *tziganes* to have travel documents – indeed, you locked up the house and the poultry when you saw them, but that was all. *Tziganes* with the *flûtiste* – that was clever; diabolically clever. Yet . . . perhaps it was just a coincidence. Who sent them? Had they come up from Naples? Were they just looking round for what scraps they could discover about the French in Italy, or were they seeking specific information – like the great operation planned for this autumn? No one could have any inkling of that – no Englishman, anyway – because the operation existed only on paper at the moment; he doubted whether any ships at all had begun to arrive in Crete. The frigates now in Porto Ercole and the two vessels supposed to join them (what were they called – bomb ketches?) were probably the first to start moving eastwards towards the assembly point, or whatever the navy called it.

The senior of these Englishmen was obviously the eldest, the fellow with the black hair and penetrating eyes and slightly hooked nose. He looked like an aristo and now that he was not acting as a gipsy he had the bearing of one. He could not hide it. With those high cheekbones, too, he was a handsome fellow; the women would have fallen for him if he had been going to live past tomorrow, or the next day. He imagined a navy hangman's noose round the fellow's neck, taking the whole weight of the body. Not as spectacular as a guillotine because you did not get that satisfying hiss and thud of the heavy blade running down the slide and lopping off the head, with the explosive spurt of blood and the thump of the head falling into the basket. Still, hanging from the yardarm was probably slower . . .

'You – where you come from?'

'England.'

'*Oui*, I know, but now, before . . . before you here?'

The damned man just shrugged his shoulders and repeated what he had answered twenty times before. 'From the hills.'

'You are spy.'

'I am not.' He said it very firmly. 'What is there to spy on?'

'Troops, the defences of Italy, the ships in the ports . . .'

'So, now I know that French officers are living at an inn in Orbetello. There are some rowing boats with fishing-nets in the lagoon. It looks as though there will be a good crop of grapes. Last year's wine should be good, too. To whom could I sell that intelligence, *m'sieur*?'

'You may find other information.'

'What is there to discover? That the French have invaded Italy? That is old information – several *years* old. That they hold Corsica or Elba? All that is old. That there are French soldiers in Orbetello?' Ramage shrugged his shoulders as best he could with the ropes holding him tightly to the chair. 'I think anyone sitting in London with a map of Italy could guess where French troops were stationed.'

'Ships then.'

Again the Englishman shrugged his shoulders. 'There are only a certain number of ports, *m'sieur*. I can tell you there are French warships in Genoa, Leghorn, Civita Vecchia, Bastia and Ajaccio. You can tell me that there are British warships in Plymouth, Portsmouth, Dover, Sheerness and Harwich. You can also tell me there are British troops in those places. It is obvious. Ports have ships – and they have to be protected by garrisons. I can go on – Toulon, Barcelona, Cartagena, Cadiz, Ferrol,

Rochefort, Brest . . . all contain French warships, and troops. I haven't been to any of them – but it is obvious.'

The devil of it is, the major thought, the thrice-damned Englishman is right. Spies were bound to be trying to find out information for their masters, and what information could they find along this coast that would be of the slightest interest to the English? Obviously there were garrisons at various towns and, as the Englishman had pointed out, any fool with a map would know where they would be. Any port of a decent size would hold warships. So . . .

Nevertheless, here were three spies. What the devil could he do with them? There was no point in getting the two sentries to knock them about – these men were not clods; any information they had would be extracted only by trapping them with words.

He took out his watch. In five hours the regiment was due to move to Porto Ercole. By then the colonel would probably still be in a drunken stupor, but it was no good starting two hours late because, faced with the wrath of a senior officer for arriving late, the colonel would have no scruple in denying he had given the order the previous night. To be fair, the old fellow often said things when he was drunk that he did not remember next morning when he was what passed for sober. Most of the time this was just as well.

Obviously there was nothing more that needed to be done at once: the spies had been caught, and they could be taken out to the frigates, interrogated again, then tried and executed. In the meantime he could get some sleep and this jail could hold the three men until they were transferred to the baggage train. They could spend the rest of the night in those chairs, securely tied up – there was no point in risking them escaping. He gave orders to the guards and said to Ramage: 'I leave you for the night. Do not try to escape – the guards have orders to shoot. Later we find out what you are doing.'

The guards changed hourly and noisily, each couple bringing a new candle with them so that they could change the one in the lantern. Ramage talked to Martin and Orsini, after making as sure as he could that neither guard spoke English. There was little to talk about and neither youngster seemed very worried because, Ramage realized just as he was feeling sick with despair, they endowed him with magic powers which would ensure their escape.

What a brief and inglorious sally into enemy territory it had all been! He had left his ship and her two prizes; he had landed on French-occupied soil for what had seemed at the time the best of reasons – to find out the destination of a possible French army and fleet; he had been captured within three or four hours; he and two of his officers were to be executed within a few hours more.

The Admiralty . . . the devil take Their Lordships. Gianna was about to lose the man she loved, and the nephew who was her heir. Of course she could fall in love again, and would, too, and produce her own heir. He shrugged his shoulders, feeling slightly silly at making such an obvious gesture while lashed to a chair in Orbetello's jail, and told himself that as far as the kingdom of Volterra was concerned, all that had happened was that the clock had stopped for a while. And for Britain? That was more serious. Their Lordships, and therefore the British government, would have no warning that the French were not only planning a new attack by land, but were busy assembling an army and a fleet, and that the target for the new attack was in the eastern Mediterranean. Ramage realized that it would be many weeks after the attack had been made that the British would learn about it, because they had effectively evacuated their ships from the Mediterranean.

Egypt or the Levant – that was where the attack was to be made. He was sure of that because of the drunken colonel's diatribe against sand. It would be another attack on Egypt, to make up for Bonaparte's defeat at the hands of Nelson and General Abercromby, or it could be an attack in the Acre area, for example, because it was the British defence of Acre that prevented Bonaparte's move northward. In either case, Egypt or the Levant, the French were using Crete as a base, and that plus the impending attack was all that the Admiralty needed to know.

Ironically, he had found the probable answers, Egypt or the Levant, within a very short time – but as the French major must have realized, information is useless to a spy if he cannot pass it on to those who can use it. Nevertheless, he had been criminally stupid in bringing Paolo along; Rossi would have been just as useful . . . and it was doubtful if he had really needed Martin.

He should have no sympathy for Rossi and Jackson, but he was grateful for their misguided attempt to help and worried about them. It seemed inevitable that they too should be captured. Well, Aitken had his orders, so he knew what to do if the Captain had not returned by midnight. He would be in command of quite a little squadron, and he would behave in the same way and have the same responsibilities as if Ramage had died on board from wounds or illness. The Royal Navy was organized on the axiom that no man was indispensable . . .

Someone hammered on the door and a moment later a key turned from the outside. As it was flung open, Ramage saw several soldiers waiting in the passage. One of them said to the guards: 'Take the prisoners out: we are about to march.'

'Are we to shoot them here in the square?' a guard asked in a matter-of-fact voice.

'No, the navy will do that in Porto Ercole, so the sergeant says. They are to go ahead of the baggage train.' As he spoke, Ramage could hear the clippety-clop of a horse's hooves and the heavy rumble of wheels rolling over cobbles as a cart approached the town hall.

'Do we keep them tied up?' the guard asked.

'Leave them as they are; we'll load them on to the cart secured to the chairs. We don't have time to waste undoing these ropes and then tying them up again, and the mayor won't mind us taking three of his chairs.'

The other guards sniggered and the rest of the soldiers crowded into the room. Ramage felt himself tilting backwards as three men picked up the chair to which he was bound and carried him out through the door. They hurried along the corridor, up the short flight of steps and along to the front door of the town hall, cursing as they banged elbows on the walls in the near-darkness and barked shins on the legs of the chair. Finally they had the chair tilted back so that Ramage was lying almost horizontally and was able to see another group of men behind carrying Martin and his chair, while more sturdy curses in English from beyond showed that Paolo had not been left behind. Ramage hoped that the French soldiers would not suddenly drop Paolo's chair, or bump him so painfully that he let fly a broadside of French or Italian oaths . . .

Outside, a chilly greyness over the far end of the square showed that dawn was approaching. Two unshaven soldiers with battered and sooty lanterns lit up a baggage wagon; about eighteen feet long with four wheels, the front pair smaller than the rear, it had a single horse pulling it, a wretched-looking animal whose ribs showed up as black stripes of shadow, its back a steep valley between neck and rump. A canvas hood protected the wagon from rain, a grotesque and tattered bonnet in the dim lantern light.

The wagon was stowed with crates and kitbags but a space the width of the wagon and about three feet long had been left at the rear end. The soldiers heaved the chair up and another man waiting inside helped them tilt it over the tailboard. A moment later Ramage found himself sitting upright in the back while more soldiers lifted Martin's chair. Finally, when the three chairs were in the wagon, the waiting soldier checked the ropes binding them and then climbed up on top of the casks and kitbags so that he could watch his prisoners. A lantern was handed up to him and, at a shout from the sergeant, the driver cracked his whip and the horse lurched forward, its harness rattling.

Ramage then saw men on horseback riding into the piazza, their plumed shakos showing that they were officers obviously waiting for the colonel and the major to appear so that they could start off for Porto Ercole. Where were the men and guns? Ramage guessed they must be camped along the via Aurelia and were yet to have their first taste of the sand on the causeway.

By the time the wagon reached the via Aurelia and turned right along it, Ramage could distinguish the features of the guard and Martin and Paolo.

'It's cold,' the boy said, 'but at least the mosquitoes haven't woken up.'

'Yet,' Martin said, 'and we're still alive. I've even got my flute, but the damned thing has slipped down so the ropes are trying to shove it through my ribs.'

'Is everything else all right under your shirt?' Ramage recalled the sailmaker making the waistcoat with the ver-

163

tical pockets, and cursed himself for not insisting on flaps being added which could be buttoned down.

'Yes, sir. I'm sorry about . . .'

'It wasn't your fault. Never trust inn tables.'

A sudden noise like a bull being strangled startled them, and a few moments later a peasant jogged past on his braying donkey, sitting astride the animal with his feet nearly touching the ground. The trees recently planted at even spaces along each side of the road to provide shade for marching troops were growing well and proving useful for the landless owners of livestock : several dozen goats had been tethered to various trees and, as was always the way with goats, most of them had gone round and round until their ropes were wound up so short that they could hardly move. As it grew lighter the guard opened the door of the lantern and blew out the candle, and the smell of the smouldering wick caught the backs of their throats.

A pair of oxen pulling a wide-wheeled cart passed going the other way and Ramage saw how each animal leaned inwards, towards the single pole between them that acted as the shaft. It was said that from the time an animal first pulled a cart and was put, say, in the right-hand position it always had to be on that side because it became used to working with an inward list. The useless information one acquires, Ramage thought sourly just as the wagon swung round to the right, rattling and bumping as it left the via Aurelia and started down the track leading to the Pineta di Feniglia, the southern causeway which ended in Argentario just short of Porto Ercole.

Looking eastward, Ramage could see that the first rays of the sun, which was still below the eastern horizon, were just catching the top of Monte Amiata and, a few minutes later, Monte Labbro, lower and nearer. There was very little cloud; it was, as Martin remarked with irritating cheerfulness, going to be a scorching day.

The track dipped downhill for a few hundred yards and as the wheels went silent Ramage knew they had reached the sand. There was an occasional shudder as a wheel hit an old tree stump. Then, as the upper tip of the sun lifted above the distant mountains and a ray shone into the wagon, Ramage glanced across at the soldier sitting among the kitbags and guarding the three Britons. He had leaned back and slipped slightly so that he was cradled between the bags; his mouth was open, his unshaven face greasy with perspiration, and he was quite clearly sound asleep. Ramage was not sure when the man had dropped off, but had been expecting him to forbid them to talk. Then he remembered that the man had been both clumsy and silent when the prisoners were hoisted on board: he was still partly drunk from the night before.

The horse ambled on; there was no cracking of the whip or cursing, and it was obvious that the driver was in no hurry to arrive at Porto Ercole: being a good soldier he knew that it was better to travel than arrive: the arrival of the baggage wagon only meant that the baggage had to be unloaded, and although he might not have to hoist out crates or toss down kitbags, he would have to rub down the horse and feed and water it, and, judging by the squeaking, put some tallow on the axletrees.

Ramage thought it curious that the man in point had cracked that whip amid a shower of curses every fifty yards or so along the via Aurelia, and for the first few hundred yards along this track. Now, as they reached the sand, he had stopped. Perhaps he too had dropped off to sleep.

Jackson's head suddenly appeared above the tailboard,

the sandy hair soaked with perspiration. The American was holding a cocked pistol.

'Morning, sir, where's your guard?' he asked quietly, loping along to keep up with the cart.

A dumbfounded Ramage nodded with his head towards the sleeping man and a few moments later Jackson vaulted over the tailboard into the wagon, reached across the kitbags and gently removed a pistol from the Frenchman's hand without waking him. He gave a sniff and showed Ramage the empty wine flask that had been in the guard's other hand.

'You must find that chair uncomfortable, sir,' Jackson said conversationally as he took out a long-bladed knife and began cutting the rope.

'A little,' Ramage said. 'We're glad to see you: we've all been sitting like this for the last six or seven hours.'

As the last piece of rope dropped free and he tried to stand up, Ramage felt as though every bone in his body had been hammered with a caulker's maul and every sinew overstretched by an inch. It must have felt like this when the Inquisition unwound the rack to give the heretic a chance to confess.

Ramage sat down on the chair again, afraid he would topple over, and tentatively wriggled his left arm. He moved it up and down until the worst of the pain had stopped and then tried the right arm. Then he moved his left ankle in a circular movement and gently bent down to massage his shin. Finally he was able to stand up without too much pain as Paolo copied him and Jackson cut through the last of Martin's bonds. The three men thanked him through their groans.

'Sorry we weren't here sooner, sir,' Jackson said apologetically as he slipped his knife back into its sheath on

. his belt. 'We came as soon as we heard.'

'Where's Rossi, then?'

'Driving the horse with one hand and propping up the driver with the other – he's asleep too. Horse seems to know the way, which is just as well, 'cos Rossi's better with a tiller than reins.'

'But how the devil did you know that – '

'That innkeeper in Orbetello, sir. He saw what happened – accidentally caused it, so he said – and guessed you were British. He and his brother belong to a sort of partisan group that fights the French when it gets the chance. Anyway, his brother owns the cantina in Porto Ercole. Rossi had already made friends with him, so that when the other brother sent word from Orbetello, we were warned. His son, a young lad of eight or nine, paddled across the lagoon with a duck punt and then ran the rest of the way. We knew the troops were due to arrive in Porto Ercole today to board the frigates, and this is the only way from Orbetello, along the Feniglia, so we waited here as a sort of ambush, because we guessed they'd have to use a cart to move you.'

'But just two of you – supposing the French had sent a platoon to guard us?'

Jackson grinned and pointed forward along the track. 'There's twenty or so of the cantina fellow's cronies waiting up there, where the pine trees come in very close to the track, like the neck of a funnel. They're armed with a weird collection of weapons – muskets that must have been intended for the Armada, billhooks, scythes, a butcher has the big knife he uses to cut up oxen . . . They're all waiting. Rossi'll give them a wave in time, so they'll know everything's all right. Now, if you'll excuse me, sir, I think we'd better wake the driver and stow him in here

167

with his mate. We can use these scraps of rope to tie them up.'

Ramage held up a hand. 'Wait a moment. If the French find our guards tied up, they'll know we were rescued, which means they'll start searching for the partisans and probably taking hostages. Innocent people will get shot in reprisal. We must make it look as though we escaped on our own.' He thought quickly for a few moments. 'Here,' he said to Jackson, 'take Martin and lodge the driver so that he stays asleep without falling off the cart. Don't wake him up. Paolo! Put that pistol back in the hand of that guard, but be careful with it.'

He realized that Paolo still had not understood the idea. 'Here, give me the Frenchman's pistol. Go with Mr Martin and Jackson and help settle the driver. When the sentry and driver wake up, they're going to think we escaped without help.'

As the others scrambled over the tailboard and dropped to the ground, Ramage leaned over and put the pistol in a fold of a kitbag an inch or two from the sleeping sentry's hand. Then he jumped down, found that his muscles were still bunched up, saw Martin, Paolo, Rossi and Jackson scrambling down from the front of the cart, and joined them as they ran towards the nearest pine trees. Once hidden by the trunks, they watched the wagon jogging along the track towards Argentario.

'Those two soldiers are in for an unhappy week or two,' Jackson said. 'It'll be bad enough for them when they wake up and find the empty chairs, but you can just imagine what the sergeant and then the major will say.'

'That damned major,' Martin said as he extracted the pistols and knives from his canvas vest. 'He's going to want to shoot them.'

'Rather shoot them than us,' Paolo said, his voice showing that he had seriously considered the point. 'Now what
do we do, sir?'

Ramage looked towards Jackson and Rossi. 'First, thank
these two for disobeying orders,' he said with a grin. 'Then
we'll get some rest.'

The Italian guerrilla group had been told that the rescue
had been achieved without a blow struck and Ramage
had formally thanked them. The five men had then walked
towards Argentario, keeping to the beach on the seaward
side of the causeway, while half a dozen partisans
shadowed the wagon. The cliffs forming the north side
of the entrance to Porto Ercole prevented Ramage from
seeing into the harbour over to his left, although he could
distinguish the frigates' masts and yards sticking up like
trees stripped by winter and canted by sudden storms.

The way some of the yards were a-cock-bill and others
were braced up as near the fore-and-aft line as possible,
showed that the hulls of the ships, with their sterns secured
to the small quay and anchors out ahead, were almost
touching each other; so close that only bracing the yards
of one sharp up stopped them locking with those of the
next ship.

Ramage found himself trying to picture the harbour as
a seagull would see it. A 36-gun French frigate is about
145 feet long on the gun deck, with a beam of 38 feet,
making a total of 5,500 square feet. Times three for the
three frigates made 16,500 plus the distance between them,
say 120 feet by ten feet, twice . . . That made nearly
19,000 square feet – compared with the top of a cask, it
was a good target for a mortar . . .

'The punt used by the innkeeper's boy is hauled out and

hidden among some bushes on the lagoon side of this causeway where it meets Argentario,' Jackson said, pointing over to the right. 'He left it there, sir, in case we wanted to pole across the lagoon to the other causeway . . .'

Ramage's orders to Aitken were to send the cutter to the spot on the northern causeway where they had originally landed as soon as it was dark. If no one arrived by midnight, then Aitken would, in official parlance, 'proceed at once in execution of orders already received'. In the meantime, Ramage thought it unlikely that many French troops would be available to make much of a search for the escaped British prisoners, for the simple reason that they would be busy loading guns, horses, ammunition, provisions and themselves on board the three frigates. Navy and army officers being the prickly men they were, there would be many arguments: majors and colonels, angry that their own thoroughbred horses were treated in the same way as baggage-train horses, would scream at ship's officers as strops were put under the frightened horses' bellies ready to hoist them on board; ship's officers would scream back, telling the soldiers to attend to military affairs and leave ship's affairs to . . . and so it would go on.

Ramage was sleepy, and so were the rest of the men; they all seemed thankful when he slowed down as they half-walked and half-paddled through the sand at the water's edge to avoid leaving footprints, and finally found a stretch of hard sand up the slight rise to the line of the pine trees, where the fallen spiny leaves of past years made the sand firmer.

They were now at a safe distance from where they had quit the wagon, Ramage considered, and they were in sight of Porto Ercole in case something unexpected happened.

It was just the place for them to catch up with the sleep they had all missed the previous night. If they started moving towards the other causeway by five o'clock, using the punt to cross the lagoon, they would have plenty of time, and by then they would be refreshed.

He brought the group to a halt, said he would take the first watch of an hour, and told them to sleep. Recalling the wine-bloated face of the French colonel warning the major of the problems of sand in the desert, he added with a grin that left them all puzzled: 'Don't get sand in your pistols.'

The sun had dipped behind Argentario, lighting up the northern slopes of the mountain, when Paolo woke them all with the announcement that it was five o'clock, an accuracy of which he could be certain because Ramage, having hidden his watch in one of his long socks before he had been captured and searched, had lost nothing of value to the French soldiers.

They all went to the water's edge and rinsed their faces in the sea.

'*Ho fame,*' Rossi grumbled.

'We're all hungry,' Ramage said sourly. 'You could have snared a few rabbits while we were sleeping.'

'Or even gone round to the cantina in Porto Ercole,' Paolo added, 'and brought back wine, bread, meat . . .'

'I might also have been captured and brought back a French patrol . . . sir,' an exasperated Rossi answered.

'Providing the lad left lines and hooks on board, you can all fish as we pole across the lagoon in that punt,' Ramage said.

'There'll be hooks,' Jackson said confidently. 'Fishing is all they use boats for on the lagoon. It's only five or six feet deep.'

There were in fact three fishing-lines and, as Rossi and Jackson poled, leaving on the right the town of Orbetello, a group of buildings hidden behind a high defensive wall and poking out into the lagoon like a mailed fist, Ramage, Martin and Orsini trolled the lines. There were some tiny scraps of fish, baked hard by the sun and the relic of a fishing expedition several days before, and, using them as bait, they caught nothing, Rossi declaring that the lake was only good for eels and every fool knew that *dentice* was the only fish worth catching.

Ramage just had a chance to see where they should land on the northern causeway when darkness fell, and by then several other punts were round them, most of them being poled by one man with another sitting in the stern handling the line. The punts had started coming out from Orbetello at dusk, as though the men, finishing with their usual jobs, liked to spend an hour or two trying their luck with fishhooks before going home to supper.

The five men hauled up the punt and crossed the causeway to the seaward side where half an hour later, as they waited amid the whine of mosquitoes and the continual buzz of cicadas, they saw the black outline of a boat rowing in fast from the north.

'Give them a quiet hail,' Ramage told Jackson. 'I wonder if they really expect to find us here?'

CHAPTER TWELVE

Ramage paced up and down the *Calypso*'s quarterdeck in the darkness, nervous, irritated and uncertain of himself. Small waves lapped against the ship's side as she swung slowly in the wind, her anchor cable creaking at the hawse. Overhead the rigging and yards were a black lattice-work against the stars while to the westward the last of the lamps in Santo Stefano went out. An occasional pinpoint of light, like a firefly close to the water, showed that a fisherman was at work, hoping that his lantern would lure fish into his net or close enough to be speared by his long trident.

Aitken had reported that no interest had been shown in the three ships during the day. With three frigates arriving in the harbour at Porto Ercole unexpected by the Italians, the equally unexpected arrival of another frigate and two bomb ketches off Santo Stefano was unlikely to raise an eyebrow whether Italian or French. Southwick pointed out that not even one boat had come over with local whores, a sure sign of the unpopularity of the French.

Ramage picked up the nightglass and looked over towards the north-west corner of Argentario, where he could just make out the extreme end, Punta Lividonia, and as he watched – with the image turned upside-down by the glass, so that it was as if he was standing on his head – he saw a small black shape moving along the horizon, slowly merging with the Point and then vanishing. The *Fructidor* had weathered the Point, following the *Brutus*, and was now easing sheets as she found a soldier's wind to carry her down the west side of Argentario and which would, if it held, let her later stretch comfortably round to anchor off Porto Ercole.

Argentarola was the only obstruction they might hit, a tooth of a rock jutting up a few hundred yards offshore past the second sizeable headland beyond Lividonia, and Jackson and Stafford remembered it well enough to be able to help Kenton if he was at all uncertain. No moon yet, but the sky was cloudless and the stars were bright enough to show up the land. Bright enough but insipid compared with the tropics, Ramage thought.

So the two bomb ketches were running with a following wind round to Porto Ercole, but for the moment the *Calypso* remained at anchor: her part was yet to come. His plan was simple – at least, as simple as he could make it. There was no complex timetable which would leave them all at the mercy of wind or current.

Doubts, uncertainty . . . should he, shouldn't he . . .? Why was commanding one of the King's ships sometimes like gambling with cards or dice, an occupation which bored him? He had just discovered information about intended French troop movements which should be sent off as soon as possible to the Admiralty, or the nearest admiral with enough ships to do anything about it. Yet if he did that, the three French frigates which were due to transport a good many of those French troops, artillery and, most important, cavalry, might well escape.

Should he bolt with the news he had, which could quite reasonably be dismissed by an admiral as wild guesses made as a result of idle gossip by a drunken French artillery colonel, or should he stay and see if he could both alter the situation and add to the information?

He had managed to get over the time he had dreaded: sending Gianna's nephew and heir off on a dangerous operation. Up to now the boy had always been within sight. Yet, he asked himself bitterly, why should it make any difference whether he was killed by a French musket ball while close to Ramage or distant? Still, the idea that he might be killed several miles away in another ship seemed like abandoning him. Gianna would never blame him – but she would be only human if she felt that the boy might still be alive if Nicholas hadn't . . .

The boy was now with Kenton and acting as the third-lieutenant's second-in-command, which was excellent experience for a young midshipman. Jackson, Stafford and Rossi were with him as an unofficial bodyguard. No one is dead yet, he told himself sourly, not a shot has been fired. In fact all that has happened is that a French colonel drank himself into a stupor and a tired French major asked a number of aimless questions of a trio of British spies who had since vanished.

Ramage snapped the nightglass shut, using the metallic double click to break the train of thought. He put the glass back in the binnacle box drawer. Count your blessings, he told himself: he had manoeuvred a frigate and two bomb ketches right up to the enemy's doorstep without them having the slightest suspicion; all they had seen were three gipsies . . .

He had played his cards, rolled his dice, or done whatever gamblers did in London for the latest fashionable game of chance, and now he had to wait for several more hours to see how good his luck was. He had many faults, and impatience was one of the worst of them. The most uncomfortable anyway, because it left him pacing up and down like a caged tiger (or a sheep trapped in a pen), feeling that he could chew the end off a marlinspike or scream like the gulls that swooped astern when the *Calypso* was under way, hoping that the cook's mate would empty a bucket of garbage and give them a good meal which they would gulp down as they fought on the wing, snatching tasty morsels from each other's beaks.

For the next hour, the ship slept. The ship's company, apart from half the starboard watch, were in their hammocks and the *Calypso* too seemed to be resting along with the frames and planks and beams whose groaning normally formed a descant to her progress through the water, with the creaking of ropes rendering through blocks and the canvas giving an occasional thump as a random puff of wind lifted a sail for a moment. The noises would return, one by one, as soon as the frigate was under way again, but now there were only the wavelets lapping at the hull as the *Calypso* swung to her anchor, the wind now ahead and then on one bow or the other. There was the occasional hail as the officer of the deck checked with the lookouts, more to make sure they were awake than to see if they had sighted anything.

Very occasionally, as a small swell wave coming into the bay made the ship roll slightly, the yards overhead creaked, and it was difficult to know if it was the wood protesting faintly or the rope of the halyards.

From time to time the two dogvanes fluttered their feathers, making no more and no less noise than one would expect from a few corks with feathers stuck in them.

It was not often that the *Calypso* was so short of officers. Wagstaffe and Martin in the *Brutus* disposed of the second and fourth-lieutenants, Kenton and Orsini in the *Fructidor* of the third and the midshipman. This left the frigate with her first-lieutenant and her master. In fact Aitken and Southwick were only too happy to stand watch and watch about because they anticipated their four hours on and four hours off ending in a brisk frigate action.

The day's rest under the pine trees had been very refreshing although it was a strange sensation sleeping amid so much noise. Several years at sea, with only an occasional night spent on shore, left you ill equipped on arriving in Italy for the continuous and rapid buzz of the cicadas which seemed to be hiding by the score in every tree, for the monotonous 'kwark' of some strange bird that regularly, at one-minute intervals, managed to keep up his doleful commentary all through the day, and for the wild boar that grunted and scratched their way busily through the trees, cracking dried branches underfoot and, as far as Ramage could make out, never going round a thicket of bushes if they could blunder through. Ramage had discovered that after he had gone to sleep, the particular man on watch had roused the others more than fifteen times during the day, uncertain whether it was wild boar or a French patrol approaching them through the undergrowth. There had even been the rapid tapping of a woodpecker, quite apart from the buzz, hum and whine of various flying insects, most of which left determined bites and itches, and the tiny varieties of ants, some of which seemed to wield red-hot pokers.

He decided as he began pacing the deck again that there was nothing, judging from the brief stay in the Pineta di Feniglia, that made him want to change a seagoing life for that of a gipsy, hunter or even a landowner: he remembered how, in a house, whether a casetta or a palazzo, there were the mosquitoes and even more vicious but much tinier flying insects called the *papatacci*, which stung like the jabs of sail needles, as well as ants that invaded furniture. Worse, if you owned a house, was the death-watch beetle that methodically clicked its way (as though its teeth were loose) through the beams and other woodwork, turning the strongest oak to powder and tunnels. Compared with all these land noises, the creaks and groans of a ship under way was faint and agreeable music . . .

He pulled his boat-cloak round his shoulders. Timing . . . minutes, perhaps even seconds, would make all the difference between a sufficient, in other words, moderate, success and a disastrous failure. Once again he seemed to be risking too much for too small a prize. Only an ass put down a single stake of a hundred guineas for a nine-to-one chance of winning a single guinea. He seemed to have read somewhere, or heard a seasoned gambler say, that the prize should match the stake and the risk. He supposed some people did in fact find themselves in a position where they could put down a stake on the green baize table with a decent chance of winning a reasonable prize at reasonable odds, and he envied them; but that must be what made a man a professional gambler – a person who would only bet if the odds were right. How nice it must be to have a choice: yes, I will bet now; no, I'll stay out of the game and come in again when the odds seem more favourable.

Ramage never seemed to have that choice; he had to put down his stake and watch the dice roll to a stop, or the card turn over, even when the odds against him were absurdly high. Yet he ought not to grumble; he certainly ought not pity himself, as he was doing at the moment, because in the past he had won when the odds simply did not exist; when there had seemed absolutely no way of winning. In other words, he had been lucky. Gamblers who relied too often on their luck instead of calculating the odds usually ended up ruined; captains of ships of war who relied on luck to bring victory instead of careful planning usually ended up dead, taking many of their ship's company with them.

Steady, he told himself. He had made a plan and worked out the odds, and the odds seemed no worse than usual, perhaps even better. The only luck he needed (the element of chance that was bound to enter into even the best of plans) was that the wind should not drop. The direction mattered little; it just had to *blow*, anything from a gentle breeze to half a gale . . . a tramontana from across the mountains to the north, a lebeccio from the west, bringing rain, a sirocco from the south, hot and searing with thick cloud, shredding nerves and nearly always lasting three days, or a maestrale from the north-west – just let there not be a calm, which stopped any movement. With the settled conditions at the moment, a clear sky, the stars sparkling, a nip in the air, and the hint of dew, with only the very slightest occasional swell wave, there could be calm an hour after sunrise. The usual sea breeze that set in about ten o'clock in the morning might decide to have a rest for the day . . .

A bulky shadow loomed up beside him and Ramage recognized Southwick.

'Just that one fishing-boat still working over towards Talamone, sir. Everyone else seems to have gone to bed.'

'Very wise,' Ramage said cheerfully. 'There isn't much to stay up for, unless you're one of the King's officers.'

'I hope all those dam' French officers are staying up late in Porto Ercole,' Southwick said, his sniff indicating that he was making a joke. 'Let's hope the navy is entertaining the army and that they all drink too much, so that in the morning they all have dreadful headaches . . .'

Southwick always amused Ramage by making 'dam' French' sound like one word. 'If it's up to that artillery colonel, they will. Argentario wine is rather special and the colonel was certainly drinking it like water when we met him in Orbetello and so were his officers.'

'So they'll introduce the navy to it,' Southwick said hopefully.

'Yes. The *vino locale* might be an unexpected ally . . .'

Southwick took out his watch and held it to the lantern kept burning in the binnacle box so that the ship's heading could always be checked against the compass. 'Half an hour to go, sir. I'd better rouse out the watch below. General quarters once we're under way?'

'Not yet,' Ramage said. 'We can wait until dawn – the men will have been at the guns long enough before the day ends.'

Soon the bosun's mates – cursed by drowsy seamen as 'Spithead Nightingales' from the shrill sound of their calls piping through the ship – were rousing out the other half of the starboard watch. Within five minutes the bars had been slid into the capstan, John Harris, the toothless fiddler, had climbed on top, and three men stood at each chest-high bar. With the bars radiating out like spokes, the capstan now looked like a horizontal wheel. A seaman walked round hitching a line, called the swifter, to join all the ends of the bars like the rim of a wheel over the spokes.

Finally Southwick gave the order 'Heave round' and Harris began scraping away at his fiddle, under strict orders not to play a traditional British song because it might be recognized by some Italian or Frenchman within earshot fishing without a light. The men began pushing against the bars, and the anchor cable slowly creaked home, the strain squeezing water from the strands like a washerwoman wringing out a sheet.

Topmen were standing by the shrouds, ready to run aloft to let fall the topsails; waisters and afterguard were also standing by, the waisters amidships at the frigate's waist, which gave them their name, and the afterguard on the poop, ready to trim the sails by hauling on the braces which controlled the great yards, or the sheets and tacks which controlled the set of the sails.

The pawls of the capstan gave their heavy but rhythmic clack, making sure that the barrel did not suddenly spin back under the strain of the anchor cable and hurl the seamen away like winnowed corn. Down below, as the anchor cable led in through the hawse, the ship's boys secured it with short lines to the endless cable revolving from the capstan barrel on the deck below to a large block right forward. Holding the lines with which they had 'nipped' the two cables together until the anchor cable arrived at the hatchway leading down to the cable locker, they quickly unwound their 'nippers', from which they received their own nickname, and ran forward to start the same process over again.

Down below in the locker several seamen manhandled the heavy cable so that it stowed evenly in concentric rings, making sure it would run out freely when the ship next anchored. It was a hot and smelly job; when stowed in the locker the rope was a breeding ground for mildew and fungus; when in the sea it became a happy hunting ground for small crabs and various little plants that grew in the water and often had a sharp sting. It picked up sand as it scraped across the bottom and worked it into the strands so that it rasped the skin of hands like the rough bark of an old tree.

Ramage waited in the darkness with Aitken at the quarterdeck rail, the young Scotsman holding the black japanned speaking-trumpet and listening for a hail from Southwick to say that the anchor was aweigh; just off the bottom and still hanging down in the water like a great pendulum yet not securing the ship to the sea bed. Away and aweigh; Ramage mused over the two words, and how often they confused landsmen. The anchor was 'aweigh', meaning it was off the bottom, when in effect it was being weighed by the cable. With the anchor hoisted on board, the ship made sail and was 'under way' or, putting it more clearly, was on her way somewhere. She 'weighed' anchor and then got under 'way' or, if she was still moving after furling sails, or was being carried along by the wind, she had 'way' on.

There was Southwick's first hail. 'At short stay', which meant that the anchor was still on the bottom but the anchor cable was taut, coming up at an angle as though it formed an extension of the forestay. More scraping from Harris's fiddle, more clanking of the pawls, more encouraging calls to the men from Southwick, which Ramage could hear quite clearly, and then the master's hail that the cable was 'up and down', which meant that the anchor was just about to lift off the bottom, and, a few clanks later, the report: 'Anchor is aweigh, sir.'

The breeze was now drifting the *Calypso* slowly towards the northern causeway, but there was plenty of room; time enough for the anchor to be hoisted and catted, stowed along the bulwark. The cable, though, would be left made up to the ring of the anchor, instead of being cast off and led back through the hawse to be stowed below, the holes of the hawse (looking like great eyes) filled with the circular wooden bucklers that fitted like old Viking shields and kept out any waves.

Ramage clasped his hands behind his back and began pacing the quarterdeck. Plans were made, all the officers had been given their orders, all timepieces checked, charts compared for accuracy, and he had made sure that both Wagstaffe and Kenton had their quadrants and accurate copies of the set of tables on which the whole success of the operation depended: a table in feet and inches which gave, as its title announced, 'The Height, above the Level of the Sea of the different Parts of French Ships of War and their Masts, according to their Rates'. In fact they had copied only the details for 36-gun frigates, and Ramage had long ago checked the table against the actual figures for the *Calypso*.

The table gave part of the answers for a whole series of right-angled triangles. To discover the range of a French 36-gun frigate it was only necessary to use a sextant or quadrant to measure the angle made by, say, the main-masthead. The height was known from the table and became the given side of a triangle – the vertical side, whereas the base was the unknown quantity, the distance or range. With the angle which had just been measured, the base could be worked out quickly and was, of course, the range.

Measuring the height of another ship's masts was a familiar enough exercise: when sailing in company and ordered to keep a certain distance, the officer of the deck used sextant or quadrant to measure the angle made by the mainmasthead and, knowing what it should be if they were the correct distance, could see that if the angle was too small they were too far away and if too large they were too near. And, of course, measuring the masthead angle was very useful when chasing an enemy ship: the slightest change in the angle indicated which was gaining.

This time though, providing all went according to plan, Southwick had done the sums, so that the table included the particular angles of a French 36-gun frigate like the *Calypso* for the cap of the mainmast and maintopmast, and the foreyard, the foretop and cap of the foretopmast, at a range of 2,000 yards. All the officers had worked at their tables and checked the figures. They found that the old master had not made a mistake. Ramage had not expected that he would, but he noticed from the hurried scribbling that Kenton and Orsini had made errors and then rapidly corrected them.

Two thousand yards ... He considered the figure; spoke it to himself and then imagined it written down, first in his own handwriting and then in type as the figure appearing in a set of tables. The first gamble was with figures. The second gamble was that the three French frigates would be secured stern to the quay at such an angle that their broadside guns could not possibly fire through the entrance. He would win that round if they were able to fire only their bow-chase guns, one each side and no bigger than 12-pounders. Six altogether, with a range of 1,800 yards at six degrees of elevation with a 4-pound charge of powder. At that range a French gunner, or any other, for that matter, would be lucky to be able to bowl a shot through the harbour entrance if his ship was anchored 1,800 yards outside, so there was not much risk from the bow-chase guns. Or from the other guns at that range, really, unless one of the frigates managed to slew round and fire off a broadside. Then there would be eighteen roundshot ricocheting off the water, and some might hit, much as a sportsman (poacher, more likely) would fire a shot into the middle of a rising covey in the hope of bringing down a single bird.

No, he corrected himself, the biggest gamble, although still concerning the 2,000 yards, was on the forts. There were two of them, Monte Filippo on the north side and high up, and Santa Catarina low down at the entrance. A third one at the southern entrance was not really a fort; simply a series of gun positions at the end of a short headland known as La Rocca and protected by stonework.

There might be 32-pounders up there in Monte Filippo, and with a 10-pound charge they could fire a shot 2,900 yards. It would be plunging fire, and at extreme range. Ricochets were always wildly inaccurate with plunging fire, bouncing all over the place. When a gun was firing on an almost level plane – from one ship at another for instance – ricochets were often quite accurate; the first graze, as it was called, could be at a third of the extreme range . . .

How often were the crews of any guns in Monte Filippo likely to be exercised? Were the gun platforms made of wood, which might have rotted? Was there wooden planking laid over stone? Or just smooth stone? Were the French gunners up in the forts conscientious men who looked after the guns, kept the powder dry, and tended the shot, keeping them well painted and making sure they did not bulge with rust flakes? Was the ropework sound, or had it gone grey, rotting in the rain and sun, so that train tackles and breechings would be useless, parting with the recoil of the first round and letting the gun career back out of control?

Questions but no answers. Was there even a garrison in either fort? Why would the French bother, because Porto Ercole was now a port of no significance whatsoever, just a haven for fishing-boats, not a port used to supply any town except perhaps Orbetello, whose wants must be slight and which probably relied on Santo Stefano. Santo Stefano – when he and Jackson had sneaked in there several years ago to rescue Gianna they had checked up on its great fort and found out the size of the guns, 32-pounders, and the fact that the gunners never fired them in practice.

One thing is certain, he told himself brutally, it is far too late to worry now; the *Brutus* and the *Fructidor* have their orders. They know the whole objective is so im-

portant that even if the forts are crammed with France's
most skilled artillerymen and bristling with excellent guns,
the bomb ketches must carry out their orders, or sink in
the attempt. You sent 'em; you get the credit if they
succeed; you get the blame if they fail.

Aitken was shouting orders. Idly Ramage watched black
figures swarming sure-footed up the ratlines of the mainmast in the darkness the moment Aitken bellowed:
'Away aloft!'

After that there was a stream of orders aimed at the
men on the maintopsail yard, Aitken's mild Scottish accent
amplified and distorted by the speaking-trumpet: 'Trice
up . . . lay out!' The men triced up the studdingsail booms
out of the way, and then scrambled out along the yard.

'Man the topsail sheets!' This was directed to the men
down on deck, and then the speaking-trumpet was aimed
aloft again. 'Let fall!'

The topmen, who had already begun to loosen the knots
of the gaskets in anticipation of the order, knowing that
they could not be seen from the quarterdeck and anxious
to save a few seconds, untied the strips of canvas and the
sail unrolled, a great canvas sheet which hissed and
scraped in the quiet night as it flopped like a curtain
before the wind had a chance to fill it.

'Sheet home!' Aitken shouted across the deck, and then
to the men aloft: 'Lower booms!' The studdingsail booms
were lowered back into place, and Aitken followed that
with the final order to the topmen: 'Down from aloft!'

There were still more orders for the men on deck. 'Man
the maintopsail halyards – now then, haul taut!' That took
up the slack ready for the next string of orders. 'Tend the
braces there, and now, all together, hoist the maintopsail!'

As the yard was trimmed sharp up the *Calypso* began to

forge ahead, slowly standing in towards Talamone, on the mainland, as the quartermaster brought the ship as close to the wind as she would sail with only one topsail. Then the mizentopsail was let fall and sheeted home and, as the jibs were hoisted, the foretopsail was let fall and the *Calypso*, gathering speed, sailed closed to the wind.

'We'll tack about a mile off Talamone' Ramage said. 'Then if anyone in Santo Stefano saw us get under way, they'll assume we're heading up to the north, unless they have the patience to continue watching . . .'

'We'll give the fishermen a scare,' Aitken commented because the *Calypso* was now heading within a point or two of the light of the fishing-boat which had been on the mainland side of the bay for the past few hours.

'They'll know we can see them,' Ramage said. 'Anyway, they're probably asleep, with their lines hitched round their big toes so that they feel the twitch the minute a fish bites.'

He bent down over the binnacle and looked at the weather side compass. The *Calypso* was comfortably laying a course of north-east, so the wind must be about north-west by north. They would clear Punta Lividonia on the next tack and then slowly bear away as they sailed down the west side of Argentario with a soldier's wind. The stars were bright enough to make the land clear; there was nothing to do now but wait – for almost twelve hours. The *Calypso* under topsails alone was, in this breeze, almost as much trouble to handle as a rowing-boat . . .

CHAPTER THIRTEEN

'We'll lose the wind here,' Southwick grumbled, shielding his eyes with his hand as he looked up in the bright sunshine at the jagged cliffs of the headland on the larboard side and then inspected the tower perched on the top, having to raise his telescope to an unusually high angle. 'Another one of those towers . . . that's the ninth or tenth since we passed Punta Lividonia. All the same design.'

'Spanish,' Ramage commented absent-mindedly. 'This one here on Punta Avoltore is the last before we reach Porto Ercole, isn't it? They should be able to see it. In the old days it would pass the word when a ship was sighted . . .'

Southwick snapped his telescope shut and walked over to the binnacle drawer, pulling out the chart and inspecting it. 'Yes, it's the last one marked on this chart, sir. We should – ah!' Once more he shaded his eyes against the bright sun as he looked over the larboard bow. 'There –' he pointed at a tiny island just beginning to show as the *Calypso* worked round the Point '– that's Isolotto. We have plenty of water to within a few yards of the cliffs over here,' he added, pointing to a long, shallow bay opening up between Punta Avoltore and Isolotto. 'There's a narrow channel between Isolotto and the shore, but it has an isolated rock at the far end and it isn't worth the risk of using it because we can just as easily go outside the island.'

Ramage nodded. He had already spent an hour going over the chart, reminding himself of a coast he had once known very well. Southwick took a bearing of the tower and looked at his watch before scribbling a note on the slate: 'We're just fifteen minutes early, sir.'

'Very good,' Ramage said. 'I assume you're keeping your fingers crossed that we don't lose the wind.'

Southwick grinned as he took off his hat and shook his head, his flowing white hair streaming out. 'We're just getting out of the wind shadow of the big mountains; it should freshen a little once we round this point. I was just afraid that we were in too close, but I think the wind is also funnelling round both sides of the island and meeting here: we'll catch the other – ah, there!' The luffs of the topsails began to flap and the quartermaster gave a hurried order to the men at the wheel to bear away. 'See, it's veered a whole point. Still, we can lay Isolotto nicely.'

Ramage picked up his telescope and examined the coast as it came into sight, the view taking him back to a land of memories. Cala dei Santi – that was the next inlet just beyond Punta Avoltore as the land began to trend round to Porto Ercole. Steep cliffs, vertically slashed grey rock, patches of soil here and there where bushes and a scattering of grass could grow, and higher up rounded hills with jagged cones of grey stone poking through. Brown, black and white specks moved slowly just above the cliffs – goats, some grazing, others jumping with surprisingly nimble grace from rock to rock and several walking sedately in line like parishioners going to Sunday matins. The water was a deep blue, white-fringed where it lapped at the cliffs. There were no beaches; it would be impossible to land from a boat even on a calm day. Apart from the towers, it seemed no one had disturbed this part of Argentario for a thousand years . . . Looked at from seaward, but never walked on.

The bay swept on until, above low cliffs, he could make

out the angular shape of Fortino Stella, old now, looking
as though it had been let go to ruin and not to be confused with the one at the harbour entrance. In the old
days, he guessed, the Spaniards had built it there well
outside the harbour to prevent any hostile ships anchoring in the lee of Isolotto to land men and attack Porto
Ercole from the rear. Or perhaps the Spaniards used the
channel between Isolotto and the shore as an anchorage,
and the small fort protected it. He shrugged, because it
was not often one came across a fortification whose purpose was not obvious, even putting the clock back two
centuries and seeing the conditions and problems existing
then.

Finally he reached the end of the land, as far as he
could see and fine on the frigate's larboard bow. That
distant point must be the little headland forming the
south side of Porto Ercole, with the harbour beyond and
out of sight. He could just make out a straight line of
stonework – that was La Rocca, the village at the southern
side, while there was another village, Grotte, in the
north-western corner. At this distance there was no
chance of seeing if there were gun barrels poking through
embrasures in that wall – the *Calypso* would have to get
a good deal closer.

Suddenly a fleck of white caught his eyes, beyond and
to the right of Isolotto, and a few moments later, as the
Calypso's course opened up the view behind Isolotto, he
saw another. Even as he watched they disappeared – for
they were sails, now being furled, brailed up or lowered
on board the bomb ketches, which were both now visible
coming head to wind and at this distance seeming smaller
than water beetles on the far side of a village pond.

Southwick had seen them and slapped his knee. 'They're
on time, too! Those two lads probably used this stretch

here to waste a little time so they weren't too early.'

Aitken came up to Ramage, squinting in the bright sunlight. 'I can't get used to those colours, sir,' he said, gesturing up at the Tricolour. Then, when he saw that Southwick and Ramage were watching the two bomb ketches anchoring, he grinned and took out his watch. 'Two minutes early. Who knows, the four of them might become admirals yet!'

He then glanced questioningly at Ramage, who nodded. 'Yes, general quarters, but leave the port lids down; don't forget we're a French frigate just paying a routine visit – probably to get fresh water. Our own colours are also bent on? Ah, I see you have them there already,' he said as he saw a carefully folded bundle of coloured cloth secured to a halyard and made up to a cleat.

The bosun's mates went through the ship, their calls shrill as they shouted to the men to go to quarters, and Ramage was thankful he had a well-trained ship's company. Normally there was one lieutenant to each division of guns, and when the *Calypso* was fighting one side – half her guns – this meant three lieutenants and a midshipman to supervise eighteen guns. Now all the broadside guns would be handled only by their captains, who were chosen because they were steady able seamen. They were going to have to be careful that in the excitement a gun was not accidentally loaded with two charges of powder. This was the most frequent reason for a gun blowing up.

He could not spare Southwick to keep an eye on the guns – an impossible task for one man anyway – and Aitken would have to take over command of the ship at a moment's notice if a roundshot removed the Captain's head. Still, the three lieutenants and midshipman would be doing more than their share in the bomb ketches, and he was far from clear what the *Calypso* would have to do, if anything. Although the bomb ketches had set roles to play, the *Calypso* was little more than a terrier lurking round to see which way an escaping rat would bolt.

Southwick was again looking at his watch, at a sheet of paper which Ramage recognized as the timetable he had written out for the *Calypso*, and then picking up his quadrant and, holding it horizontally, looking over at Isolotto and adjusting the vernier screw. Then he examined the angle shown, the horizontal angle made by each end of Isolotto. Again he consulted a piece of paper and nodded to himself, obviously satisfied at the distance it revealed. Ramage managed to restrain himself from asking the old master if they would arrive on time; if they would not, then Southwick would be doing something about it – requesting topgallants to be set if they were late, asking for permission to clew up the maintopsail if they were too early.

The slowly increasing tension was making Ramage look for faults, and he realized that any minute now he would start asking Aitken quite unnecessary questions – was this all right, had he forgotten that, what about the other? He leaned against the quarterdeck rail, in defiance of his own rule that no one ever rested his elbows on its capping, and told himself that it helped steady the telescope. It did, of course, but there was no earthly reason why he should be squinting through the glass; he had already examined the coast, and they had not gone far enough to make any appreciable difference to the appearance of the walls and embrasures at La Rocca. The hills on the south side of the harbour were, from this angle, too high for him to be able to glimpse the masts of the frigates – supposing they were still there.

He felt perspiration soaking into the band of his hat at the sudden thought that they might have left, and used the back of his hand to wipe some away from his upper lip. The three frigates could have sailed during the night. They might not have gone into Porto Ercole. Don't be such a damned fool, he told himself, you saw them there yesterday as you walked along the Feniglia. But they could have sailed at sunset, after he and his motley quartet had punted across the lagoon. But why should they? They could not have embarked the troops in that time. Supposing they had brought, or received, new orders, to leave the troops there and go on to join this fleet, wherever it was?

He felt himself flushing with annoyance and embarrassment together, angry both for his nervousness and his stupidity: the two bomb ketches had anchored in what seemed to be the exact spot and at the exact time. He had not put anything in his orders to cover the fact that the frigates might not be there because it had never occurred to him, but Wagstaffe had initiative. If the harbour was empty he would never have anchored the *Brutus*, and Kenton would certainly not have disobeyed any order from Wagstaffe. Anyway the *Calypso*'s second-lieutenant knew that the frigate was close, and in an emergency he would have turned back to report.

So, Ramage told himself angrily, all is well; stop fretting. The ship's company always boast about how calm you are going into action (which only proves what a good actor you are), so try to live up to your reputation. If battle is an opera, then the orchestra is now just beginning to tune up for the overture, with some of the players still arriving late with their instruments.

Instruments reminded him of Martin and his flute. The lad was likely to have been giving the *Brutus*'s men a tune or two as they sailed round Argentario. How did 'Heart of Oak' sound on a flute? The men would love some of the more popular tunes like 'Black-eyed Susan', because they seized any opportunity to dance. He must encourage Martin to play more often, especially in these long summer evenings, so that the men could dance. They were bored with John Harris's fiddle; the man had a complete repertory of about a dozen tunes, at least four of which were fore-bitters, played when the capstan was being worked. Always supposing, he thought with a touch of bitterness, that Martin, the *Brutus*, and the *Calypso* survive the next couple of hours. Then, ashamed of the dark thoughts that scurried about his mind like a North Sea fog suddenly springing up off the Texel, he hoped that Martin had stowed his flute somewhere safe, so that a French round-shot would not splinter it.

He glanced up and was startled to find that they would be abreast of Isolotto in a few minutes and La Rocca was just beginning to open up beyond it. He swung the telescope slightly – the muzzles of two or three guns poked through the embrasures, but they did not glisten from blacking recently applied, nor could he see any heads wearing bright shakos beyond them or behind the wall. There were just goats this side of the wall, scrambling nimbly along the rocky face of the cliff – goats which would run away if there was sudden human activity. He walked back to the binnacle and glanced down at the compass, up at the luffs of the sails and then across at the nearest dog-vane.

The wind was steady from the north-north-west and the *Calypso* was slipping along easily on a heading of north-east, which would take her a hundred yards or so to the east of the anchored bomb ketches. He found Southwick looking at him, a satisfied grin on his face. The master gave a cheery wink. 'On course and on time, sir.'

'Luck or judgment?' Ramage enquired innocently.

'Best not enquire too closely, sir,' Southwick said modestly. 'But as best as I can make out, the lads have anchored those two bombs perfectly, and because no one is firing at them, I presume no one in the Port of Hercules is at all suspicious.'

Ramage could not resist looking at his watch yet again. Twenty minutes to go. In that time the *Calypso* would stretch across in front of Porto Ercole as though heading for the Feniglia, passing close to the sterns of the bomb ketches, which by then should have springs on their anchor cables so that they could turn to the precise degree necessary to train the mortars. As soon as the leadsman was reporting six fathoms and shallowing as they approached the Feniglia, the *Calypso* would either wear round and make for the harbour entrance, or heave-to, keeping up to windward of Porto Ercole, ready to pounce. It all depended on the guns of Monte Filippo and Santa Catarina, the three frigates, the two bomb ketches, and the chart. There might be a rock or two, even a shoal, to the north-east of the harbour, where no ship would normally sail but where the *Calypso* now had to go to get up to windward, but it was not marked on the chart. Nor would anyone expect it to be marked there, although the fishermen would know all about it. The Secca Santa Catarina was shown, a shoal just off the north-east end of the harbour entrance, and the chart said it had a least depth of twenty-one feet over it. No threat to the *Calypso*, whose maximum draught at present was just sixteen feet.

Suddenly he could see into the harbour entrance and there, like three plump black crows perched on a bough, were the three frigates. They were just as he had expected: each had two anchors out ahead and their sterns appeared

195

to be secured to the quay. The telescope showed clearly that tucked between them, on each side of the middle frigate, was some kind of raft, so that the guns and horses could be run down from the quay on to a raft and then hauled forward to be hoisted by a yard tackle. In fact the northernmost frigate was hoisting a gun carriage at this very moment. The gun had been removed – probably hoisted a few minutes ago – and now the carriage was following.

No signal flags were flying, so obviously the senior officer of the three frigates was waiting to see who commanded the *Calypso* before giving any orders – the *Calypso*'s captain might be the senior of them all. Not only that, Ramage thought maliciously, but they do not have the faintest idea of the name of the frigate anyway because we are not flying her pendant numbers. There were no signal flags hoisted anywhere, and no boats making for the bomb ketches to ask the sort of questions that could give the whole game away . . .

Southwick tapped his arm and Ramage saw the master pointing at a faintly brownish-green patch in the water over on the larboard bow. 'That'll be the shoal, sir, Santa Catarina. Won't interfere with us . . .'

By now the leadsman standing in the forechains was beginning to chant the depth as he heaved the lead, hoisting it with the water streaming down his leather apron, reading off the marks and coiling the line again. Four fathoms . . . five fathoms . . . six fathoms . . . five fathoms . . . Ramage watched the chart with Southwick and noted that the shape of the sea bottom being revealed by the leadsman's shouts was corresponding to the soundings on the chart. The pines lining the Feniglia were now beginning to stand out as individual trees rather than a dark green band at the back of a strip of golden sand which was almost blinding in the bright sun. Through the gap formed by the next bay, peaks showed up like the leaves of an artichoke.

Five fathoms . . . six fathoms. Ramage ignored the 'and a half' and 'and a quarter' or 'and a quarter less'; he was not interested in anything less than a whole fathom; the *Calypso* was merely getting into a good position, not trying to find her way through a difficult channel. Five fathoms . . . four fathoms . . . He glanced back to Porto Ercole, now over on the frigate's larboard quarter, and at the two bomb ketches, and then he looked at Aitken and nodded. The first-lieutenant put the speaking-trumpet to his lips and shouted the first of the orders that would wear round the frigate so that she would be steering back almost along the reciprocal of the course that had brought her some three thousand yards off Porto Ercole.

CHAPTER FOURTEEN

Paolo was angry because his hand trembled as he held the quadrant. It was a one-handed job with the quadrant already set at a particular angle, and all he had to do was to watch the centre of the three French frigates and warn Kenton when the mainmasthead made the correct angle. Finally he used his left hand as well, not to stop the slight tremor of the right – the left did not help because it too was shaking – but because he did not want to make any mistakes. Both the Captain and Kenton had been emphatic that the angle must be correct within a few seconds of arc; any error would mean that the frigates were nearer or farther away, and that could be disastrous.

He would not have been so cross with himself if his

hands were trembling because he was frightened – he was not; it was simply that he was excited. Who would not be excited in this situation? Here were a couple of captured French bomb ketches, once again French according to their colours, just nosing up to an enemy harbour under a flying jib and mizen, making perhaps a knot . . . Captain Ramage had been very emphatic in saying that it must all look quite normal, as though the two bomb ketches were just anchoring normally off the harbour, and the senior of the two commanding officers would be coming in as soon as his ship was properly anchored, ready to report to the senior of the frigate captains and receive any new orders that might be waiting for him. The ketches must not waste time and fiddle about so that the French had any idea that they were in fact anchoring exactly 2,000 yards from the frigates . . .

Kenton was watching him, speaking-trumpet in his hand; Jackson, too, standing forward ready to let the anchor run, was watching him. Everyone seemed to be watching him. Guiltily Paolo took a hurried look through the quadrant eyepiece. He saw thankfully, after being frightened for a moment that his inattention had taken the *Fructidor* too far in, that the frigate's masthead in the mirror was not level with the waterline that he could see through the plain part of the glass. Almost, but not quite.

'How far, do you reckon?'

Kenton's voice was harsh. It was hard to guess. He had not heard the *Brutus*'s sails flapping as she luffed up to let go the anchor, and he could just see her out of the corner of his eye, seemingly fixed on the starboard beam not a hundred yards away.

'About a cable, I reckon, sir.'

Two hundred yards . . . how the devil was he expected to translate in his head a few seconds of arc measured by the quadrant into yards along the surface of the sea? That was for people like Southwick, who could work out mathematical problems in the same way that a child's ball goes down a staircase – it starts at the top and bounces down, step by step, until it reaches the bottom and stops. And that, *ecco*, is the answer . . . Southwick made it all seem very logical when he was explaining it, but the minute he stopped explaining and asked for an explanation, the ball seemed to want to bounce upwards, or miss three steps . . .

'A hundred yards to go, sir,' Paolo said firmly, but realized that in addition to his hands trembling, his knees felt shaky too. He was not frightened, but they should not have given this job to someone who did not understand mathematics. 'Twenty-five yards, sir!'

Everything happened at once: he saw the *Brutus* turn into the wind, sails flapping; Kenton shouted at the helmsman; seamen let halyards go at the run and the flying jib sheets flogged for a moment before the sail began sliding down the stay. Porto Ercole, the frigates and the big fort up on the hill, Filippo, which seemed to be watching them like a crouching animal, suddenly slid to starboard. He turned quickly for a last check – yes, the turn into the wind meant the ketch was still sailing along the 2,000-yard radius from the frigates, so by the time she lost way and the anchor cable began to run, the distance would still be exactly right.

Accidente, his hands were trembling even more now, and the muscles in his knees seemed to be turning to water, and yet he had made no mistake; he had done exactly what Kenton had told him; the ship would be anchored exactly right. He put the quadrant down on the binnacle box and caught Kenton's eye. The third-lieutenant winked, and Paolo saw that he too was holding a quadrant – he had checked at the last moment.

'Good lad,' Kenton said. 'Now get forward. I want that spring clapped on the anchor cable as soon as we've veered ten fathoms.'

These French galliots were clumsy things, but one could hardly expect too much; they were little more than heavily built boxes which in peacetime would probably be plying between places like Calais and Havre de Grace with cargoes of potatoes or casks of salt fish; perhaps even carrying stone, from somewhere like Caen, which was needed for building a new breakwater at Boulogne. Stone-blocks, so Rossi said, were a cargo which most seamen dreaded. The great weight for a small bulk meant that masters tended to overload and if the ship sprang a leak it was usually impossible to shift the heavy blocks down in the hold to get at the source to make repairs. After a few hours' threshing to windward with a stone-block cargo, Rossi had said, and his experience had been in carrying marble from Carrara, even the toughest sailor began to imagine that with all the violent pitching the blocks were lifting and dropping on to the hull like an enormous mallet, forcing the planking . . .

'Yes,' he said hurriedly as Jackson reported that ten fathoms of cable had been veered, the anchor was holding, and they were all ready to clap on the spring.

Paolo looked round at the spring, a heavy rope which came in over the bow but which had been led aft right along the starboard side outside of all the rigging, secured temporarily with lashings to stop it dropping into the water, and coming in over the starboard quarter.

'Right,' he said to Stafford, Rossi and two other seamen, who were waiting at the bow, just beyond the mortar. 'Secure the spring. A rolling hitch, of course,' he added airily.

'Of course, sir,' Jackson said politely, and Paolo blushed.

It had not been necessary to tell *them* what knot to use, but at least they now knew that *he* knew, and come to think of it that was about the only reason for saying it.

The five men seized the spring, a rope of perhaps a quarter of the diameter of the cable, and quickly secured it to the anchor cable with the rolling hitch, Jackson using a length of line to seize the end to the cable. 'Always worth doing, sir,' he explained to Paolo, 'just in case the rolling hitch takes it into its head to slip.'

He turned aft and called to Kenton: 'Spring is made up, sir; shall we prepare to veer?'

'Aye, veer enough to take the strain.'

Paolo turned to give the men the order but Jackson's glance made him pause. The American was staring along the starboard side, obviously trying to warn him about something – the lashing!

'Cut the lashings . . .' He watched as the men went along the ship's side, slashing at the lines with their knives, so that heavy rope dropped down into the water with a splash.

'Right – Jackson, you and Stafford stand by to get the hitch over the side; Rossi and you two, veer away on the cable . . .'

The seamen knew well enough what to do, but it was part of a midshipman's job and training to give orders. Jackson and Stafford stood by at the rolling hitch, the knot making a bulky lump in the anchor cable which, in the bomb ketch, went over the bow through a fairlead in the bulwark, not through a hawsehole, so that if they were not careful the knot would jam.

Jackson nodded to Rossi and the Italian seaman let the anchor cable suddenly go slack; as it ran out through the fairlead Jackson and Stafford pushed upwards and then pulled on the spring so that the knot flicked out and disappeared over the bow. Rossi snubbed up the anchor cable to stop any more running out.

Paolo turned aft and called to Kenton: 'Spring made up and ready for veering, sir!'

Kenton, who had been watching the *Brutus* as well as inspecting Monte Filippo with his telescope, said: 'Very well, leave a couple of men there to veer the cable and bring the rest of your party aft to handle the spring.'

Kenton had to admit that he had not liked the idea of leaving Orsini to check the mast angle and distance off when they anchored: his complete inability to understand mathematics was a joke in the *Calypso*, although fortunately he could handle a quadrant well enough, and even Southwick had to admit that he had never found the lad make a mistake in the actual sight.

The youngster had been cool enough; he had stood there watching the centre frigate through his quadrant eyepiece as though admiring the view, and when asked he had given quick and accurate estimates of the remaining distance. Kenton knew the Captain would be pleased to hear about that.

Now the *Fructidor* was anchored in precisely the right place, and the spring was on the cable. He suddenly had a slightly absurd picture of what they were doing to the ship. Or, since this was the first time, trying to do. The anchor and cable over the bow was as if a bull was tied to a tree (the anchor) by a rope through the ring in its nose. Then a thinner line was tied to its tail and taken to the rope and secured well in front of the bull's nose. By heaving on the line to the tail (the spring that went to the *Fructidor*'s stern) the bull could be turned round to make it face a different direction.

Fortunately, the *Fructidor* was more tractable than a bull which, not unreasonably, would object to being pulled round by its tail. Now all that remained to do was veer away more anchor cable and spring so that the hitch holding the spring was farther ahead, to give more leverage. Then, by heaving in on the cable *Fructidor*'s stern would come round.

The men would haul and veer, haul and veer the spring until he had the ship lying at the angle which meant that the two mortars were aimed at the frigates. The spring, in more precise language, would make sure they were traversed correctly (the only time the words 'left' and 'right' were used in a ship). They were already elevated, and the gunpowder charge calculated for a range of 2,000 yards.

He pulled out his watch. Time was skidding past; they had twenty-five minutes left. Suddenly he remembered the *Calypso* and looked back towards Punta Avoltore. There she was, stretching up towards them under topsails, hull glistening black, gunports closed although he knew the guns would be loaded and the crews staying hidden below the bulwarks, ready for action. From ahead there was no mistaking that the *Calypso* was of the same class as the three frigates anchored over there in Porto Ercole. It gave him a strange feeling to think that he had been serving in her for the past year or more, and here she was bowling along on a wind with the Tricolour streaming out, to a stranger so obviously a French ship of war; belonging to a country with whom Britain had been at war for as long as he could remember.

They had reached what Mr Ramage had dubbed the 'Gambler's Half Hour': he reckoned that the French frigates would not be in the slightest bit surprised at the two bombs coming in and anchoring a couple of thousand yards or so off the harbour entrance: they were expecting to see the bombs, and two thousand yards out was an obvious place to anchor. That part of the operation would be of no interest to the French officers in the frigates; indeed, apart from someone routinely reporting the fact to the senior officer, no interest would be shown: the senior officer would wait for the senior of the two bomb ketch lieutenants to have himself rowed in to report and receive fresh orders.

The gamble would come, Mr Ramage reckoned, from the time the spring was put on the cable and the bombs were slewed round, so that they were not lying head to wind to their anchors. At a casual glance someone on board the frigates might think that the two bombs were lying to a different slant of wind; that the high hills round the harbour deflected the wind outside. But if someone in the frigates was curious and put a glass on them, he might well spot the spring, even though it came on board on the side away from the harbour, because it had to be hitched to the anchor cable well ahead of the ship, otherwise there was not enough leverage to turn the ship round. But each bomb was showing a Tricolour, so there was nothing to show they were not French. And who knew much about bomb ketches anyway? Mr Ramage had made the point that the frigates might well think that bombs often anchored with a spring on the cable . . .

So from the time the two bomb ketches started hauling round until the operation really began, precisely at half past eleven, there was a chance that the French might . . . Mr Ramage had shrugged his shoulders at that point: if the French realized their danger, they might cut the lines holding their sterns to the quay and rely on the weight of their anchor cables to pull them out so they could swing round enough to fire off a few broadsides, even if they ended up drifting on to the rocks on the south side of the harbour. Or one of them might cut everything and try to sail out of the harbour. Or the alarm might be given to Monte Filippo, Santa Catarina and La Rocca – no one knew if those guns could be used.

Kenton crouched down, sighting along the complicated mechanism with its spirit level which formed the mortar's sight. 'Heave in – handsomely now!'

Eight men began heaving at the spring as it came through the aftermost gunport on the starboard side; a gunport which had long ago been lined along the two sides and bottom with thick copper sheeting, to take up the chafing of a rope being used in just this way, a spring to aim the ship and the mortars.

It took several minutes of heaving before the ship began to turn: there was slack in the anchor cable and slack in the spring. Finally, Paolo, watching the ship's head against the Feniglia, and Kenton, looking through the sight, saw the first movement. It was slight, and would remain so until the seamen could get a steady pull on the spring, but Kenton knew that once he let the ship swing past the exact bearing so that he had to order the men to veer, not haul, they might get flustered and the ship's bow would start swinging like the pendulum of a clock.

He told them to stop and belay and waited a couple of minutes, using the time to check that the *Calypso* was still approaching fast, coming clear of Isolotto and bearing away to head for the beach at the Feniglia, where she would turn and . . . Yes, another ten degrees would do it. He ordered the men to haul in ten feet of cable. The difference was so slight he could hardly measure it. Another ten feet . . . ten . . . ten . . . ah, better. Ten more feet. Now he had the few houses in Grotte, the village at the northern end of the harbour, showing clearly. Another ten . . . ten more . . . just a fathom now, and there was the first frigate. He had to line up on the middle one

– although the three of them looked like one enormously beamy ship. Another fathom . . . and one more . . .

'Belay that without losing an inch,' he growled and remained crouching, watching through the sight, until Orsini reported: 'It's belayed, sir.'

Kenton snatched up his quadrant, checked the angle made by the mainmasthead of the centre frigate, found that veering the extra cable had made no perceptible difference, and stood up. The muscles of his thighs hurt so much that he realized he had been crouching for longer than he thought. Damn, the *Calypso* was closing fast!

He gave a string of orders and by the time the *Calypso* hissed past a hundred yards away, the shells were ready: a carefully measured charge had been poured into each mortar, a wad had followed, and then the shell had been lowered on top, its fuse cut to exactly the right length.

To one side of the two mortars, away from the piles of shells, there was a low tub of water. Notches had been cut round the lip of the tub, and now lengths of what looked like thin grey line hung down from the notches like dried snakes. Faint wisps of smoke rose up from inside the tub, showing that the slow matches had been lit and the burning ends were hanging down safely over the water. Jackson was holding a short rod which ended in a Y, a linstock, and Stafford had another. As soon as Kenton gave the word, each would take a length of burning slow match and wind it round his linstock, arranging the burning end so that it was held by the fork.

Kenton looked at his watch once more. Two minutes to go. Suddenly he realized that he was soaked with perspiration and that he had cut it very fine. The *Calypso* was ahead of the schedule! He snatched a telescope from the binnacle box drawer and looked across at the *Brutus*. They were all ready – there were Wagstaffe and Martin, standing still, two men close to the mortar, and four or five more farther aft, all motionless. Now Wagstaffe was looking at his watch and then picking up his telescope and looking at the *Calypso* – here she came, beginning to wear round . . . Captain Ramage could be wrecking his own plan by being four minutes early. There was only one thing to do – would Wagstaffe do it? Kenton felt his telescope wavering.

He looked across at Paolo and Jackson. The American said: 'Early, isn't she, sir?' Kenton nodded; his throat felt dry and he was afraid it would show in his voice if he spoke. The *Calypso* was supposed to pass northward across the harbour entrance and then turn southward again as soon as she reached the Feniglia to cross the entrance a second time ready to prevent any of the French frigates escaping. Being too early meant that she would pass too soon and the French might escape astern of her . . .

'Is Mr Wagstaffe going to open fire early to make up for it, sir?' Jackson asked.

Kenton looked at the smoking slow match. 'Drop the French colours and hoist ours . . . Now stand by to fire,' he said, and both Jackson and Stafford snatched up slow matches and in a moment had them coiled round their linstocks as a seaman hoisted the British colours and made up the halyard on the cleat.

'Fire both!' Kenton said and clutched his hands over his ears as Stafford reached over with his linstock and lit the fuse of the shell, jumping back as Jackson bent down to touch the glowing end of the linstock in the pan. A moment later the mortar gave an enormous, asthmatic grunt. By then both men were running aft with their linstocks, heading for the second mortar, and Rossi was busy organizing the sponging and reloading of the forward mortar, which looked like an enormous cast-iron bulldog squatting open-mouthed in the midst of a smoky bonfire. A moment later there was a heavy grunt from aft as the second mortar fired, and from the starboard side a sharper crack as the *Brutus* opened fire.

Kenton cursed because in the excitement he had forgotten to follow the flight of the first shell. Now he looked over towards the French frigates.

CHAPTER FIFTEEN

As the *Calypso*'s bow swung round and Aitken gave orders that steadied her on a course which would take her across the sterns of the bomb ketches – but far enough away not to interfere with them – Ramage heard a distant bark of a gun. It seemed to be a heavy gun, and immediately he looked across at Monte Filippo, but there was no sign of smoke, and at that moment there was a second bark.

Southwick saw his head turned and nudged him, pointing across at the *Fructidor*, which was now almost hidden in yellowish, oily smoke, the top of which was just being caught by the breeze and twisted into strange shapes.

Ramage pulled out his watch, flipped it open and cursed: the *Fructidor* had opened fire early. But the *Calypso* was much too early: he realized he had been so confident that everything was going according to plan that he had forgotten to check the time for the past several minutes. But young Kenton had been smart enough. A double explosion and more smoke showed that the *Brutus* had followed suit and opened fire. Ramage held the watch to his ear to listen for the tick – a useless gesture. Southwick said : ' 'Tisn't your watch, sir; the wind's freshened and we're going to be too early. We've come out of the lee of those damned hills. But the bombs have made up for it.'

Ramage could not see into the harbour yet but his eye caught the flight of one of the shells as he suddenly saw that the fault was his own. His plan was wrong. He had misjudged distances. He had explained to Wagstaffe and Kenton what he hoped would happen when the bomb ketches opened fire, and that the *Calypso* would be waiting off the entrance to attack the first frigate that came out and somehow force her to block the harbour, her bow aground on one side, stern on the other.

He thought for a few moments longer, realizing that he had lost sight of the shell as it curved over towards Porto Ercole. If the bomb ketches had waited until exactly half past eleven before opening fire, the *Calypso* would have been out of position because he had made a number of little mistakes, all of which added up. The *Fructidor*, which meant young Kenton, had noticed this and, what is more, had had the guts to disobey orders and open fire two minutes early to retrieve the mistake made by his captain. Kenton had taken a bigger risk than he probably realized, Ramage thought grimly, because the third-lieutenant was not to know if his captain had changed the *Calypso*'s task at the last moment, so that by prematurely opening fire the bomb ketches could wreck some new plan.

Well, Lieutenant Kenton was right and Captain Ramage was wrong, but for the moment all that mattered was that the two pairs of mortars were keeping up a high rate of fire: first the *Fructidor* and then the *Brutus* fired their second pair of shells, and the fact that they were firing as fast as they could reload meant, or Ramage hoped it meant, that the mortars had been accurately aimed right at the beginning.

'Clew up the maintopsail,' Ramage snapped at Aitken: the *Calypso* was still sailing too fast as the breeze increased, because the harbour was just coming into sight. No shots from Filippo, none from Santa Catarina – and nothing from the bow-chase guns of the three frigates.

Seamen were running to haul on ropes; gradually the lower corners of the great maintopsail, the clews, were pulled up and in towards the middle, a quick way of reducing the area of the canvas and the *Calypso*'s speed.

Suddenly there was an enormous drumroll, turning into a reverberating explosion inside the harbour which hurt the eardrums and echoed and re-echoed among the hills, punctuated by the shrill screams of startled gulls, and, a moment later, while the noise was still rolling and rumbling like thunder, Ramage saw a great cloud of oily smoke streaming up from the middle of the harbour, as though from an enormous bonfire.

A few moments later the *Calypso* had sailed far enough for him to be able to see into the entrance. The southernmost frigate had blown up: one of the shells must have landed in her magazine. All that could be seen of her were her masts poking out of the smoke: some spars had toppled over across the next frigate, festooning her with rigging, yards sticking out at crazy angles like pins in a pincushion and several with sails still attached and beginning to burn. The weight of the wreckage was making the centre frigate heel to the south, over the spot where as the smoke drifted the hulk of the exploded frigate could now be seen amid a white froth of water. All over the harbour there were splashes, like leaping fish: it was raining wreckage . . .

A ball of smoke appeared above the hulk as another mortar shell burst in mid-air; a second one landed close in the water and exploded a moment later, stirring up the wreckage. A third landed well beyond, over the quay, and then a fourth burst high in the air, the fuse obviously cut too short. Then Ramage spotted a movement: the northernmost frigate was making a desperate attempt to get out of the harbour: obviously all the lines holding her stern to the quay had been cut and she was being pulled forward by the weight of her own anchor cables; being pulled clear of her consort, which was likely to catch fire at any moment from the wreckage of the third ship.

At this moment the *Calypso* was in a perfect position, but every passing minute carried her southwards across the harbour entrance, so that she would have to tack back and then wear round again . . .

'We'll heave-to, Mr Aitken,' Ramage said. 'Trice up the port lids and run out the guns. Warn boarders to stand by and – ' he glanced round, looking for Renwick ' – I want the Marines ready, first as sharpshooters and then perhaps as boarders.'

The *Calypso* began swinging again, to head into the wind as she hove-to, turning back towards the Feniglia and then lying stopped in the water like a resting gull as backed foretopsail pressed the bow to starboard and mizentopsail pushed it to larboard, so the two forces balanced.

Ramage continued watching the French frigate. His telescope revealed men now swarming up the rigging and out on to the yards. On the fo'c'sle men were struggling to load the two bow-chase guns. The drooping curve made by the anchor cables was shortening as the weight of the ropes sinking into the water pulled the ship forward and towards the harbour entrance. Ramage expected to see them vanish the moment the two cables were hanging down vertically from the hawsepipes, cut on board and freeing the ship.

So far the northerly breeze had not begun to push her over to the southern side of the entrance, to the rocks at the foot of the headland forming La Rocca. If her captain had remembered to put the wheel over to make use of the little way the ship had from the drag of the anchor cables, he might manage to keep her over to larboard long enough to get a sail set. Any squaresail would help; the foretopmen, for instance, should be streaming out on the yard slashing with knives at the gaskets which kept the sail furled.

Then he caught sight of frantic movement on the frigate's starboard quarter: she appeared to be towing something – it was the raft which he had seen between her and the next frigate; the French had been using it as a ramp to load the horses and guns. Now they were trying to cut it free – and there was a gun carriage perched on it, like a cat adrift on a box.

The foretopsail dropped like a huge napkin being shaken, there was a pause as the yard was hoisted, and almost at once Ramage saw the movement as the yard was braced sharp up and the sail sheeted home. The main course was then let fall and sheeted home – and a splash at the bow showed that the anchor cables had been cut, snaking out of the hawseholes and splashing down into the water.

As the main course was trimmed, so the fore course was let fall, and by now the French frigate was getting clear of the harbour entrance. How far did those rocks run northward from La Rocca? Ramage watched tensely, conscious of a slight tremble as he held the glass. The frigate came on; there was no shudder, so she had not bumped a rock. She had plenty of way on now, and as he watched the masts he realized she was managing to turn slightly to larboard, away from the rocks and more into the centre of the channel out of the harbour.

With topsails and courses set she would move fast the moment she was clear of the harbour and able to bear away to the south. It was time for the *Calypso* to get under way again, wearing round and running down to meet her.

He gave a stream of orders to Aitken, who began bellowing through the speaking-trumpet. Southwick had produced his great sword from somewhere and was buckling it on: Silkin, his steward, was offering him pistols and a cutlass and belt. Ramage took the pistols as Silkin assured him they had been carefully loaded, and took off his hat for a moment as the steward slipped the cutlass belt over his head and settled it across one shoulder. He tucked the pistols into the band of his breeches, after assuring himself they were at half-cock, thanked Silkin and watched as the *Calypso*, foretopsail now drawing, wore round to head down towards the two anchored bomb ketches. That maintopsail was drawing again – Aitken did not have to be told that one did not chase after escaping French frigates with the maintopsail still clewed up.

A shout from Aitken and there was a heavy rumble across the decks as the starboard-side guns were run out; then, after a pause as the guns' crews ran across to the other side of the ship and took up the side tackles, another rumble as the larboard guns were hauled out so that their muzzles stuck out through the ports, stubby black fingers.

Closer to him there was a grating noise and a series of thuds as the carronades were run out on their slides. Thirty-six 12-pounder guns, eighteen a side, and six carronades, three a side . . . all loaded and ready.

A pillar of water spurted up vertically just astern of the French frigate, and smoke was mixed in the shower of water droplets: one of the mortar shells had just missed and burst in her wake: extraordinary that the fuse should continue burning under water. The Board of Ordnance always claimed that they would, but he was never quite sure what sort of tests the soldiers were likely to make to prove the point. What an explosion it had made . . .

An orange flash turned into oily brown smoke just ahead of the French frigate, and Ramage realized that his lads in the bomb ketches were shooting with quite fantastic skill; they needed just a little more practice at firing at a moving target . . . A little more, he thought ruefully; they had never fired a mortar at a moving target in their lives, and he doubted if there were any officers serving in the Navy who had.

Now the *Calypso* was beginning to move fast through the water with the wind on her starboard quarter; the French frigate was quite clear of the harbour and for the moment appeared to be heading straight for the two bomb ketches, as though determined to sink them in revenge. On the other hand she might be trying to make sure she had enough offing to run clear without getting close to Isolotto. French charts might not be very accurate.

An isosceles triangle, he thought: that's what we make. The Frenchman is one corner, the bomb ketches another, and the *Calypso* at the top, on a course which should cut the triangle in half. Bisect it, he corrected himself, and found he wanted to giggle.

A puff of smoke from the French frigate's bow showed that one of her guns had been fired; then another puff warned that a second had gone off.

Southwick looked across at Ramage and shrugged his shoulders.

'Nowhere near us or the bomb ketches,' he said. 'They must be excited over there. They're going to bear away — they might try a broadside.'

Ramage could see the stubby black muzzles of the frigate's broadside guns: whoever commanded her was doing a remarkably good job of recovering from the surprise attack: he had his ship under way and in a few minutes – it might even be seconds – he would be ready to exchange broadsides. Had there been time to load those guns? Ramage thought of the rush to get the key to the magazine, the line of powder boys waiting to collect the powder charges . . . But of course the French might have left the guns loaded . . . No ship of the Royal Navy would lie alongside a consort with loaded guns, but perhaps the explosion on the other frigate showed that the French considered the risk worth taking.

The French frigate now had headsails drawing and was beginning to bear away to the south. She would pass very close to the *Fructidor* and, Ramage guessed, would give her a raking broadside which would probably blow her out of the water. The British colours flying from the two bomb ketches looked defiant but the frigate was moving fast now and the bomb ketches had nothing to defend themselves with; they had no cannons, not even muskets. Kenton and Orsini probably had pistols – which meant only that they were free to shoot themselves if they wanted to deprive the French of the honour.

Ramage glanced down at the compass, across at the dog-vanes and then ahead again to the frigate and the two bomb ketches. There was no time to use men needed at the guns to let fall the topgallants: the *Calypso*'s topsails were rapfull of wind and that was that. He gave a quick order to the quartermaster, who had the men at the wheel bring the *Calypso* half a point to starboard.

'Will we make it, sir?' Aitken muttered, doubt obvious in his tone.

'We might,' Ramage said shortly. He was heading the

215

Calypso for the invisible point where the French frigate
would probably turn away to starboard to begin her run
clear of the whole harbour and the point where she would
fire her larboard broadside into the *Fructidor.*

The *Calypso* had two choices: Ramage could either
bear away or round up short of the Frenchman, firing a
broadside at her and hoping to scare her captain into
turning away prematurely, or he could stay on his present
course and try to ram or to get alongside the Frenchman.
In any case the penalty for being a few moments late
would be seeing the *Fructidor* destroyed. He tried to think
of it as just the destruction of a bomb ketch, deliberately
trying to keep the picture of young Paolo, Jackson, Rossi,
Stafford and young Kenton from his mind . . . why in
God's name had he ever let them all serve in the same
ship? They were part of his own life. Now the *Calypso*
and the French frigate were in a dreadful race, one to save
and one to destroy them.

'We stand a chance,' Southwick said, giving a sniff that
betrayed his own doubt. 'We could try a ranging shot with
the bow-chase guns . . .'

Ramage shook his head. 'A waste of time, and we don't
want smoke obstructing our view.'

The *Calypso*'s bow wave was hissing and the men at
the guns, coloured strips of cloth bound round their heads
to stop the perspiration running into their eyes, were beginning to cheer as they scrambled up on to the guns for a
better view of the desperate rush to rescue the little bomb
ketch.

They began to cheer and shout defiance and dreadful
threats at the French frigate, and Ramage guessed that at
least the *Fructidor* would hear the voices carried across
the water by the wind. That might be a tiny grain of
comfort for the little group of men watching the French

frigate bearing down on them and waiting for the turn away which would bring all her guns to bear.

'She has a hundred-yard lead on us,' Southwick said bitterly. 'She'll just get across our bow, turn and fire and then bolt before we get there . . .'

'Why's he risking it?' Aitken asked, obviously puzzled. 'Just to sink a bomb ketch!'

'Revenge,' Southwick said promptly.

Ramage pointed towards Isolotto. 'He has to come out this far before he can turn away – he daren't try to pass between Isolotto and the shore, and the *Fructidor*'s unlucky enough to be anchored just where he turns . . .'

Ramage bent over the compass again and once more called out a slight alteration of course. The Frenchman was not increasing speed; it was just . . .

'He has a hundred yards' lead,' Southwick said again, this time his voice angry. 'That's all.'

'Less,' Ramage said quietly. 'I estimate less than two ship's lengths. He'll be able to fire as he bears away, and by the time he's on his new course we'll be about seventy-five yards astern of him, just sitting in his wake, and only the bow-chasers will bear . . .'

It would all be over in two or three minutes. By now it seemed that every man in the *Calypso* was screaming threats and defiance at the French, completely ignoring training and discipline. Ramage's only regret was that he could not join in. The French frigate's hull was becoming shiny as spray made wet patches on the dull hull to reflect sunlight from the waves. She was slightly grey at the bow, like the muzzle of an old black dog, but it was just dried salt crystals. Her sails had been patched time and time again, but they were all cut well, and properly trimmed: the man commanding her knew his job.

All the guns were loaded: Ramage was sure of that

because he could see a face or two at each gunport; men watching and waiting for the target to come into view. He swung his telescope across to the *Fructidor*. The men were grouped round the mainmast. There was nothing they could do except wait for that dreadful broadside.

CHAPTER SIXTEEN

The shell that crashed down on to the southernmost of the three frigates, bursting a few moments after missing the main yard and rigging and hitting the ladder leading down to the mainhatch, exploded in a confined space, so that the blast and flame swept through the canvas-and-lathe bulkheads and reached the hanging magazine, breaking the windows that allowed light to shine in from the outside, and flashing across an opened cask of powder from which the gunner and his mate were filling cartridge cases in readiness for the resumed voyage to Crete.

Both men, thankful to be away from the neighing and cursing on deck, wore the regulation felt slippers instead of boots or shoes, so that they would not make any sparks with their feet; both men used copper ladles and the cask was bound and lined with copper, because copper against copper made no sparks.

They knew nothing of the impending attack; the two bomb ketches had been expected, and their arrival had been reported to the frigate's captain, who, after checking that the senior captain's frigate had already sighted them, did nothing more. The only unusual noise that penetrated the magazine had been the occasional terrified neighing of a horse which found itself suddenly swung high into the air from the raft, and occasionally there was the sharp drumming of a horse's hooves on the deck as it kicked out wildly before it could be calmed down after being lowered.

The gunner was a mild-mannered little man, once an artilleryman who had deserted from the royal service and, swept up by the Revolution, had joined the navy, where his knowledge of guns had brought him rapid promotion. He had enjoyed the promotion but not service at sea. His only previous knowledge of water had been watching the Loire flow past his little home at Tours, on the Quai d'Orléans almost opposite the Ile Aucard, just where the ferrymen came alongside the rickety wooden jetty, usually drunk and always cursing – not at anything in particular, but because the Loire flowed strongly on its way down to Angers and Nantes, before emptying into the Atlantic. In fact the Atlantic was usually the target of the ferryman's curses; the Loire, he complained, was always in too much of a hurry to get swallowed up by the Atlantic.

The shell which exploded blasted through the bulkheads with the result that in a fraction of a second the half-opened cask of powder went up and sent off the rest of the magazine, nine tons of powder. Not all of it was meant for the ship; five tons were for the flagship which they were due to meet in Crete, and one ton was for the garrison. They were due to embark another ton which the artillerymen were supposed to be bringing with them; in fact, it was the knowledge that more casks of powder were due later in the day that had made the gunner call his mate to help fill some cartridge cases: the arrival of more casks would so restrict the room in the magazine that the work would be twice as difficult.

The shell was the third fired by the *Fructidor*. Although Ramage thought she had fired without interruption,

Kenton had watched the fall of the first shell from the forward mortar and even as Jackson and Stafford were touching their linstocks to the powder at the after mortar and Rossi was beginning to swab out the forward one, Kenton had ordered the spring to be slackened away two fathoms.

This meant that when the mortar next fired the shell burst a few feet more to the south. The first shell had burst to the north of the frigate which was now heading for her; the correction made by Kenton had been a little too much – one fathom would have been enough – and the effect was that the shell landed on top of the southern frigate, not the northern one, reducing her magazine to a smoke-filled void into which the gunner and his mate had vanished. The two-fathom correction had, in fact, led to the northern frigate escaping and, in her rush for the open sea, steering to pass close to the *Fructidor,* to destroy these scoundrels who captured French bomb ketches, sailed and anchored them under French colours, and then suddenly ran up British colours and opened fire.

As the French frigate raced towards them from the west and the *Calypso* came thundering along from the north, the men grouped round Kenton and Orsini at the mainmast.

'Yer know wot?' demanded Stafford, and when no one answered he continued : 'It's like standing at a crossroads, wiv a highwayman galloping towards you from one direction, and a cavalryman coming along another to rescue you.'

'What about the other two roads?' Rossi asked. 'The difference is you can't escape up the other ones.'

'That's true,' Stafford said philosophically. 'In fact I'm a beautiful woman tied to the tree, and there's my true love on his white 'orse –' he pointed towards the *Calypso*

'– and there's the 'orrible villain wot wants to kidnap me.'

As he pointed at the French frigate Orsini said, in the deepest voice he could produce: 'I'm afraid the 'orrible villain is going to get you first.'

'Yus,' Stafford agreed equably. 'I shall give an 'orrible girlish scream, wave to my distant lover (that's Mr Ramage, of course) and get swep' orf to a fate worse than death. I can't akshully imagine a fate worse than death, but that's wot they always say.'

Orsini produced his pistol and said firmly: 'I shall fire at the frigate just as she hits us, or opens fire.' With that he cocked the pistol and Jackson leapt to one side, 'Steady on, sir,' he exclaimed nervously. 'You'll kill someone if you're not careful.'

The American began to laugh when he realized the significance of what he had said. 'Well, I'm sure none of us is in any hurry, sir.' Then he added, after looking at the two approaching frigates: 'This is such a good race I don't want to miss any of it.'

'Nah,' said the irrepressible Stafford, 'it's the first time you've ever been a prize, I'll bet. If this was Newmarket 'eath, I'd say you'd be worth your weight in guineas.'

Paolo was rather angry. Not entirely angry, but he knew that if he was still living in the palace at Volterra he would be curt with the servants. Not an angriness of the *fegato*, or in other words induced by the liver, just anger that, having unexpectedly blown up one enemy frigate, they were about to be blown up by another.

The English had a phrase for it, 'tit for tat', but the English were hopelessly impractical about this sort of thing. He had been surprised to find out from the Captain that the English regarded Machiavelli as 'rather a scoundrel', and tended to get sentimental about their enemies after they had won a victory. If the French won this war, then they would set up guillotines in every town in Britain, and execute anyone who had two pennies to rub together on the grounds that he was an aristo. If the English won, or rather *when* they won, they would probably dance in the streets with the French and tell them how naughty it was of them to have executed their royal family.

Surprising how time slowed down at moments like this, Paolo thought to himself: the enemy is steering straight for us at six knots or more and fear slows things down so that you can have quite complicated thoughts. Still, as the frigate got closer the thoughts became less complicated. Aunt Gianna would be proud of the way he had died. But she would probably never know, because the Captain would not have seen that it was a shell from the *Fructidor*'s mortar that blew up the other French frigate.

He wished, as he stood under the hot Italian sun, that he had studied mathematics more carefully with Mr Southwick, who was such a patient man. It was a pity Mr Southwick did not have a son, because he would make a wonderful father – or grandfather rather. Anyway one could only hope that he knew that Paolo Orsini was grateful.

The Captain was just a few hundred yards away: he would be standing at the quarterdeck rail, his deepset brown eyes sunk even deeper, the skin of his face taut, almost tight over the high cheekbones, his nose like an eagle's beak (though not so curved, of course) as though he was about to peck. His voice would be calm and *he* would be calm. He would tell Aunt Gianna what had happened – at least, as much as he knew of it.

Who would rule Volterra after Aunt Gianna died? Would she marry the Captain and have a son who would become the ruler? He hoped so. A boy who had Aunt Gianna for a mother and the Captain for a father would grow up a man among men and fit to rule.

He turned, intending to shake hands with the rest of the men, starting off with Kenton, but he stumbled over the thick rope of the spring. As he regained his balance he looked at the French frigate. Her masts now beginning to tower high so that all the mountains beyond were lower. Then he looked at the *Calypso*. Her masts were lower, too, which meant that she was just that much farther away. Not much in it – he knew that from his very recent experience of measuring the heights of masts with the quadrant.

'Can't be a hundred yards in it,' Kenton murmured. 'I think now is the time to say goodbye, so thanks, men, at least we took a French frigate with us. But we've run out of surprises . . .'

The spring. Paolo looked at the pile of rope. Twenty fathoms or more of it, more than a hundred feet. The spring was holding the *Fructidor* well over to the northeast of where her anchor was lying; holding her so that the wind, instead of blowing from the bow, was almost on the starboard beam.

He turned to Kenton, after a quick glance at the French frigate, which was now steering almost directly at them, making sure that, when she turned, her broadside would be fired at less than fifty yards' range.

'If we let the spring go, we'll swing right across the Frenchman's bow,' Paolo said calmly, but louder than he had intended. 'Either he'll ram us or have to bear away suddenly. If he has to bear away his gunners are likely to miss because she'll be swinging . . .'

But Kenton was no longer standing there: with a bellow of 'Quick, men!' he had leapt at the spring and begun flinging the turns off the kevel. Jackson was the first to react, and within moments the rope, like a coiled snake, was free and beginning to race out of the gunport, with Jackson bellowing at them to kick and pull out the kinks and bights in case it all twisted into a tangled mess and jammed in the port.

Paolo stood up and looked across at the *Calypso* and then at the Feniglia beyond her. For several moments the *Fructidor*'s bow remained steady, as though the ship had run aground; then he thought he detected a slight movement just as he heard a splash when the last of the spring slid into the water. It was too slight and too slow; he could already hear the thunder and hiss of the French frigate's bow wave and the occasional thump as a sail flapped.

CHAPTER SEVENTEEN

Ramage knew that not only had he made a grave mistake but he had probably killed Paolo, Kenton, Jackson, Rossi and Stafford, and the rest of the men whose names he could not for the moment remember. He had probably killed them all because he must have measured the distance from the harbour entrance to the Feniglia and back wrongly. He was unlikely to have done that, he decided, so he must have relied too much on a chart which he knew could not be accurate to a few hundred yards. Not accurate for longer distances like those, although it would be accurate enough in giving the width between the headlands forming the harbour, or the length of Isolotto . . .

He should have allowed for chart error of up to a cable. Two hundred yards would have been enough; two hundred yards would mean that at this moment the *Calypso* would be between that damned French frigate and the *Fructidor*. Not just between them, but forcing the Frenchman to turn away and fight, ship to ship. The fight would have been the fairest ever fought in the Mediterranean, or anywhere else for that matter, because they were identical ships.

He looked again at the French frigate, her mastheads beginning to tower high fine on the starboard bow, waiting for the tell-tale flap of the luffs and leeches of her sails or the rush of men to sheets and braces that would warn him the moment she began to turn away. Two hundred yards to go, one hundred and seventy-five, one hundred and fifty, one hundred and twenty-five . . . That was curious, it was still about one hundred and twenty-five . . .

'The bomb's swinging! She's swinging!' Southwick was bellowing. In his excitement he slapped his captain on the back. 'Oh, just look at her, sir!'

'She's slipped her spring,' said Aitken, matter-of-factly. 'That's surprised those Frenchmen!'

'Aye, the *Fructidor*'s swinging right across her bow! Will they dare ram the bomb? One of her masts might whip one of their yards out! By God,' Southwick shouted, 'we'll have them yet!'

Ramage snatched the speaking-trumpet from Aitken's hand, put it to his lips and was startled when a roaring voice he did not recognize as his own hurled itself at the seamen at the guns below him.

'Stand by down there!' he bellowed. 'There's just a chance we'll save 'em. Starboard guns, there: open fire as the target bears, and keep on firing until she strikes her colours!'

The men cheered and yelled in reply as he handed the speaking-trumpet back to Aitken, who said excitedly: 'They're beginning to turn away, sir – '

They could turn before they had intended and yet still give the *Fructidor* a broadside; that much was obvious. But although the race to interpose the *Calypso* between the frigate and the bomb ketch was over, there was time for a quick sidestep.

He snatched back the speaking-trumpet, yelled at the men at the wheel to turn four points to larboard and, speaking-trumpet to his mouth, turned again to the men at the guns. 'Listen down there!' he roared. 'You're going to see that Frenchman for less than a minute, and the range will be about a hundred yards. Aim for the hull, otherwise the *Fructidor* will get their whole broadside!'

He turned away. Damnation, this was like the Mall with three horses bolting at once: to come round to larboard far enough for the *Calypso*'s starboard-side guns to bear meant that he would have to shave under the *Fructidor*'s stern the moment the guns had fired . . . Still, there was no choice!

The Frenchman was broad on the bow as the *Calypso* swung one way to bring her guns to bear and the Frenchman turned the other in a desperate last-moment attempt to dodge the broadside they now saw would hit them.

'Here they come!' Ramage found himself roaring into the speaking-trumpet and it seemed from all round him there was the popping of muskets as Renwick's Marines fired at the Frenchman's quarterdeck. The 12-pounders thundered in a rippling fire one after the other down the starboard side, but Ramage hardly heard them because of the blood beating in his ears. He saw puffs as the guns fired, and then thick clouds of oily-yellow smoke as the puffs merged and began to stream out of the ports . . .

An enormous cough, another and then another as the carronades almost beside him fired, flinging the lemon-sized grapeshot into the French ship.

He glimpsed the *Fructidor* only a few yards away and almost dead ahead. 'Hard a' starboard,' he bellowed at the men at the wheel.

Smoke and noise – the heavy thudding of roundshot hitting solid wood, the whine of splinters being thrown up in swathes, the bell-like clanging of roundshot ricocheting from metal . . . the Frenchmen had let go their broadside at the *Calypso*, tit for tat. Now the men were scurrying around reloading and – hellfire and damnation, any moment the *Calypso* will be so far round she would be taken a'back – no, the men were spinning the wheel, almost climbing up the spokes in their urgency – and Aitken was standing beside them, looking as calm as if he was just checking that the gillie's gralloching knife was sharp enough before they cleaned the deer he had just shot.

Where was everyone? The French frigate was squaring her yards to run off before the wind, smoke streaming from the larboard gunports as though she was on fire, and the *Fructidor* was sliding past on the quarter. Every man in the *Calypso* who was not busy loading the guns or steering the ship was standing at gunports or even perched on the hammock nettings cheering as the frigate swept by.

'I saw young Orsini,' Southwick said gruffly. 'And Kenton, and the rest of them. No damage to the ketch; I don't think they had any casualties. The Frenchman was more concerned with firing at us.'

Ramage nodded and looked away because the old master seemed to want to have a good weep from sheer relief and Ramage felt like joining him. The French frigate was now five hundred yards ahead . . . the turn to bring the *Calypso*'s broadside guns to bear had cost her dearly in distance.

'Mr Aitken,' he said, 'let fall the topgallants, and set the stunsails. Not the courses; I'm not fighting under courses. That Frenchman's lucky they didn't catch fire. We'll cut the stunsails adrift when we get alongside him.'

Southwick pointed at the *Brutus*, which was setting sail. 'What's Wagstaffe up to, then?'

Ramage thought for a moment. 'Going into Porto Ercole to see what he can find, I suspect, and Kenton will be close in his wake.'

Southwick lifted up his quadrant and carefully measured the angle made by the Frenchman's mizentopmasthead. He then looked at his watch and, after putting the quadrant down carefully, noted the angle and the time on the slate. 'It'll depend on which of us has the cleanest bottom,' he said to no one in particular. 'So if he's been growing barnacles in Toulon, we'll beat him providing the Toulon barnacles are bigger than the ones we brought over from the West Indies.'

Ramage changed his mind, and to gain a knot or two gave the order to set the fore and main courses, the largest sails in the ship. While they were being let fall he reflected that a stern chase is a long chase . . . That had been dinned into him from the days when he was a young midshipman. The frigate's name was *Le Furet*. The Ferret. He had forgotten to look until this moment, but it showed up well in the telescope. The letters were carefully painted in blue on a red background; indeed, the whole transom was carefully painted. Not at all like the usual French ship of war, especially of the size of a frigate. There was always a shortage of paint in any dockyard, but he knew that in French dockyards these days it was critical, and no French captain was going to spend his own money on the extra few tins of paint that brightened up a ship . . . To spend money on gold leaf would be an anti-Revolutionary act, he supposed. Anyway, the *Furet* looked a good deal smarter than most French frigates he had seen. Still, he had a feeling that by the time this day was over he was going to be heartily sick of the sight of the *Furet*'s transom; her captain obviously knew how to get the last quarter of a knot out of his ship.

Southwick picked up his quadrant, twiddled the vernier and, after consulting his watch, noted his findings down on the slate. He pondered for a minute or two and then looked up at Ramage with a cheerful grin. 'We've gained a few yards, and we haven't got the stunsails rigged out yet.'

By now the courses had been trimmed, the studdingsails (in effect long strips of canvas to be hoisted up alongside each of the squaresails to make them wider, the tops held out by the stunsail booms, which slid out to form extensions of the yards) had been brought up on deck from the sail room and the special halyards were ready.

Aitken took the speaking-trumpet while Southwick continued keeping a watch on the *Furet*.

'Starboard stunsails ready, there!'

The first-lieutenant ran his eye over the three bundles now resting on the deck abreast each of the masts.

'Hands aloft rig out the booms!'

The topmen streamed up the rigging and along the yards, sliding out the pole-like booms which they normally had to lift up while they were working on the sails. These booms, now poking out like fishing-rods, seemed too flimsy for the job they had to do.

'Haul taut the tacks, and belay!'

Ramage stopped listening to Aitken's sequence of orders

as he tried to guess the *Furet*'s destination. For the moment she was obviously intent on escaping, but where would she have gone with the other two frigates and the two bombs, had everything gone the way the French planned? To Crete, of course, but where after that?

What was the *Furet*'s captain intending to do? If he managed to stay ahead of the *Calypso* until nightfall, he would need to have a lead of a couple of miles or more to stand a chance of dodging in the darkness – unless there was thick cloud. But a clear night with stars meant the *Furet*'s sails would be easily seen by the *Calypso*'s lookouts. Supposing he *did* escape completely though – which obviously he was trying to do, escape without fighting – where would he go? The next couple of hours might show – by then he would be clear of any possible wind shadow from Argentario, and the *Furet* would either turn to the west-south-west if he intended going back to Toulon, planning to pass through the Strait of Bonifacio between Corsica and Sardinia, or carry on to the south if he intended rounding Sicily and turning eastward towards Crete. Of course, he might make a bolt for Civita Vecchia, now only a few miles to the south along the Italian mainland, hoping to find safety there, but a wily fox never bolted for its lair when the hounds were in really close pursuit . . .

By now the stunsails were set and trimmed, and as the *Calypso* seemed almost to surge along Southwick said: 'The wind's freshening, sir. A cast of the log?'

Ramage shook his head. 'It won't make us go any faster. Our only concern is catching up with that blasted frigate – and the angle shown on your quadrant will tell us more exactly than the log.'

'Well, we gained a little when you set the courses, but lost it when the *Furet* set her stunsails – she had them up and trimmed before we did. Now we might be gaining a little, I'm waiting a few minutes for our halyards to settle, and Mr Aitken's busy with the sheets and braces: a foot here and a foot there makes a difference . . .'

The Italian mainland, now flattening in the great plain and marsh that led to Rome, was sliding past as though the *Calypso* was a bird flying south to a warmer climate. The Torre di Buranaccio, where he had first met Gianna, had already dropped below the horizon on the larboard quarter; soon he would be able to see the hill towns of Montalto di Castro and then Tarquinia, standing behind their walls beside the via Aurelia like massive sentries from the days of the Caesars guarding the long road to Rome.

Ramage started as Southwick gave a cross between a bark and a chuckle as he put down his quadrant.

'We've gained a little . . . perhaps a quarter of a ship's length.'

'We're not exactly ready to range alongside and board her in the smoke,' Ramage said irritably. 'The wind hasn't freshened; it's easing if anything.'

'Aye, sir,' Southwick agreed soberly. 'We both have the same sail set, but if that French captain doesn't want to turn and fight, it could take us a couple of days to catch him.'

'Obviously he doesn't want to fight,' Ramage snapped. 'Can't say I blame him: he just saw one of his squadron blow up almost alongside him, and the second ship is probably wrecked.'

'But we're still even, sir, ship against ship,' Southwick pointed out reasonably.

'Ship against ship,' Ramage said sarcastically, 'doesn't mean very much unless they're in range of each other.'

Southwick knew his captain's temper was getting short

because of the frustration of having the *Furet* out of reach and range ahead of him. He was not a man with enough patience to sail in another ship's wake for very long.

'We need something to surprise him,' Southwick said complacently, being himself quite prepared to take a couple of days, gaining inch by inch, providing he could eventually get alongside, or at least within range. 'He must have had a surprise when that mortar shell burst in his wake! Still, we need something else.'

'Yes, we need Martin sitting on the end of the jibboom playing tunes with his flute,' Ramage snarled. 'A male siren on the rocks. Or perhaps you'd like to go and make nasty faces at him?'

'Wind might drop, sir,' Southwick said. 'He might run into a calm patch while we still have a breeze – that'd gain us a few ship's lengths.'

'And it might just as easily work the other way, with the wind dropping from astern, so we lose it first and *he* gains the distance.'

'True, sir, very true,' Southwick said hastily, recognizing warning symptoms. First the Captain would rub the upper and older of the two scars on his right eyebrow vigorously; then the skin of his nose would seem to get taut and bloodless, as though it was shrinking; then he would have trouble pronouncing the letter 'r', turning it into a 'w'. After this, Southwick knew well, although he had seen it happen only a few times, and usually in frustrating circumstances like these, God help the poor fellow who fell across the Captain's hawse. It was likely to be himself this time, he realized, and wished Aitken would come aft : the more live bait the better . . .

Ramage picked up his telescope and spent the next three or four minutes examining the *Furet*. Southwick measured the angle of the mizenmast once again and noted the angle and the time on the slate. The small island of Giannutri was fading away on the starboard quarter and already Argentario was beginning to shrink over the horizon astern as though shrivelling in the heat of the sun.

Finally Ramage put down the telescope and walked right aft to the stern-chase ports. Southwick was startled to see him kneeling down and, hands gripping the sides of the port, hang out, staring down at the *Calypso*'s wake. He stayed there for several minutes, hauled himself back in again, picked up his hat, which he had left to one side of the port, and jammed it on his head.

'I want five hundred shot brought up on deck from the shot locker,' he told Southwick abruptly. 'See to it immediately.'

The master promptly passed the order to the bosun's mates, and at once dozens of men left the guns and streamed below.

It might work, Ramage thought. He could, of course, start twenty or thirty tons of water from the casks and pump it over the side, so that the ship, lightened by that much weight, might be able to gain a few yards. If he still lost the race, however, he would run out of water weeks before the period his orders lasted, and he would have to go back to Gibraltar with his tail between his legs, defeated by thirst, not the enemy. He could equally well hoist a few guns over the side – each of the 12-pounders weighed a ton – but for every ton he gained he was weakened by a gun, and it still might not do the trick if the Frenchman copied him. There were dozens of other ways of lightening a ship; the trouble was that every one of them also weakened her fighting ability.

Now the men were coming up from below, each clutching four or five 12-pounder roundshot in their arms.

'It might work,' Southwick admitted. 'It did for the bomb ketches on the way down to Argentario. But – forgive me asking, sir,' he added warily, 'what makes you think we're not properly trimmed now?'

The question was a fair one because the ship's trim was the master's responsibility and as provisions and water were consumed he had to make sure that the casks, sacks and barrels were taken from parts of the ship that ensured she remained floating level, to the marks set down by her designer.

'We may well be properly trimmed,' Ramage said, 'but from the day we captured the ship we've never had anything official to go on, only the references in the French logs noting her draught forward and aft whenever the French master could be bothered to have a look and note it down.'

'But she always seems to sail well enough,' Southwick protested, feeling that his professional skill was being criticized.

'Yes, she always seems to sail well enough against another British frigate of roughly the same size, but this is the first time we've sailed her against an *identical* French frigate.'

'We don't seem to be doing too badly either,' Southwick grumbled. 'She hasn't gained a yard on us . . .'

'And we haven't gained a yard on her, either,' Ramage said grimly.

'No, sir, but we've spent a season in the tropics; we've a lot more barnacles than she has, I'm sure.'

'I'm not,' Ramage said shortly. 'The French dockyards are overworked and have next to no materials.'

'But what are you going to do now, sir?' Southwick asked anxiously, gesturing at the crowd of seamen now gathering round the mainmast with their arms full of roundshot.

Ramage pointed to a telescope. 'Look at the *Furet*. She's griping. They're having to use the rudder every few moments to keep her on course. You can see the white feathers of water it pulls up, like a hen scratching in the dust.'

'But so are we, sir,' Southwick said defensively. 'A ship always yaws when running like this, and the stunsails are out to starboard. 'Tain't as though we're running dead before the wind so we have stunsails set both sides.'

'Go on, look,' Ramage said firmly. 'She's not yawing, she's griping. She's down by the bow. Every time her rudder goes over it stirs up the water like an egg whisk.'

He waited until Southwick had the telescope to his eye, and then added: 'Now you can see . . . Aft she's floating a foot or more too high; the blade of the rudder isn't deep enough. Instead of turning the ship, it's slowing her up, like a paddle held out sideways. Not much, but it must add up to half a knot. And we're doing the same – I guessed as much and that's why I had a look.'

Southwick, still staring through the telescope, muttered in near-disbelief: 'There . . . there . . . there . . . and there . . . and there . . .'

At the same time Ramage watched the men at the *Calypso*'s wheel. They turned the wheel a few spokes and let it run back as though they were working in unison with the men at the *Furet*'s wheel.

'We're just the same,' Ramage said as Southwick turned away and put down the telescope. 'You never get the best out of a ship unless you have a trial of sailing against a sister ship.'

'I know,' Southwick said miserably, 'but I'd have sworn

this ship couldn't be sailed any faster than we've sailed her up to now. Thousands of miles . . .'

By now there were a hundred men gathered round the mainmast, each cradling roundshot. A hundred men each weighing an average of, say, eleven stone and holding sixty pounds of shot . . . Ramage struggled with the mathematics. That meant each man totalled 214 pounds, and a hundred of them totalled 21,400 pounds, which divided by 2,240 gave the answer in tons. Nine tons, in fact.

'Distance!' he said curtly to Southwick who, immediately grasping what Ramage had in mind, hurriedly snatched up the quadrant and then noted the angle and the time on the slate.

Ramage picked up the speaking-trumpet, which had been left beside the binnacle. 'You men holding shot – move over to the lee side.'

He waited until the group was close against the bulwarks on the larboard side.

'When I give the word, I want you to walk aft in pairs, up the quarterdeck ladder here on the lee side and go as far aft as possible. You can sit against the taffrail with your shot. Don't drop 'em; I don't want them rolling around the quarterdeck like a children's marble alley. Right, start coming aft!'

He called across to the men at the wheel and the quartermaster, who had overheard the conversation with Southwick and understood the purpose of the experiment: 'Once all these men are aft, you might find the ship handles slightly differently. You, Quartermaster, watch for it; and you men at the wheel, I want you to feel it through the spokes – or not, as the case may be.'

Two by two the barefooted seamen came tramping up the wide treads of the ladder, all of them grinning broadly, and most of them beginning to perspire with the weight of the shot.

They passed Ramage, passed the carronades, and as the first pair reached the taffrail subsided on to the deck with groans. The rest of the men followed and within two or three minutes they had occupied one side of the deck and taken up most of the room round the two aftermost carronades.

Ramage waited a couple of minutes and then walked over to the men at the wheel. 'Do you feel any difference?'

Both men nodded their heads eagerly. 'Yes, sir, she's a lot lighter to the touch. She always seemed to be wanting to gripe before but now – well, she's almost sailing 'erself.'

'S'fact, sir,' the quartermaster said. 'She ain't yawing now, either.' He looked at the wheel and whispered to the two men. 'Yes, sir, she takes just a quarter of a turn on account of the stunsails up to weather, and then she's as good as steering 'erself.'

In a minute or two, Ramage guessed, Southwick would report that the *Calypso* was beginning to catch up on the *Furet* . . . In the meantime he had most of the guns' crews squatting up here holding roundshot which, the moment they let go of them, would roll back and forth, cracking ankles and spoiling the whole trim once again.

He snatched up the speaking-trumpet and bellowed to the men left in the waist of the ship. 'Quickly, you men: each grab a hammock and get up here!' He stood there impatiently and suddenly blared: 'Don't worry about the blasted hammock cloth – we're expecting an action, not an admiral's inspection.'

It was not fair, and anyway the men were quite right because the long hammock cloth – a strip of canvas covering intended to keep the lashed-up hammocks dry – would get in the way of the guns, but the guns' crews could get that clear when they were back at their posts.

As men came running up the quarterdeck ladder with hammocks over their shoulders Ramage called to the boatswain, who was one of them, 'Undo the hammock lashings and put in shot, then lash them up into bags, so the shot won't roll all over the place. Stow 'em as far aft as you can.'

While the men dropped the shot into the hammocks and joked as they hurried to make up the bags, some of them recognizing their own hammocks by the numbers painted on them and groaning at the thought of scrubbing out the blacking from the shot that was already making the flax look like zebra skin, Ramage was conscious out of the corner of his eye that Southwick seemed to be doing a jig just forward of the binnacle.

'Well,' Ramage demanded. 'What's this – the beginning of the Helston Floral Dance?'

'Could be, could be, sir,' the master said, grinning as he pointed to the slate. 'We've caught up a hundred yards – leastways, what I mean is we're now overhauling them.' He snatched up his telescope and after examining the *Furet* said: 'Take a look, sir. Three heads along the taffrail, all officers, like starlings on a bough. The third one is using a quadrant. I can almost hear him reporting that the angle is greater . . . *and they don't know why . . .*'

As soon as the seamen aft put down their shot they returned to their guns, all taking a good look forward as they went down the quarterdeck ladder. Normally when serving at the guns their view forward was limited by the after side of the fo'c'sle, but now, probably for the first time in their lives, they had had a good look at the opposition; a captain-on-the-quarterdeck eye view, Ramage thought, just as he realized that the weight of a hundred men was now moving forward again, leaving only the roundshot. Too late to worry now . . .

Guns loaded and run out on both sides; the starboard side manned for the moment. It would be nice to have enough men to fight both sides at once but he doubted if there was a ship in the Navy with a full complement that could do that. Anyway, the *Calypso*'s men were now so well trained that if he had the chance to get both broadsides fired into the French, the enemy would think both sides were manned.

He would attack the Frenchman's larboard side. With the wind from the north-west and on this course, it meant that if the Frenchman tried to bolt he would have to turn away to leeward – and the *Calypso* would be there to stop him.

By now Aitken was back on the quarterdeck, looking with amusement at the white bags covering the larboard after corner of the quarterdeck.

'Looks as though it's done the trick, sir,' he commented. 'But it's going to be a pounding match once we get alongside.'

'Pound her well and then board her. We're short of officers to lead boarding-parties.'

'Aye, sir: Wagstaffe, Kenton, Martin, Orsini – we could do with them now.'

The *Furet*'s hull was entirely black: the only colours were the dull buff paint used on the masts and yards, and the inside of her gunports, which were red: that was traditional. And the name on the transom. The Revolution, Ramage thought, seemed to be against colour. Perhaps if equality was a colour, it was black, while fraternity was buff. The French Navy seemed to have run out of colours when they came to liberty – unless you include the blood red used inside the gunports . . . The Royal Navy issued no more colours than that; but neither did their writing-paper have '*Liberté*' and '*Egalité*' printed on the top. It was hard to imagine Their Lordships in the Admiralty administering a navy with a Tree of Liberty planted in the forecourt in Whitehall.

He stopped his train of thought for a moment and reached for his telescope. It was curious the amount of water suddenly flowing over the side from the *Furet*'s scuppers and scattering into droplets like smoke as the wind caught it. They must be wetting the decks to put down more sand in anticipation of battle. There was enough heat in the sun to dry the planking very quickly, but one would have thought a few buckets of water slung over them from a tub would be enough: with this amount of water the sand must be sluicing over the side too.

So much water, he thought, putting the telescope to his eye, that they must be using the deckwash pumps. No, it could not be that: both ships were sailing too fast for deckwash pumps to draw, even if lead piping went down the side to the water instead of canvas hose.

Hell fire! The water was not just a spray now; it was running in a stream through the lee-side scuppers – in spurts, rather like blood pulsing when a man lost a leg. The *Calypso*'s pump dale was also on the lee side, a wooden trough which carried the bilge water over the side from the great chain pump.

It must be the chain pump. He pictured many men turning the big cranked handle to rotate the sprocket wheel which turned the endless chain and brought each leather disc up the pipe casing with its quota of water, emptying it into the trough of the pump dale as it came over the top and started its downward journey again.

Then he cursed himself for his stupidity: the French captain was trying to lighten his ship in just the way Ramage himself had considered starting fresh-water casks, throwing a few guns over the side and jettisoning a couple of the boats. Very sensibly the French captain had decided to sacrifice the fresh water, so that now there were thousands of gallons of water in the *Furet*'s bilge which his men were busy pumping out. The *Calypso*'s bilges were pumped every morning, on Ramage's orders; not because she had a leak but because water left in the bilge soon began to stink. He had been in some ships of the line commanded by men who should know better whose bilges smelled like the Fleet Ditch at a midsummer noon. Anyway the chain pump leathers wanted wetting daily if they were not to dry and crack.

Southwick looked round at him and nodded cheerfully. His latest reading with the quadrant showed the *Calypso* still gaining. 'That ship is about five hundred yards ahead of us – from our jibboom to his taffrail, sir.'

'It's still going to take a long time to make up that distance,' Ramage said gloomily. 'Half an hour, anyway. Still, the men can have their dinner; it's long overdue.'

It was as if the *Furet* was towing the *Calypso*, Ramage thought irritably; despite his recent gain, the distance hardly changed now – not perceptibly, anyway; just two identical frigates surging southwards with a quartering wind, one flying the Tricolour, the other British colours. The *Calypso* was by far the smarter, Ramage thought; but paint did not make a ship fast nor did scrubbed decks stop barnacles and weeds growing on the bottom. No doubt the copper sheathing was by now wafer-thin in places, no longer keeping the growth away, and it was equally certain that many thin sheets would have ripped off, leaving only the stubby sheathing nails sticking out like the heads of pins pressed into a pincushion.

He would give anything to see the face of the *Furet*'s captain, just to know what the man looked like. The

Frenchman knew his business, that much was certain. Ramage would bet that the fellow had learned his profession under the old navy and, having no aristocratic attachments (and no enemies to accuse him falsely), had received well-merited promotion. Ramage felt that if he could catch a glimpse of the man's face he might be able to guess what his next move was likely to be, like a prize-fighter watching his opponent's eyes for a warning of the next punch.

He lifted his telescope and saw the three heads facing aft at the taffrail, obviously watching the *Calypso* racing along in the *Furet*'s wake. In the tropics one would expect to see flying fish making their graceful waltzes over the wavetops, but they were nearly twenty degrees too far north ...

Suddenly men were climbing up the *Furet*'s starboard shrouds, going to the stunsail booms at the ends of the yards. Perhaps the French captain knew a trick to make them draw better. Curious that so much water was still pouring through the scuppers on the lee side – the men working the pumps must be getting tired.

'How long ago did you take the next to last altitude?' he asked Southwick, who consulted his slate and then looked at his watch.

'Seven minutes, sir. I've been taking one every four minutes.'

He had first noticed the pumps going just before Southwick took that sight. Say eight minutes. That was a long time to have the men pumping at that rate, because there was no doubt they were making that cranked handle spin, probably with a couple of bosun's mates standing over them with starters ... Suddenly his thoughts froze as if a highwayman had jabbed him in the stomach with a pistol and demanded: 'Your money or your life.'

The *Furet*'s pumps were going, and now there were men gathered at the starboard end of each of her yards, about to do something with the stunsails. What trick was that captain up to? No answer, no hint of a reason, came to mind.

'Stand by sheets and braces,' he snapped at Aitken, who snatching up the speaking-trumpet and bellowed through it, although he was clearly startled by so unexpected an order, which would sacrifice the *Calypso*'s stunsails and booms.

'Stand by at the larboard guns – yes, *larboard*, blast it!'

Again Aitken bellowed as he repeated the order, while Southwick hurriedly snatched up his quadrant and once again moved the vernier a fraction, noted the time and wrote the figures on the slate. All this Ramage saw only from the corner of his eye because he was watching the *Furet* through the telescope again.

Suddenly the head of the *Furet*'s maintopgallant stunsail dropped a few feet and then streamed forward along the starboard side, flogging and twisting like the tail of a kite, and a moment later the rest of the stunsails were cut adrift, canvas and rope threshing in unison. She was going to turn suddenly to starboard, Ramage was certain of that and he was going to turn first to cut her off. If he was wrong he would lose a few hundred yards, but he had to gamble.

He shouted the order to Aitken and pointed at the quartermaster. An eight-point turn meant the men had to spin the great wheel several revolutions, and the quartermaster crouched ready over the binnacle, watching the compass and the dogvanes as well as glancing up at the luffs of the sails, which were beginning to flap as they lost the wind, although the yards were already being braced up.

'Larboard guns to fire as soon as they bear on the

target,' Ramage said to Aitken, who again shouted the order through the speaking-trumpet, although from the sound of the Scotsman's voice and the look on his face he probably thought his captain had suddenly gone mad because the *Furet* was still sailing on the same course with the *Calypso* astern of her.

Then the *Calypso*'s bow began to swing to starboard, the *Furet* seeming to slide away over to the larboard bow, like an ice-skater . . . Ramage had guessed wrongly. Already the *Calypso*'s sails were slatting overhead as seamen struggled with the sheets and tacks controlling the sails and braces which trimmed the yards, the stunsails tearing adrift and the stunsail booms breaking with a noise like fresh carrots snapping.

The guns' crews, having raced from one side of the ship to the other, busied themselves with side tackles, train tackles and trigger lines. The gun captains stood ready with the trigger lines slack in their hands; second captains checked the powder in the pans and waited the order to cock the locks.

Ramage opened his mouth to give the order that would bring the *Calypso* back into the *Furet*'s wake when the French frigate's transom disappeared, suddenly narrowing as gradually Ramage saw the whole length of the ship's starboard side appear: gunports open, stunsails slatting like streamers from each yard, sails flattened and fluttering as the yards were hurriedly braced sharp up.

Now the two ships were racing along side by side, perhaps two hundred yards apart, both heading west, both with sails flogging as men struggled to trim them, and from forward in the *Calypso* came the first bronchitic coughs as three forward guns fired. A red eye winked once abreast the *Furet*'s foremast, followed by three more farther aft. Smoke began to stream from the ports and Ramage felt a heavy thump nearby as a roundshot crashed into the *Calypso*'s hull.

Rapidly, because the ship had turned fast and suddenly brought the enemy into view, the rest of the *Calypso*'s guns fired in a ripple of thunder, and the guns rumbled back in recoil, the men poised for them to stop so they could begin the ritual of sponging and reloading.

More of the French guns winked and smoked; behind him and to one side Ramage heard the crack-crack-crack of the Marines' muskets as they tried to shoot down the officers and the men at the wheel on the *Furet*'s afterdeck.

He noted that the *Furet*'s stunsail booms had all carried away, snapped by the long strips of sail blowing forward and wrapping round the braces, which would jam in the blocks when they tried to trim the yards.

The *Calypso*'s fourth 12-pounder on the larboard side suddenly spun off its carriage, and a moment later Ramage heard a loud clang and a shriek of pain: a French roundshot had hit and dismounted it.

By now all the rest of the guns had been reloaded. Steadily each fired its second round at the *Furet* and Ramage, with nothing to do but await the outcome of the pounding, examined the French ship.

They were taking their time getting the sails trimmed; so much so that the *Calypso* was slowly drawing ahead. The *Furet* seemed to be heeled to larboard – but naturally, she was on the starboard tack. But – now she seemed to be heeled to starboard; in fact she was rolling, and rolling heavily enough to overcome the press of sails to leeward. They were rapidly clewing up the courses – but why reduce speed at a time like this? Now the topgallants were being furled. And the topsails.

Her gunports seemed to be nearer the water than one

would expect, too. Then Ramage turned open-mouthed to Southwick, who was now standing beside him, and both men exclaimed simultaneously: 'She's sinking!'

'Aye, we must have had a lucky shot,' Aitken cried jubilantly but Ramage said: 'No, they've had the chain pump going for the past ten minutes, but I didn't realize what was happening.'

The *Calypso* had fired another broadside before Ramage noticed that several seconds had passed since the last French gun had been fired. He told Aitken to pass the order to cease fire.

'Watch her colours,' he told Southwick, and then snapped at Aitken: 'Stand by to heave-to and be ready to hoist out boats. Renwick, stand by with your men. I'll be calling away boarding-parties in a few minutes.'

He turned to Aitken. 'Clew up the courses – use men from the guns if you need 'em because the topgallants will be next.'

There was nothing more dangerous and unnecessary than fighting with too much sail set; topsails were quite enough, giving complete control of the ship, and keeping the canvas high enough above the guns so that the muzzle flash would not start fires. For the first time in his life, he realized, he had been forced to fight under all plain sail. At least, he had stunsails and all plain sail set to the topgallants when he had to fight, because the *Furet* suddenly bore up . . . Now the men were busy cutting away the torn stunsails and halyards and clearing the booms.

The French frigate was sinking all right: she had that slow, ponderous and ominous roll of a ship with many tons of water slopping around inside her, sluicing first to one side and then to the other. In a few minutes it would be too risky to put the *Calypso* alongside her in case she rolled so much that their yards locked together. Indeed, the way she was going, the whole ship might well capsize.

'They're trying to heave-to,' Southwick said, 'but I think the foretopsail braces have been cut. Ah, down they come! She's struck her colours, sir!'

Ramage was almost numbed by the speed of events. What had started off as a regular battle was turning into a scrap-bag of different experiences. And Southwick was right, the *Furet* had been trying to heave-to – what in God's name was going on now? He swung his telescope along her deck. Men were slashing at ropes with axes – several of them chopping with tomahawks as though frantically trying to drive home nails with hammers.

Suddenly the main yard slewed round drunkenly and the foretopsail yard, its halyard obviously let go at the run, the lifts parting, came crashing down across the foredeck. The rest of the sails and yards began to drop, swing, cant or flog as the men on deck slashed through sheets and braces, bowlines and tacks, halyards and lifts.

'We'll heave-to on the larboard tack, if you please, Mr Aitken,' Ramage said, 'and I want boats hoisted out.' He looked at the *Furet* again. 'Make sure the ship's company have pistols or muskets; we're going to have more than two hundred prisoners on board in an hour or so – less, probably. If she sinks, we'll need to sling over hammocks for the survivors to hold on to until we can fish them out. Not a good day for hammocks,' he added, gesturing to those used as bags to hold the roundshot. At that moment one of the masthead lookouts hailed that a xebec which he thought he had earlier seen leaving from the direction of Porto Ercole was now catching up fast and seemed to be flying a flag or pendant from the upper end of the yard.

CHAPTER EIGHTEEN

Exactly fifteen minutes later Ramage leapt from the stern
sheets of the *Calypso*'s red cutter to seize a rope trailing
over the larboard quarter of the *Furet* and scramble up,
while the bowman tried to hook on and the rest of the
boarding-party grabbed at other ropes and began climbing the sinking frigate's side.

Ramage was unarmed; knowing that he would probably have to climb a rope he had taken off his cutlass belt
and then, as an afterthought, remembering their presence
when he bent over slightly, had taken the two pistols
from the band of his breeches and put them down on
deck.

The rope, hanging from the mizentopsail yard, was thick
enough for climbing but worn smooth with use. Finally he
reached the bulwark and swung himself inboard to land
on the quarterdeck, where two officers were waiting for
him, two rigid figures among a swirling crowd of men
who were shouting with excitement and fear and obviously
not far from panic.

'Which of you is the captain?' he demanded in French.

An officer with a bloodstained left leg unbuckled his
sword and offered it with a bow. 'I am . . .' but in the
chatter and yelling Ramage did not catch the name, hearing only the end of the sentence, '. . . and surrender the
ship to your captain.'

'I am the captain,' Ramage said and asked abruptly as
his boarding-party came swarming over the bulwark:
'You've scuttled the ship, eh?'

The officer looked startled. He was a grey-haired man of perhaps fifty years of age: his mouth was that of a man given to worrying. He wore trousers and a plain shirt, but he was freshly shaven, which was unusual, Ramage thought sourly. He seemed to be bleeding badly from the leg wound.

'No, not scuttled! It was you!' he said accusingly.

'Nonsense,' Ramage said angrily. 'You were sinking before I opened fire! I warn you, if you've scuttled her I shall leave you all on board.'

'That damnable mortar shell that burst in our wake as we left Porto Ercole,' he man protested bitterly. 'It seemed not to do any harm at the time, but suddenly – you saw our pump starting – we began leaking. It was just as you suddenly increased speed – how you did it we could not understand – and we knew you'd eventually overtake us. I think the explosion must have strained our planking. Anyway, the butts of several planks began to spring and our speed through the water was just opening them up more and more, beating the pumps.

'We tried to stop the leaks but the more we jammed in hammocks to caulk them the more the planking opened. Finally we had to bear up, but slowing the ship did not slow the leaks: we were obviously doomed. You opened fire, we fired back . . .' He held his hands out, palms upwards. 'The rest you can see.'

Ramage saw Renwick scrambling over the rail and signalled to him to take charge of the two officers who, hatless, white-faced and frequently pushed aside by hurrying seamen, reminded Ramage of children lost in a country market among the bleating of sheep, the mooing of cows and the shouts of buyers and sellers.

'That leg wound: go down to my cutter. My surgeon will soon be treating it. What happened to your surgeon?'

The man shrugged his shoulders and gestured towards his own men, who were still running about aimlessly.

Ramage beckoned to a couple of Calypsos and ran down to the captain's cabin. It was a curious feeling because it was a replica of his own in the *Calypso* – except that it was far more comfortably furnished. Heavy blue velvet curtains were held back on each side of the stern lights; two large brass-covered mahogany trunks were secured against the bulkhead; the desk was of heavy and highly-polished mahogany. The wine cooler was carved from a block of a heavy, dark wood but the lid had come off, exposing the metal lining.

Ramage went straight to the desk and began ransacking drawers. The three on the left were unlocked and contained various items usually kept in the drawer of a trunk. The lowest drawer on the right was locked.

'Here, open this with your cutlass,' he told one of the seamen excitedly. There was a chance, just a chance, that in the panic . . . The wood splintered and suddenly the drawer catapulted open, sending the seaman lurching across the top of the desk as he tried to recover his balance.

Ramage grabbed the drawer. It was heavy. Inside, fitting snugly as though made to rest there, was a plain wooden box which Ramage saw as he removed it had several holes drilled in the top and a sheet of lead riveted to the bottom. It was locked, and there was no sign of a key in the drawer. Now Renwick appeared at the door, and as he spoke Ramage realized that the whole movement of the ship was changing. She was beginning to wallow sluggishly, all life gone from her.

'You'd best come up on deck, sir,' Renwick said breathlessly. 'I think she's going to capsize any minute and more than half the Frenchmen have already jumped over the side.'

Ramage nodded to the two seamen, who hurried out through the door. Ramage gave Renwick the box to carry, warning him to conceal it as much as possible, and then followed him up the companionway. 'What have you done with those two officers?'

'Down in the red cutter, sir. The wounded one is in a lot of pain. I took the liberty of telling the cutter to stand off until I gave the signal: I'm afraid these Frenchies in the water will capsize it. The green cutter from the *Calypso*'s nearly here, and they're hoisting out the jolly boat, but I can't get any of these dam' Frenchmen to do anything about hoisting out their own boats: they've got five sitting on the booms . . . And I bet not one in four of the dam' fools can swim.'

As Ramage climbed the steps of the companionway, he tried to think what had struck him as odd about the cabin he had just left. There was something strange about it, but as he was thinking he felt the frigate roll to starboard with a terrifying slowness, stay there for what seemed to be minutes, and then begin the slow roll back to larboard. From beneath his feet the noise coming up from the lowerdeck was of water swirling and bubbling, sounding like a mill stream to a poacher leaning down to tickle trout.

Then he was in bright sunlight with Renwick standing on the hammock nettings, waving to the red cutter. There were few Frenchmen on the *Furet*'s decks now; most of them were in the water, clinging to hatch covers, yards, the greyish sausages of lashed-up hammocks, mess tables and forms, and other pieces of wood. Two men stood up in the bow of the cutter, beating back the Frenchmen

trying to scramble on board, and as soon as it was alongside Ramage slid down the rope into it, following Renwick and the two seamen. He grinned; even in an emergency the regular routine must be followed: the seamen
and Renwick had all gone down the rope before him without argument: a senior officer was always the last one into
a boat and the first one out. Renwick had wrapped the box
in a piece of torn sail; it looked more like a round object
than a rectangular one and the Marine officer went down
one-handed, the box tucked under his arm.

Halfway back to the *Calypso*, Ramage looked first at
the French ship, and then at the British. The French
frigate looked as though she had been hit by a sudden
storm; most of her remaining yards were a-cock-bill, as
though the ship was in mourning, the yards forming
crosses. Other yards had fallen to the deck or swung over
the side. The ship was rolling from side to side even more
slowly now in her massive death throes.

By contrast the *Calypso* sat in the water like a gull,
foretopsail backed, guns still run out, and – he counted
carefully – three shot holes caused by the French. They
showed up as rusty marks in the hull, although the real
damage would be inside, where the shot hit, spraying up
great splinters of wood or ricocheting.

He looked back at the French ship to count her shot
holes. There were eight in the hull between the fore and
mainmasts, so the *Calypso*'s shooting had been good. So it
should have been; conditions and range were ideal.

Then the red cutter was alongside and Ramage scrambled back on board the *Calypso*, followed by Renwick,
whom Ramage signalled to go down below with the can-
vas-wrapped box. Ramage waited at the entry port as the
Marines brought up the two French officers. He told them
to help the wounded one down to Mr Bowen, the *Calypso*'s

surgeon. After that he paused and saw that the *Calypso*'s green cutter was now among the Frenchmen struggling in the water or clinging to wreckage, picking up survivors, and the jolly boat was only a few yards away, while the launch was still being hoisted out. The wind was slowly drifting the *Calypso* down towards the men, who were struggling towards her, those that could not swim kicking out as they held whatever was keeping them afloat.

As he watched, the extra seamen in the green cutter helped the Frenchmen on board, and as soon as the boat was full the men at the oars bent their backs and sent the boat surging towards the *Calypso*, pursued by shrill shouts from the survivors left behind.

He looked at Aitken, who was waiting patiently, knowing how Ramage would hate what he had to say. 'We have three dead from the shot that dismounted the gun, sir, and five wounded – from splinters.'

'How many badly?'

'One, sir. Bowen says he'll probably be all right, though. The other four will be back on duty in a week.'

'The dead?'

'Instantaneous, sir. Cut down as the gun spun off the carriage.'

Surgeon Bowen could be relied on: he would come up to the quarterdeck later to report in detail on the wounded men. He had served with Ramage long enough, and together they had suffered enough casualties in battle, for him to know the routine.

Aitken said: 'The xebec the lookout reported earlier, sir: she's closing us fast. Seem to be three or four men in it, and there's a flag or something flying from the upper end of the lateen yard. Might be local fishermen out for some pickings,' Aitken added, but Ramage shook his head.

'They'd arrive after dark . . .'

'The sea's calm enough,' Southwick commented, knowing the exact moment when to interrupt his captain's thoughts and stop him brooding. 'We'll save these Frenchmen. But their ship hasn't much longer to go . . .'

'When I left her I didn't think I'd get off before she capsized,' Ramage said. 'The rolling doesn't look too bad from here, but on board . . .'

'The way her masts snatch on the shrouds – you just look at it,' Southwick said, looking round for Ramage's telescope and passing it to him.

He saw that either the *Furet*'s rigging had not been set up very tight with the lanyards in the first place, or her hull was distorting, because her masts were like tall pines buffeted by gusts of wind. As she rolled to larboard the masts gave an enormous twitch and tightened all the shrouds on the starboard side with another violent jerk which Ramage thought would have parted them.

Even as he watched the ship, the frequency of the roll seemed to be slowing down but it was increasing in amplitude, the masts swinging like inverted pendulums.

'All that water swilling round as though it was inside a bladder,' Aitken said miserably. His love of ships and the sea made him hate to watch a ship die, even if she was an enemy. 'Fancy scuttling her . . .'

'They didn't,' Ramage said. 'She sprang the butts of some planks just as we started to catch up. Seems a mortar shell burst in her wake as she came out of Porto Ercole, so one of the bomb ketches can claim her. The French didn't find any damage – until we started closing up on her and they began to drive her hard. Then she sprang a butt, then more went . . . That was why she suddenly luffed up – the water was pouring in.'

'Those bomb ketches earned their pay today,' Southwick

commented. 'Whew, just look at that!'

The frigate rolled towards them and, for a moment, seemed about to capsize : the remaining yards came swinging round the masts like flails, again to hang vertically, and they could see several guns dropping across the deck, ripping away the bulwarks on one side as the train and side tackles and breechings tore out the eyebolts, and then falling to crash through the other. As the *Furet* staggered back again, like a drunken man making an enormous effort to stay on his feet, they could see that the bulwarks, jagged where the guns had fallen, were now like the smashed-in battlements of a besieged castle.

The red cutter was back among the survivors, picking up more men as the jolly boat and then the launch returned to the *Calypso* and sodden, spluttering Frenchmen climbed up the side, to be met by seamen who marched them forward to the fo'c'sle while others kept them covered with muskets.

Southwick waved down at the bosun, who called back: 'That makes seventy-three, sir. I reckon there's another couple of hundred left.'

'Looks like it from up here,' the master said, 'but there's no rush, they've all found floating wreckage or hammocks. She had a full complement, from the look – '

He broke off as the *Furet* rolled slowly to starboard, so that for a few moments he was looking down on to her decks, the view of a bird hovering seven or eight hundred feet above her when she was floating normally. Now he saw more guns breaking loose from the larboard side and falling across the ship, smashing their way into the sea through the bulwarks.

Water pouring into the ship through the starboard gunports, now immersed, built up the air pressure down below and water spurted up through unexpected holes like whales spouting; suddenly a dozen or more casks popped out of the hatches like, as Southwick commented, peas rolled out of a measuring mug. Still the great masts continued to heel; several of the yards dropped so that once again they were perpendicular to the masts; then the tips of the yards touched the water as she continued rolling over, her larboard side rising like a surfacing whale as the starboard sank. With a graceful but despairing slow movement she turned upside-down, the black planking vanishing as she capsized, to be replaced by the coppered bottom of the ship. The copper was reddish here and green there and tried to reflect the sunlight; whole sections were missing, and there the teredo borers would have riddled the wood . . . The ship paused for a minute or two, white swirls of frothing water showing where air was still forcing its way out of the hull as water poured in and looking, from this distance, like grotesque whirlpools swirling round a half-tide rock.

Suddenly they were all looking at a great smooth patch of sea, and while they absorbed that shock, dozens of pieces of wood came to the surface, some of them long topsail and topgallant yards which shot up several feet like leaping swordfish before dropping back to float as if it were kindling tossed into a village pond. Great bubbles of air belched up and slowly the wind waves covered the smooth patch where the *Furet* had been.

Ramage turned away and saw the unwounded French officer standing at a gunport abreast the mainmast, a Marine behind him. Obviously Renwick had allowed him to watch his ship die while the other one was being treated by Bowen.

While the rest of the survivors were being picked up he had work to do, Ramage realized, and the first task was to see what was in that weighted box. Renwick had, as instructed, left it on Ramage's desk, watched by the sentry. It was the usual type in which most ships carried the secret papers unless their captains preferred a canvas bag. It would sink quickly when thrown overboard, but in the case of the *Furet* the man responsible for making sure it was thrown over the side when the colours were struck had, fortunately, failed in his duty. Perhaps, in the excitement, his first-lieutenant had forgotten it or been killed. Unless there were *two* boxes? That might well be the case, Ramage thought. The second box, with the secret papers, orders, signal book, challenge and private signals for the next three months, might have been put down beside the binnacle and, as the colours came down, thrown over the side. Or, he realized with dismay, it might still have been there as he stood talking to the French officers; it might just this moment have sunk with the *Furet*.

He shook the box but the weight of the lead prevented him from guessing if it was empty. He looked around for the Marine sentry at his door and said: 'Use your bayonet to open this box, please.'

When he saw the impatient look on Ramage's face the man put his foot on the box, pinning it to the deck as he inserted the bayonet point into the tiny gap between lid and box just above the lock.

Suddenly the box sprang open and a bar of lead, which had been inside it, slid across the deck and startled the Marine who, never having seen such a thing before, made a leap for it as Ramage hurriedly grabbed the box and looked inside, seeing that there were several papers.

He sat at the desk and put the battered box in front of him. All at once he felt so weary that he would have liked to sleep for the rest of the day. One French frigate blown to pieces in Porto Ercole by a mortar shell, another sunk, alongside the *Calypso*, a third looking badly damaged in the fleeting glance he had given her as they passed the harbour entrance. Two out of three accounted for. Considering that they were formerly sister ships of the *Calypso*, a superstitious man might feel a chill. Yet perhaps not . . . the fourth, the *Calypso*, flew different colours and had a different loyalty . . .

What *was* it about the cabin in the *Furet* that had looked odd? The memory nagged him. The cabin was the same shape as this one, although the furniture was better. The lid had come off the wine cooler. The left-hand drawers were full of the bits and pieces that a man tended to accumulate in extra drawers.

A jacket had been slung down on the settee. Not a captain's coat because the epaulets were wrong. He knew very little about French naval uniforms but could recognize the coat of a French captain, and that was not one. Based on that one glance, when he was thinking of something else, and his present memory of it, that frock coat belonged to someone senior, probably a rear-admiral.

That would make sense, he thought sleepily: the senior officer of a squadron of three 36-gun frigates could be a senior captain; but three frigates which were going to transport a regiment of artillery, cavalry and infantry, and escort two bomb ketches to a distant port might well be carrying a rear-admiral to a new command.

A rear-admiral would of course occupy the captain's cabin, and in turn the captain would move down a deck and take over the first-lieutenant's cabin in the gunroom, the first-lieutenant displacing the second, and so on . . . The captain's secret papers would have been in his temporary cabin, leading off the gunroom, one deck down . . . which meant, Ramage realized as he stared at the box in front of him, the shock bringing him wide awake, that these might well be the rear-admiral's papers. But where was the rear-admiral?

There had been only two officers left alive on board the *Furet*, the oldish fellow with the wounded leg and a pimply youth; the rest had been killed. Both were wearing trousers and shirts, as though disturbed before dressing in uniform for the day. Yet the wounded man was well shaven; Ramage had particularly noticed that because usually French officers seemed to favour shaving the night before, so that one never saw them just shaven; always shaven twelve hours earlier, like innkeepers and ostlers.

He reached for the box, flipped open the lid and took out the contents. The first few papers were addressed to a Rear-Admiral Jean-Paul Poitier. A more reliable source of information, Ramage thought sourly, than a drunken artillery colonel boasting in an Orbetello inn.

CHAPTER NINETEEN

Twenty or thirty documents of varying sizes, and most of them bearing the now-familiar oval symbol with the anchor in the middle and the words *Fraternité* and *Egalité* printed at the sides. What happened to *Liberté*, Ramage wondered. They were arranged in date order, the earliest on top.

The first was addressed to Jean-Paul Poitier, '*capitaine de vaisseau*' and telling him, in bureaucratic French so complicated that Whitehall clerks would have envied the prolixity, platitudes, irrelevances and redundancies, that the Minister of Marine and the Colonies had been pleased to advance him to the rank of '*contre-amiral*'. The letter gave the date when the promotion would take place and added that further orders would be sent to him 'in due course'.

Poitier was in Toulon at the time, Ramage noted, commanding a ship of the line; probably one of the fleet that spent most of its time at anchor, yards sent down, sails stored on shore in rat-proofed buildings, cordage hanging in coils, and, he suspected, always fearing that Nelson would return.

He had to wait three months – 'due course' seemed to be as long in Revolutionary France as it was in Royalist England – before being told he was to command a squadron 'to be employed upon a special service'. There was no indication of which ships would form the squadron, nor any hint of the nature of the 'special service'.

Three successive letters concerned pay and allowances for his new rank; a fourth instructed him to report to the prefect of the province to swear a new oath of allegiance upon his promotion. The government of France must be uncertain of itself if its officers had to swear oaths of allegiance at various stages of promotion, Ramage thought. British officers had to take the Test Act oath, but that was more a question of religion than of allegiance. Britain was lucky, he realized; the nation was not split, so that brother could find himself fighting against brother. One tended to forget after all these years that the French war had started with Frenchmen revolting against Frenchmen.

The next letter acknowledged notification that 'Citizen Jean-Paul Poitier, rear-admiral', had taken the oath and was to command a squadron comprising two frigates which would later join another frigate and two bomb vessels and form part of a fleet 'now being assembled' and which was 'intended for a special service'.

Poitier's natural hope for an independent command must have suffered an unpleasant shock when he received that letter, Ramage thought. He was to be the third or fourth junior admiral in a fleet; at best he would be commanding a small squadron attached to the fleet. But what was the 'special service'?

Poitier was then told to take two frigates under his command, hoist his flag in the *Furet* after she was commissioned, and as soon as both ships were provisioned for three months, to report the fact to the minister. Further orders arrived telling him that the frigates would be transporting cavalry, infantry and artillery, and although they were not to be armed *en flûte*, he was to draw extra hammocks and blankets from the army depot in Toulon, and take on an extra month's provisions, which the army would also supply.

Ramage read that with a smile, the chances of Poitier getting even one blanket out of the army depot in Toulon were nil, and only a bureaucrat in Paris could imagine that any army depot would have a supply of hammocks.

That was obviously a point made by Poitier in a letter to Paris, because a reply, signed by the minister himself, brushed aside 'these minor supply problems' and said that a third frigate would be added to his squadron.

The minister told him to put to sea as soon as the third frigate was commissioned. He was to sail for Porto Ercole, in Tuscany, and there embark the 156th Regiment of Artillery, the 47th and 67th squadrons of cavalry and the 19th and 75th regiments of foot. Two bomb ketches, the *Brutus* and the *Fructidor*, which were also intended for the 'special service', would join his squadron there, having previously watered and provisioned. They would be under his command and could embark any troops for whom there was no room in the frigates.

The letter gave Poitier the day by which his frigates should arrive in Porto Ercole and the date when the whole squadron, including the bomb ketches, should sail, but there was no mention of the destination. However, Poitier was assured that the bomb ketches had received relevant orders and been warned that they must not be late arriving in Porto Ercole. The commanding officers of the various army units involved, the minister added, were being informed 'by the other Ministry'. This phrase led Ramage to guess that the navy was having a quarrel with the war ministry. Events in Paris probably ran parallel to those in London, where at times a serving officer could be forgiven for thinking that the enemy was another ministry, rather than the French.

The war ministry in Paris had done its job, however, and its orders had been obeyed, because the troops had arrived in Porto Ercole on time.

There were a dozen documents left in the box, but it was obvious that none was going to mention the objective. The destination of the squadron and the fleet, and the nature of this 'special service' were obviously closely guarded secrets. The French were wary enough not to commit anything to paper, never sure that ministry officials or others who might see written orders were not secret royalists, or British spies. Ramage finished reading through the remaining papers but they covered only routine matters.

It was getting hot and stuffy in the cabin, and Ramage remembered that the *Calypso* was still hove-to. Although he had gone through the papers in less than half an hour, there had not been enough time yet to complete the rescue of all the French survivors.

He locked the documents in a drawer of his desk and put the broken box in another, which he left unlocked. He picked up his hat. The sentry came to attention as he walked through the door, and halfway up the companionway he began to squint in the bright sunlight. The ladder was canted to starboard and the rays of the afternoon sun heated the woodwork, so that he could smell the paint as he went up.

The carpenter and his mates were repairing the damaged gun carriage while the gunner made checks with his callipers to ensure that the gun itself had not been damaged. Aitken was on the quarterdeck and pointed to the xebec, which was barely a mile off. Southwick was scanning the wavetops with a telescope and moving across to the other side of the quarterdeck when he saw Ramage.

'Just making sure we aren't missing any survivors, sir,' he explained, and Ramage saw that the wreckage now covered a large area. 'The boats are going to everything that's floating. One silly fellow clinging to a yard hid himself under a piece of the sail – apparently thought we were cutting everyone's throat, until some of his mates shouted to him. He bobbed out quick enough then!'

Ramage nodded and left Southwick to his search as he walked forward to where all the French prisoners were herded together on the fo'c'sle. They would soon be taken below and a gun loaded with canister shot trained on the hatch, but for the moment it was easier to guard them up in the bow.

They were a classic cross-section of seamen serving in a man o' war, whatever their allegiance, but Ramage thought that among the pinched faces, sea-soaked and bedraggled hair, and torn clothing, he could hear various regional accents. One man grumbled in the deep, slow accents of the Camargue; another, excited, angry, and frightened, came from the north, probably Artois, among the flat fields of Flanders. A third, from his behaviour a petty officer trying to restore discipline, was almost certainly from Alsace or Lorraine.

Ramage knew he was deliberately wasting time: there was only one Frenchman he needed to talk to and he would be down below, being patched up by Bowen, who had so few wounded to attend to that he had turned the gunroom into a surgery, with a piece of canvas stretched across the table with short lengths of rope ready, if necessary, to strap down a patient if the pain became too bad: there was no rum yet distilled that could deaden the rasp of a saw if a limb was being amputated.

As Ramage walked into the gunroom he saw that the tub, conveniently placed to hold 'wings and limbs', was empty. There were perhaps two dozen wounded Frenchmen waiting outside the gunroom door, but they were patiently sitting on the deck.

The sheet of canvas was soaked with blood; Bowen, the man who had been one of Wimpole Street's finest surgeons until his practice was ruined when he became a drunkard and was forced into the Navy – to be cured of drinking by a ruthless Ramage – looked up, apron stained red, as Ramage spoke to him.

'Ah, sir; a most successful action: my congratulations. A frigate sunk and hardly any work for me. One funeral for you, and there's a young Frenchman I'm worried about.'

Ramage nodded, already experiencing the familiar nausea that always made him feel faint at the sight of all the medical instruments laid out on another piece of canvas stretched on the deck, with a loblolly man kneeling beside it, ready to pass in a moment whatever Bowen called for.

'Let me have your report when you've finished treating everyone. Now, that French officer . . .'

'Ah, leg wound. Nothing serious – lacerations of the gastrocnemius and the tibialis anticus muscles. Pieces of splinter – I've extracted them all. Plenty of blood at the time but he's been bandaged up and given a stiff tot of rum. Apart from changing the dressings in a day or two, he's quite all right. He can walk, but I've put him in Martin's cabin until I had time to get orders from you, sir.'

'Very well, Bowen, thank you. I'll take him away because I want to talk to him.'

'He's still weak from the loss of blood, sir,' Bowen said cautioningly. 'I must still consider him my patient.'

'I have a terrible reputation for torturing wounded prisoners,' Ramage said dryly, and Bowen grinned. 'I know, sir; you tortured me enough!'

'But you can give a man a tot of rum now, and never feel the need . . .'

'Oh yes, sir, the torture was effective enough!'

'Right, now which is Martin's cabin?'

He walked over to the tiny hutch Bowen pointed at as he called for an instrument and turned back to the seaman lashed down on the table. 'Keep still, you oaf,' he said in appalling French. 'Because of my skill you will keep the arm. But not, certainly not, if you wriggle like an eel.'

The little cabin was lit only by the gunroom skylight, and Ramage saw the man lying in the cot, the lower part of his left leg swollen by the dressings and the trouser leg cut away almost to the crotch. The grey-haired man was lying almost at attention, but he looked defeated. Not defeated in battle, Ramage thought, but defeated by life. He had good, almost fine features, and Ramage wondered whether he was what the Revolutionaries would have called an aristo who, to save his life, land or because of a change of heart, had joined the Revolutionaries but had never become *of* the Revolution because someone who had not fought or shouted at the barricades or howled at the guillotine platforms was never fully accepted. What, apart from losing his ship, which was a risk any naval officer took, made his face sag and his body look, even recumbent on the cot, as though it had just received five hundred lashes?

'Admiral Poitier,' Ramage said quietly from the doorway, 'can you walk up to my cabin or shall I get a couple of men to carry you?'

The man had gone rigid for a moment, a movement which brought another stab of pain to his leg, but he slowly relaxed when he realized that there were many ways by which Ramage could have learned his name and rank.

'I can walk slowly,' Poitier said, sitting up in the swinging cot and putting his right leg on the deck as he looked round for something to grip. Ramage held out a hand and a moment later, with a deep grunt, Poitier was standing beside him. He was not as tall as Ramage remembered, and there was the smell of rum on his breath, but he was sober enough.

'Your surgeon,' he muttered, 'he did a fine job. Just cuts, from splinters. No permanent damage – if I understood his French correctly.'

Ramage stood back as the man hobbled from the cabin, glanced at the seaman stretched on the table and murmured a few words of encouragement, and then made his way up the companionway, able to walk more easily than Ramage expected because the kneecap had not been damaged.

Ramage led the way to his cabin, then stood back at the top of the companionway, noting Poitier's obvious familiarity with this type of ship: the duck of the head at the fifth step of the companionway to avoid a deck beam, sharp turn aft at the bottom to enter the captain's cabin, the nod to the Marine sentry who came to attention and was obviously about to challenge Poitier until he saw Ramage following.

Inside the cabin, Ramage twisted the armchair round until it faced the desk, and gestured towards it. Poitier sat down carefully, as though expecting it to be some trick chair with arms that would seize him, and then he sighed as it gave him relief from the pain in his leg. Ramage tossed his hat on to the settee and sat in the straight-backed chair at the desk. He took a key from his pocket, opened the lower drawer and took out the documents, putting them squarely in front of him on the desk.

'Admiral,' he said quietly, 'I must congratulate you on your recent promotion –'

Poitier inclined his head in acknowledgment. This too was information the Englishman had obviously obtained from some of the men.

'– which I imagine you never expected. You are a Breton, no?'

Poitier nodded. 'You speak very good French, Captain. Fluent, in fact. I would have –' he paused for a moment, his eyes searching Ramage's face warily. 'Do you come from Paris? Are you a royalist?'

Ramage shook his head. 'You flatter me. No, I am English. I must apologize for not introducing myself: my name is Ramage, Nicholas Ramage.' He pronounced the name in the French way, and Poitier seemed to freeze.

'Lord Ramage?' he asked, seeming breathless, his hands grasping the arms of the chair as though he expected to be tipped out of it at any moment.

'Yes – why? Is my reputation so bad?'

Admiral Poitier shook his head. 'Not bad in that sense . . .'

'What sense?' Ramage asked, curious but at the same

time flattered that the French in Toulon had even heard of him, let alone given him an assessment.

'Well, talk from the West Indies . . . that you abandoned drowning men after sinking their ships – that sort of thing.'

Ramage thought back over several years in the Caribbean; he remembered the trouble and risks he had taken to rescue the survivors – scores, indeed hundreds of them – in the action in which he had captured the *Calypso*. Risks, because the rescued were so numerous they could have seized the ship from the rescuers, and that had led to a warning from his own admiral. In crossing the Atlantic the story had undergone a radical change . . .

He looked directly at Admiral Poitier. 'Do you believe such stories now?'

Poitier shook his head vigorously. 'I do not believe them now and I did not really believe them then. You understand that newspapers like *Le Moniteur* have to print stories of British atrocities.' He gave a short, dry laugh. 'Now I think about it, I should really have been able to say: "Yes, Captain Lord Ramage?" when you came down to me in the cabin and addressed me as "Admiral Poitier". The attack on Porto Ercole, the sinking of one of my frigates using one of my own bomb ketches . . . yes, it has the Ramage touch.'

'You flatter me,' Ramage said, thinking that Admiral Poitier's compliment meant a good deal more than the grudging treatment he had recently received from the commander-in-chief on the Jamaica Station. 'However . . .' he said, his tone changing to indicate that the conversation was now taking a different turn, 'I believe you were engaged upon "a special service", with your frigates and the bomb ketches.'

'Of course not,' Poitier said slowly, as if considering each word. 'Just a routine cruise.'

'With bomb ketches?'

'I met them by chance.'

'But three frigates and two bomb ketches – an unusual squadron to be cruising in the Mediterranean, you must admit. What targets are there for bomb ketches? With few ships of my own country – this one is almost an exception – in the Mediterranean, is not a squadron of three frigates rather large?'

Poitier could not see that the documents on the desk came from his own cabin in the *Furet*, Ramage realized. Most British naval officers would know that such grey-tinted paper would not be used by the Admiralty or commanders-in-chief, but, after years of war, a Frenchman would have forgotten that really white paper still existed.

'Admiral,' Ramage began, tapping the small pile of documents, 'I have been – '

He heard someone clattering down the companionway and now the sentry knocking on the door interrupted him. 'Captain, sir : Mr Aitken would like to see you.'

'Send him in.'

Aitken had a broad grin on his face and Ramage realized that the Scot was a handsome fellow, a fact which was usually disguised by his sombre expression.

Noting Poitier's presence, the first-lieutenant said : 'May I report to you privately, sir?'

Damn! Ramage had spent some time leading up to the right moment – creating it, in fact – when he would confront Poitier and force the secret of the expedition out of him. Now Aitken had arrived at the wrong moment. Yet Aitken would not have intruded unless . . . Ramage picked up his hat and followed the Scotsman from the cabin, telling the sentry to latch back the door and keep an eye on the prisoner.

Halfway up the companionway Ramage hissed up at Aitken: 'What's happened?'

'That xebec, sir: Wagstaffe sent it. Orsini's brought news of what happened at Porto Ercole.'

Ramage stopped climbing. 'What happened that we don't know about?'

'Well, nothing really important, sir,' Aitken said lamely. 'I just thought –'

'Very well, tell Orsini to wait: I want half an hour with this French officer ...'

Aitken acknowledged the order and Ramage went down the companionway, apologized to a startled Poitier for the interruption, and sat down at his desk after dropping his hat on the settee once again.

'We were discussing your orders,' he reminded Poitier, 'and you claimed you were on a routine cruise.'

'Yes,' Poitier said, obviously becoming bored, as well as tired and shaky from his leg wound. 'A routine cruise. We'd sighted nothing; we needed wood and water ...'

'Why choose Porto Ercole and not a large port like Leghorn?'

'Light winds,' Poitier said smoothly. 'It would have taken days –'

'But you arrived off Argentario from the direction of Leghorn,' Ramage interrupted. 'I saw you.'

'That is true,' Poitier admitted. 'I like Porto Ercole. The wine, plenty of wild boar from the Maremma, as much fresh water and wood as we need ...' The Frenchman's voice had a confidential note, as though he was confessing to Ramage that he had a weakness for roast boar.

Ramage nodded understandingly but then the Frenchman saw his eyes narrow, the skin over his cheeks and nose tautening, and his left hand slap down three or four times on some papers, the heavy signet ring on the little finger banging on the desk top.

'Admiral, you were engaged in some secret operation. I want to know what it was.'

Poitier held out his hands, palms upwards. 'Yes, I admit it, of course. The bomb ketches give that way. The details I do not know: they were secret, you understand – probably only the Minister of Marine and a few others would know the details. Nothing was in writing – except for assembling some of the ships. Only the senior army commanders and the admirals received verbal orders about the destination. You do the same in England.'

Ramage did not bother to contradict him; there was no point in telling him that the details of most secret operations were usually the talk of fashionable London drawing-rooms for days and weeks beforehand. The idea of a secret operation being mounted from Britain was almost ludicrous, unless only one or two ships were involved.

'Nevertheless, because your role in this operation is now over, Admiral, I should be interested to know what it was.'

Poitier eased his wounded leg and nodded. 'Yes, I suppose there can be no harm in telling you: the seamen in all three frigates knew – the regular ship gossip, of course. We were to embark cavalry, infantry and artillery at Porto Ercole and carry them elsewhere. We were doing that when my – when your,' he corrected himself, 'bomb ketches attacked.'

'Where were you to transport them?'

Poitier shrugged his shoulders most convincingly. 'I do not know: I was expecting a messenger hourly from the Minister in Paris with further orders. He had not arrived when you attacked.'

Ramage saw that the Frenchman had been quick with his story and it was convincing enough for Poitier to be able to keep to it. The messenger from Paris . . . delayed as the frigates prepared to sail . . . so likely, so readily understood by an enemy officer. Poitier might be feeling weary and his leg might hurt, but he was thinking quickly and clearly. Very well, the pressure must be applied; another turn taken up on the rack.

Ramage said quickly but firmly, his fingers tapping on the papers as though it was a nervous habit: 'I must know your ultimate destination, Admiral. It affects the safety of my country and the lives of my countrymen.'

'I am sorry I cannot help you, Lord Ramage,' Poitier said regretfully. 'I am a prisoner and no further use to my own country, but I was told so little.'

The Frenchman had changed in the last few minutes – from the time that Aitken had come in. His complexion was less grey, his face less lined, and he was sitting upright in the chair now, as though this was his cabin and Ramage merely a tiresome visitor. Ramage felt instinctively that the longer he kept the admiral sitting there in the armchair the less chance he had of wringing any secrets out of him. The Frenchman's confidence had imperceptibly returned. Now was the time for gentle threats – and perhaps some that were not so gentle.

'I have no wish to be burdened with so many prisoners,' Ramage said conversationally, 'so I am proposing to land all of you at Porto Ercole, providing each of you signs the usual agreement not to serve again until regularly exchanged. You agree to that?'

Poitier nodded eagerly, wincing as the movement jerked his leg. 'Yes, of course. It is generous of you. You can go into Porto Ercole under a flag of truce.'

'Very well, we shall do that. However, there is one small question. Small for me,' he said, tapping the papers again, 'but of more consequence for you.'

Poitier looked at him warily. 'What is it? I've agreed to

the exchange – which takes nearly three hundred prisoners off your hands. They could rise and take your ship.'

'They could not,' Ramage said shortly. 'We rescued them from drowning, but any sign that they are not suitably grateful means that they get a whiff of canister shot fired into the middle of them. No, I was thinking of your own particular position.'

'My *own* position? Well, if I sign an exchange agreement, presumably you will put me on shore with the rest. You will have my parole.'

'Yes,' Ramage said carefully, 'and at the moment, only two people know that you did not dispose of your most secret papers – you, and me.'

Poitier went white, making a curious grasping movement with his hands, as though afraid he would fall from the chair. 'What . . . what do you mean?'

'If your Minister of Marine and Colonies knew that you had not destroyed these papers – even though the *Furet* had been overtaken by an enemy ship, had hauled down her colours and was sinking – I think we know what would happen to you. You recognize them' – he held them up and when he had put them down he reached for the box and held it up ' – and the weighted box? Bottom right-hand drawer of your desk?'

When Poitier made no answer Ramage said: 'The guillotine, I imagine.'

Poitier nodded dumbly. 'Yes, they would suspect a plot. Collusion, in fact. My family in Britanny would be punished. Our land would be confiscated. There would be no end to it.'

'Exactly,' Ramage said, hating what he was having to do but knowing that he had no choice. 'That young lieutenant of yours knows nothing and suspects nothing. I presume the captain disposed of his papers?'

'I don't know,' Poitier admitted. 'I did not see him, but anyway it hardly matters now – he is dead and the ship is sunk and obviously you do not have them. Had I seen him throwing them over the side it would have reminded me, but the ship was beginning to sink so fast and you were so close in our wake . . . we were concerned –'

'With staying alive,' Ramage interrupted with deliberate cruelty, trying to make it easier for Poitier to agree to what he was about to propose. 'A broadside *pour l'honneur du pavillon* and then a hurried surrender.'

'It was not like that,' Poitier protested. 'We had to bear up to slow the ship – her speed was ripping away the planks . . .'

Ramage shrugged. 'You will have to convince your minister about that, not me. But the affair of the secret papers – that is the thing which could send you to the guillotine.'

'*Will* send me to the guillotine,' Poitier said.

'Yes, if it becomes known in Paris I am sure it will.'

Poitier glanced up at the word 'if', caught Ramage's eye and said frankly: 'You are offering me some kind of exchange? What can I bargain with?'

'You can have all these papers –' Ramage pushed them towards him across the top of the desk ' – in exchange for one piece of information. Once I have it, you will be free to go out to the quarter gallery and throw them over the side. Or you can put them in your pocket.'

'What piece of information?' Poitier blurted out.

'What is that "special service"?'

Poitier's head dropped and his eyes closed. For a moment Ramage thought he had fainted. With a great effort he pulled himself together, sat upright and, looking directly at Ramage, said: 'There is no "special service" now. I doubt if you will believe me but it has been cancelled. One of the minister's aides came to tell me, and the fleet – ' he broke off, as if deciding to keep the rest secret.

Ramage pulled the documents back across the desk and began straightening them up, so that their top edges were level. 'I think you had better prepare yourself for the guillotine, Admiral. I'm sorry.'

Poitier looked Ramage straight in the eye. 'There is no reason why you should believe me, but I hope you will listen for a moment. The "special service" is cancelled – not just postponed but *cancelled* – so I suppose there is nothing treasonable in my telling you about it.

'A fleet was being assembled in Toulon and Cartagena – there were to be several Spanish ships of the line accompanying us, but no Spanish troops – with transports. Troops were collecting from all over France, but to make up the required strength it was decided to use some forces from the Army of Italy – the men I was to collect at Porto Ercole. They were stationed at various places in the local province – at Grosseto, I think the town was called.

'As you have read in those letters, I was to sail from Toulon with three frigates, meet two bomb ketches at Porto Ercole, embark all these soldiers, and then sail for the rendezvous with the fleet.'

Ramage held up his hand. 'Where was the rendezvous?'

'At Candia. The fleet was to have sailed for Crete soon after me, although it was due to arrive there first, because I was expected to lose time embarking the troops at Porto Ercole – the army,' he said without malice, 'is rarely punctual.'

He paused for a moment, as though collecting his thoughts. Or, Ramage realized, hurriedly making up more of a story, or ornamenting it. Up to now the story rang true though: certainly it seemed likely, and it was borne out by the letters.

'Where was I? Oh yes, the rendezvous at Candia. That was arranged, and according to the orders I had already received my three frigates provisioned and watered in Toulon for three months. You understand that provisions are difficult to obtain in France these days, and I had a struggle to get even a small amount of cordage and canvas to have as a reserve. I still had to get the extra month's provisions for the troops we were to embark in Porto Ercole.

'Then the minister's aide arrived in Porto Ercole yesterday, while we were loading troops, with the news that the whole operation had been cancelled. The admiral was told that half his ships of the line (five out of eleven) were to be laid up in ordinary, and all the seamen from those five ships with less than a year's experience at sea were to be handed over to the army.

'The orders for myself were that I should pick up the troops in Porto Ercole as arranged, and proceed to Candia. There I was to land the troops, who were to take up garrison duties in the island. The two bomb ketches were to remain there to give some protection to what is otherwise a poorly defended anchorage. Having escorted the bomb ketches and disembarked the troops, I was to return to Toulon with the frigates.'

Ramage asked: 'Where was the fleet to land this army?'

Poitier paused for a good minute, obviously weighing up his answer. Finally he said: 'I cannot tell you. You could guess. There is only one place for which Bonaparte might again consider risking an army and a fleet.'

Again? Ramage realized that Poitier wanted him to guess. 'Egypt? Where he's already lost an army and a fleet?'

Poitier looked away and in his own mind had not mentioned the word. 'The point of the great rendezvous of the fleet in Candia was that we did not think you British would look there, should you learn that we were assembling ships.'

Ramage was about to comment that the *Calypso* comprised about the entire British force in the Mediterranean but held his tongue and gathered up the secret papers. 'The letter cancelling the main operation and the orders that you should carry on to Candia are not here.'

Poitier looked startled, as though just discovering a theft. But he was also quite clearly trying to remember something. Suddenly he began taking a few folded papers from a trouser pocket. He sorted through them and found letters which were still folded.

Poitier pulled them out with a smile on his face. 'These were given me by the minister's aide yesterday: I forgot to put them away with all the other papers, otherwise you would have read them. They belong with the others. Perhaps you will allow me . . .' With that Poitier tucked them under the pile, so that they were in date order.

Ramage, admiring the man's subtlety, picked up the pile again. The extra letters were blood-stained and creased.

'Assure yourself of their genuineness and then read them,' Poitier said.

Ramage took the first one and examined the seal again, holding the paper against the light to see the watermark, although given the circumstances in which he had obtained the papers, there could be no trickery. He unfolded the letter and read it. Blood had dried across one corner but had not blurred the writing.

It was a copy of a letter from the War Minister himself and addressed to General Bruiton, commanding the French forces at Candia. It said that the attempt on Egypt, of which he had been apprised and for which he had been ordered to prepare provisions and fresh water, had been cancelled, and instructed him what to do with his ships and men. However, because General Bruiton's force had suffered such losses from sickness and desertion in Crete, the troops at present embarked in the vessels commanded by Admiral Poitier were to be landed in Candia to form part of the garrison. The two bomb ketches were to remain at Candia and form part of its defences, the navy instructing the army in the use of the mortars, and once this was done the crews of the two vessels would be put on board 'whichever of the frigates Admiral Poitier specified'.

Ramage read the letter a second time. Yes, this would be the way the minister would inform people like Poitier. He reached out for the second document, addressed to Poitier and from the Minister of Marine. It said, almost word for word, what Poitier had related – that he was to take his force to Candia.

Poitier had been honest. Ramage slid the documents back into the pile. 'I have to leave this cabin for a few minutes.' He walked over to the door of the quarter gallery to starboard and pushed it open before going out through the main door, acknowledging the sentry's salute.

Egypt, he thought; Bonaparte must be off his head. At any rate, the drunken artillery colonel need no longer worry about sand.

As Ramage climbed the companionway he remembered bitterly what the French major had known in the prison cell at Orbetello: that information was only valuable if it could be passed on to someone in a position to make use of it. By a combination of luck and blackmail, he had discovered that the French were, at least until a few days ago, assembling a fleet and an army to invade Egypt. The only way he could warn the Admiralty was to sail the

Calypso a thousand miles to Gibraltar, and that involved abandoning the most potentially exciting orders he had ever received. The alternative was to send one of the bomb ketches with the news. But it would take weeks to get there . . . He admitted that the Admiralty would be justified in bringing him to trial for allowing such delay . . .

CHAPTER TWENTY

As Ramage stepped out on deck, almost dazzled by the sunshine, he saw a small xebec lying astern, a line serving as a painter leading out through a stern-chase port and made fast round her mast. The lateen yard, with its furled sail, was curved like a bow. The hull had not seen a coat of paint for a couple of years but like most of her type she was fast.

He was just turning to go to the rail, expecting to find Aitken, when he almost bumped into a small figure with a cutlass belt across his shoulder and giving a salute that made up in keenness what it lacked in martial correctness.

'Report from Mr Wagstaffe, sir,' Paolo Orsini said, trying to keep the excitement out of his voice. 'He gave me command of the xebec, and I have Jackson as my second-in-command, and –'

'You made a fast passage: we were watching you,' Ramage interrupted briskly. 'Where is the report from Mr Wagstaffe?'

Paolo looked embarrassed and Ramage, noticing everyone within earshot had stopped whatever he was doing, said: 'A verbal report?'

'Yes, sir.'

'Good news?'

'Oh yes, sir, very!'

'Out with it then!'

'Well, sir, we captured the second frigate! We cut her out of Porto Ercole. Well, perhaps not cut her out because all the French had bolted, but we towed her out and anchored her out of range of any shore guns.'

'Congratulations,' Ramage said, and added with a smile: 'In fact it is the *third* frigate.'

Paolo looked puzzled, and Ramage realized that Jackson, Stafford and Rossi were standing nearby. 'The first was the one we blew up with the mortar shell, the second –'

'Was the one we sank an hour ago,' Ramage interrupted. 'So the one you've towed out is the third.'

Paolo now looked very disappointed, as though only the two bomb ketches had a right to sink frigates in these waters and that ships like the *Calypso* were little better than poachers.

Ramage gestured to Southwick and Aitken to join them. 'Mr Orsini brings news from Mr Wagstaffe: they've towed out the third frigate and anchored it out of possible range of the batteries.'

'Hah! Three out of three,' Southwick exclaimed. 'But Mr Orsini doesn't seem pleased. Is anything wrong? A lot of men killed?' The old master reminded him of everyone's favourite grandfather, always fussing over the grandchildren.

Ramage raised his eyebrows questioningly, and when Paolo shook his head he said: 'Mr Orsini thinks the bomb ketches had a lien on the three frigates, and I believe he regards us as poachers over the *Furet*. You'd better tell him.'

Southwick gave a great bellow of laughter and Ramage

joined in when he saw the startled expressions on the faces of Paolo, Jackson, Stafford and Rossi.

'The *Furet*,' Southwick explained, 'can be shared between the bomb ketches – unless you know which one exploded a shell in her wake as she came out of Porto Ercole.'

'Did that sink her, sir?' Jackson asked disbelievingly.

'No. In fact we had a long chase after her – right down to here. But for a long time we just could not overhaul her enough to let go the broadsides. Then Mr Ramage noticed something – you remember both bomb ketches were sailing down by the bow as we came down to Argentario, and what he shouted to you to do?'

The four nodded their heads vigorously.

'Well, this was the first time that the *Calypso* has had a trial of sailing against a sister ship, and although she wasn't drawing ahead, we weren't overhauling. Leastways, not until Mr Ramage spotted that both of us – the *Furet* and the *Calypso* – were griping too much, even though we had stunsails set only on one side. He spotted why and cured it in the *Calypso*, with the result that we suddenly started overhauling the *Furet*.

'They tried to drive her faster – but although that mortar shell of yours hadn't done any damage that showed when she was driven hard, as soon as they tried *extra* hard – or it may have been a coincidence: I reckon it was – she sprung a plank or two, and the tremendous pressure of water just opened her up, like peeling a banana. She luffed up – we thought to engage us, of course – and we both got off a few broadsides, but she sank . . .'

By now Orsini was grinning, but Ramage suddenly remembered Gibraltar. Perhaps he could leave the bomb ketches to carry out his orders. Even stay with them and send Aitken in the *Calypso* to Gibraltar with a dispatch.

No, the Admiralty would not stand for that. He half-heard something Paolo had said to Aitken.

'What was that about the frigate?'

'The one we towed out, sir: I was saying that she's hardly damaged.'

'But there was wreckage hanging from her masts and yards when we passed – some of it seemed to be burning.'

'Yes, sir, but once we had her anchored, we cleared most of that while we were getting the xebec ready.'

'Do you mean to say this frigate – the one you towed out – is seaworthy?'

'Oh yes, sir: Mr Wagstaffe told me particularly to tell you he'd have her ready for sea by the time you returned to Porto Ercole. By noon tomorrow, anyway.'

'Thank you,' Ramage said sarcastically. 'So far telling me about it had slipped your memory.'

'Sorry, sir,' the boy said. 'Might we have a drink of water, sir? We had no time to get water or provisions before we sailed to try to catch you up.'

Ramage nodded to Aitken.

'Get them fed – I have to go below to write a report to the commander-in-chief at Gibraltar. Tell Renwick to send a Marine to guard the French admiral and then you join me in my cabin. Orsini, what's the name of this other frigate?'

Ramage signed the dispatch, found the ink was drying fast from the heat so that he did not need the sand-shaker, and then looked up at Aitken. 'Well, I'm sorry I've been able to give you only ten minutes, but have you made up your mind?'

The Scots first-lieutenant nodded. 'Aye, sir, and don't think I'm not grateful for the offer to command her, but if it's all the same, I'd sooner stay with you in the *Calypso* and perhaps you'd agree to Wagstaffe taking the other frigate, this *Tortue*, to Gibraltar. It might lead to him being made post.'

'You'd definitely be made post,' Ramage said. 'I'm sure the admiral will buy her in and give you the command.'

'Aye, sir, I know; but there'll be more chances for me later, but maybe not such a good one for Wagstaffe. And to be honest, sir, I'm enjoying this cruise; it seems – if you'll pardon the familiarity – to have the Ramage touch.'

Ramage was startled to hear a phrase in English which he had heard in French not half an hour earlier from another man sitting in the same chair.

'Very well, I appreciate it. You'd better warn Orsini and his scoundrels that they've got to beat us to Porto Ercole with this dispatch. They can sail as soon as I've written orders for Wagstaffe. In this light wind that xebec will beat us there by hours . . .'

'Aye, sir, and if the lads know what the orders are then the *Tortue* will be out of sight over the western horizon long before we get there. Should Martin take over command of the *Brutus*, sir? Perhaps Orsini could have the *Fructidor* . . . we're very short of officers . . .'

He was just getting up to leave the cabin when Ramage motioned him to stay. 'Pass the word for Renwick to bring the French admiral and that other officer to this cabin.'

While the first-lieutenant gave the order, Ramage took the admiral's sword from the locker in which Silkin had stowed it, and gave the scabbard a wipe with the corner of a curtain.

Within a few minutes he would return the sword to Poitier. In fact, Ramage thought sourly, Poitier has not done much to deserve it, but it was very important that the French government had no hint that the British knew of Bonaparte's plans for Egypt, because cancelled plans could be brought into use again.

The formal return of his surrendered sword, the warrior's age-old tribute to a gallant but vanquished foe, would be reported back to the Minister of Marine in Paris as soon as Poitier and the other prisoners were landed under a flag of truce in Porto Ercole. This would indicate that the British considered that Poitier had fought a brave fight. There would be no gossip about papers not destroyed – only two living men knew about them. Ramage went to a drawer in his desk, took out the lead-weighted box with its smashed lid, and went out to the quarter gallery. He dropped it over the side. The letters would have sunk long ago.

Dudley Pope

'Takes over the helm from Hornblower . . . Dudley Pope knows all about the sea and can get the surge of it into his writing.' *Daily Mirror*

'An author who really knows the ropes of Nelson's navy.' *Observer*

'The best of the Hornblower successors.' *Sunday Times*

RAMAGE 85p
RAMAGE AND THE DRUM BEAT 80p
RAMAGE AND THE FREEBOOTERS 85p
RAMAGE AND THE GUILLOTINE 80p
RAMAGE'S DIAMOND 85p
RAMAGE'S MUTINY 85p
RAMAGE AND THE REBELS 85p

Fontana Paperbacks

James Jones

FROM HERE TO ETERNITY £1.75
The world famous novel of the men of the U.S. Army
stationed at Pearl Harbour in the months immediately before
America's entry into World War II. 'One reads every page
persuaded that it is a remarkable, a very remarkable book
indeed.' *Listener*

A TOUCH OF DANGER 95p
A superb first thriller by the author of *From Here to Eternity*
set on an Aegean island where the sun and sex are corrupted by
violence and drugs. 'A believable private eye at last—not too
tough, not too lucky—and a plot built with loving care.'
John Braine, Daily Express

GO TO THE WIDOW-MAKER £1.50
A superb novel about the war between the sexes, set in the
world of rich men and those who cater to them. In Jones's
tale of dangerous living, love is for men and women are for
sex. 'Jones is the Hemingway of our time . . . There is savage
poetry in his descriptions of spear-fishing and treasure-
hunting.' *Spectator*

THE MERRY MONTH OF MAY £1.00
Paris in the spring of 1968: students on the rampage and their
effect on a wealthy American family living in Paris. 'Very
gripping . . . a novel of our time which takes the reader into
the heart of the Revolution. The atmosphere is splendidly
conveyed.' *Financial Times*

Fontana Paperbacks

Geoffrey Jenkins

Geoffrey Jenkins writes of adventure on land and at sea in some of the most exciting thrillers ever written. 'Geoffrey Jenkins has the touch that creates villains and heroes— and even icy heroines—with a few vivid words.' *Liverpool Post* 'A style which combines the best of Nevil Shute and Ian Fleming.' *Books and Bookmen*

A BRIDGE OF MAGPIES 85p
A CLEFT OF STARS 70p
THE RIVER OF DIAMONDS 85p
THE WATERING PLACE OF
  GOOD PEACE 75p
A TWIST OF SAND 75p
HUNTER-KILLER 85p

Fontana Paperbacks

Fontana Paperbacks

Fontana is a leading paperback publisher of fiction and non-fiction, with authors ranging from Alistair MacLean, Agatha Christie and Desmond Bagley to Solzhenitsyn and Pasternak, from Gerald Durrell and Joy Adamson to the famous Modern Masters series.

In addition to a wide-ranging collection of internationally popular writers of fiction, Fontana also has an outstanding reputation for history, natural history, military history, psychology, psychiatry, politics, economics, religion and the social sciences.

All Fontana books are available at your bookshop or newsagent; or can be ordered direct. Just fill in the form and list the titles you want.

FONTANA BOOKS, Cash Sales Department, G.P.O. Box 29, Douglas, Isle of Man, British Isles. Please send purchase price, plus 8p per book. Customers outside the U.K. send purchase price, plus 10p per book. Cheque, postal or money order. No currency.

NAME (Block letters) ———————————————————

ADDRESS ————————————————————————

————————————————————————————

————————————————————————————

While every effort is made to keep prices low, it is sometimes necessary to increase prices on short notice. Fontana Books reserve the right to show new retail prices on covers which may differ from those previously advertised in the text or elsewhere.